THE VAMPIRE LOVER

By Juliette N. Banks

COPYRIGHT

Copyright © 2022 by Juliette N. Banks. All rights reserved.

No part of this book may be reproduced in any form or by any means, electronic or mechanical, including photocopying, recording, or by any information storage and retrieval system without the written permission of the author, except for the use of brief quotations in a review.

This book is a work of fiction and imagination. Names, characters, places, and incidents are either products of the author's imagination or are used fictitiously. Any resemblance to actual persons, living or dead, events, or locales is entirely one of coincidence. The author acknowledges the trademarked status and trademark owners of various products and music referenced in this work of fiction, which have been used without permission. The publication and/or use of these trademarks is not authorized, associated with, or sponsored by the trademark owners.

Author: Juliette N. Banks
Editor: Jen Katemi
Cover design by: Elizabeth Cartwright, EC Editorial

DEDICATION

To my late grandfather, Jack, who we called *Bobby*. Apparently, as a toddler, I kept calling him Bobby like the character inside my favorite book—go figure! And it stuck.

He worked at the Ford Motor Company here in New Zealand all his life, so I named a side character after him. You'll spot him along the way.

ALSO BY JULIETTE N. BANKS

The Moretti Blood Brothers
Steamy paranormal romance
The Vampire Prince
The Vampire Protector
The Vampire Spy
The Vampire's Christmas
The Vampire Assassin
The Vampire Awoken
The Vampire Lover
The Vampire Wolf

Realm of the Immortals
Steamy paranormal fantasy romance
The Archangel's Heart
The Archangel's Star
The Archangel's Goddess

The Dufort Dynasty
Steamy billionaire romance
Sinful Duty
Forbidden Touch
Total Possession

THE VAMPIRE LOVER

CHAPTER ONE

Two weeks ago

Oliver sat in the driver's seat of Piper's car as they drove through the dark streets, with one hand on the steering wheel, and the other hand ready to grab her.

Or protect his balls.

It could go either way with her.

"So, kidnapping and now theft?" Piper snarled at him, her arms crossed and her long, dark hair falling around her shoulders. "Your rap sheet is getting longer, asshole."

Oliver shook his head.

"For a journalist, you're pretty stupid," he snapped, darting a quick look at her and trying to ignore how plump her breasts were. Piper Roberts was far from stupid, but she *was* fucking pretty.

Correction. She was fucking gorgeous.

If she wasn't Sage's sister, and a goddamn pain in the ass, he'd take her home and fuck her until she lost her voice.

But Piper *was* a pain in the ass, and an all-round annoying human. First, she had followed him back to the mansion after seeing him leave Sage's house a few days ago, and tonight she'd turned up again demanding to see her sister.

Who was now a vampire.

So, yeah, that meeting wasn't going to happen any time soon.

Actually, Sage was in transition, and they had no idea when she would wake. Oliver had been instructed by Ari, Sage's mate and the director of The Institute, to return Piper home and wipe her memories.

So, just another day at the office.

"I'm stupid for letting you take my car," Piper said, shaking her head at him. Or herself—he wasn't sure.

Oliver rolled his eyes. "For God's sake, let me spell this out to you. I haven't *taken* your car. You are *in* it."

"Without my permission," Piper stamped out.

Like she could stop him.

He was a powerful vampire and assassin at The Institute. Recently, he'd been promoted to head assassin after his friend and colleague, Ben, had mated and moved to Italy. Ben was now back in Seattle with them, along with the Moretti royals.

Oliver was looking forward to catching up with him for a few drinks, but this time they wouldn't be ending the night with one, two, or five females and a handful of sex toys. When a vampire mated, he was mated for life to that one person. If the mate was a human, the vampire turned them. Simple as that.

Of all the vampires he'd expected to mate, Ben had not been on his list. The guy was lethal, charming and sex-driven. Which, okay, fine, described Oli as well. That's why they were such good friends.

Giving and taking pleasure with beautiful women was Oli's favorite pastime. Well, that and killing baddies with a shiny AT308 rifle.

"I didn't kidnap you. Alex and I took you back to your place after you *followed* us, and then we restrained you." He realized how dodgy that sounded.

"Usually when that happens to me, it's for much more pleasant reasons," Piper said, and Oliver's cock responded.

No. Fucking, no, no, no.

"I'm sure they gag you, too. I would," Oliver said, only half under his breath.

"You won't. Ever. Because you aren't touching me again," Piper said, and ripped open the door when he parked outside her house.

Again?

It had been Alex who had restrained her last time, although, sure, Oliver taken her arm and pulled her inside.

Okay fine, yes, he remembered every millisecond of it because Piper's soft warm skin had burned into the palm of his hand, sending electrical sparks through his body.

But he wasn't thinking about that.

No.

Not thinking about it.

Oliver shook his head and got out of the car, following her to the front door where she punched in a code to open the door.

"Keys!" she demanded when it opened, holding out her hand.

"Inside," Oliver said, lifting his chin.

"I don't fucking think so." Piper crossed her arms.

Oliver picked her up and threw her over his shoulder, kicking the door closed with his foot and stomping up the stairs.

Meanwhile, Piper shrieked in his ear like a banshee. "Put me down." She yelled as he deposited her on the sofa in the least gentle way he could.

Well, he could be way less gentle with her, and his cock was very interested in that idea.

Never happening.

"Let's get down to business," Oliver said, squatting in front of her and placing his hands on her knees.

"Oh my God, are you going to rape me?" Piper retreated on the sofa.

The fuck?

"No!" He growled. "I don't rape women. Do I look like I need to rape women?"

Piper shrugged.

Shrugged!

Oliver stood and glared down at her.

"Well, you don't exactly look like an accountant with all those tattoos and leather!" she exclaimed, then shrugged again. "You could be a rapist."

Oliver ran a hand through his hair.

This wasn't cool.

He bent down in front of her again. "Piper, I am not going to harm you," he said more gently. "We don't do that."

She narrowed her eyes at him. "Who is *we?* I just want someone to tell me where Sage is and if she's okay."

The emotion from earlier was back in her eyes and her fight subsided. She was tired. Not surprising, given it was nearly eleven at night. She had yelled and screamed for hours at him while he had hidden her in his room, and they'd waited for Ari to join them.

That she was still sassing him was admirable.

In fact, he much preferred being aggravated with her. Then he could pretend she was just a pain in his ass, and not a woman he'd been thinking about for days since they first met.

Because there was no way he was mating.

Ever.

Not fucking ever!

"I promise you; she is fine," Oliver said, taking her chin in his hand as their eyes connected. "Now, Piper, you sexy little pain in the ass, I want you to focus on my words."

"What are you doing?" she asked in a whisper, already half under his vampire hypnosis.

He took in her startling blue eyes as his hand rested on the bare skin of her thigh. God, she was too fucking beautiful.

"I'm making you forget," Oliver said.

Mostly.

CHAPTER TWO

Present time

Piper turned off the shower and dried herself with her favorite kabillion-thread Egyptian cotton oversized bath towel. She may not be wealthy, but it was little luxuries like this that made her feel less unhappy about the fact.

One day.

She brushed her teeth, swept her facial moisturizer across her clear creamy skin and pulled her long dark hair into a pony.

Walking into the bedroom, she noticed she'd left her large window open. The sheer curtains were billowing about like she was in a romantic suspense novel, which was kind of cool. However, there was a little patio outside, so she was conscious of security. That and the latch was coming loose.

She pulled it closed and shivered.

Thing was, she had been feeling uneasy for the past two weeks. Like she'd forgotten something or had to remember something.

As someone who relied on her sharp mind in her role as an investigative journalist, it was frustrating as hell.

Okay, fine, she was *just* a journalist. But one day she'd be an investigative journalist working for one of the big media names.

Piper Roberts: Investigative Journalist.

It sounded amazing, and maybe she'd end up working for the *New York Times* or Reuters.

She knew she was capable of it and her MBA in Media and Communications, where she'd achieved honors, went some way in proving that.

Still, the qualification hadn't been enough to impress her father.

Nothing she'd ever done had been enough for that man.

Piper pulled on a pair of red boxers and matching singlet top with spaghetti straps, grabbed her laptop and hopped into bed. It was a bad habit she was trying to break, but tonight she had an excuse.

She was looking for her sister.

Sage had gone on holiday with her boyfriend, Ari Moretti. They were due back today, and she hadn't heard from her the entire time. Not a single post on social or a text.

The truth was, the two of them were no longer close. When they were younger, they had been extremely close and perhaps it was because there was only a year between them, but it didn't matter anymore. Piper had fucked everything up.

She chewed the side of her mouth — something she did every time she thought about that one stupid mistake.

Colin.

Small cock, Colin.

Not the point, Piper.

She let out a long sigh. If she could turn back time, she would without question.

Colin was Sage's college boyfriend, and the two had been in love. Well, Sage had loved him—that part was true.

What her sister didn't know was Colin had been sleeping with at least two other girls that Piper knew of.

And she ended up being another one.

Stupid, stupid, stupid.

Not only had she destroyed her relationship with Sage, and broken her sister's heart, but it had added another nail in the coffin of her relationship with her father.

All she wanted was his love and acceptance. Like he gave Sage. But instead, she got judgment and rejection.

Her sister was smart as hell. A scientist. She was working for one of the largest pharmaceutical companies in the world and *was going to change the world,* or so her father always said. Quite how he thought she would do that, Piper wasn't sure, but for as long as she could remember their father was constantly telling her and everyone how incredible Sage was.

And what a disappointment Piper was.

When Sage finished high school with honors their father insisted on throwing a big party where he surprised her with a car. The following year when Piper did the same, it was like crickets. Well, they went out for dinner, but that night have been one she would rather forget.

"Piper, you would do well to follow in your sister's footsteps when you get to Brown," Simon Roberts had said. "I want to hear you're focusing on your studies, not ending up one of those kids who spends their college years drunk and at parties."

By then she had been used to his imbalanced judgment of her and simply pressed her lips together.

"And get those grades up and you might actually end up doing something decent with your life."

That she couldn't let go.

"I passed with damn honors!" she had spat, slamming her drink down.

"See what I mean, Maryanne? Attitude and lacking in brains."

The insult had sliced through her.

When they arrived home and simply headed to bed, she stood in the hallway ready to scream. There was no car in the driveway, no dangling of keys in front of her face.

"Excuse me!" she'd said, crossing her arms. It was as if a light had turned off inside her heart.

Her father had turned and looked at her. She threw out her arms. "Where's my damn car?"

"What car?"

"Sage got a car for finishing high school. Where's mine?"

He let out a cold laugh, and walked away, calling out over his shoulder—not even bothering to give her the time of day. "Your sister worked hard. When I see that same work ethic from you, I'll get you a car, but I'm not holding my breath."

Piper had stood gaping at his back and eventually tears had poured down her face. Sure, she had been more social than Sage, but it wasn't like her studies had suffered. For goodness' sakes, she'd ended up with honors, regardless. Socializing and building friendships were an important part of a person's development. Not that she'd had the wherewithal to say that to him at the time.

In fact, it was at high school she'd met her friend Kara, who was still her best friend today. They worked together at *The Seattle Times*, and Kara had single-handedly kept Piper from going into depression when she and Sage had fallen out.

When her father had found out what the rift between the two of them was about, he had looked at her like she was dead to him. And he still, to this day, treated her as such. He spoke the bare minimum to her.

But she deserved it in many ways. She had slept with her sister's boyfriend. It was the lowest of lows.

She hardly knew why she'd done it herself.

Sage had been studying late one night in the college apartment they shared, so she and Colin had decided to get something to eat. There was nothing unusual about that—the three of them hung out regularly and Colin and Piper often found themselves alone waiting for Sage after class, or meeting first at the library.

That night, they ended up having a beer while waiting for their takeout and decided to eat at the restaurant to give Sage some space to study.

Everything was fine up until the third beer.

Three senior guys from the football team showed up and slid into their booth, joining them. Piper knew Chad, the captain, had a thing for her—aka wanted to fuck her—and while he was extremely hot, she was sick of all the one-night stands.

She wanted a boyfriend.

Like Sage had.

Especially after the dig her father had made during their last visit back home, asking when she was going to get herself a real boyfriend.

Asshole.

If he knew Colin slept around, he might not be so cocky, but Piper wasn't going to hurt her sister just to shut her father up.

When she'd found out, Colin had assured her it was just a phase he was going through, and he loved her sister. And begged her not to say anything. After the second time, she gave him a warning: do it again and I'm telling Sage.

Turns out she was the third, and Sage had busted them anyway.

The night it happened Chad was getting all handsy with her under the table. Colin had stepped in and after a whole bunch of testosterone ranting, she had dragged him out of the venue, and they'd started walking home.

"You okay?" Colin had asked.

"Yeah. Chad is an idiot."

"He is. If he had any brains, he'd take you on a date. Not feel you up."

Piper snorted. "Thanks."

"I'm not joking. You're hot *and* smart. What guy wouldn't want you?" Piper had glanced up at him, blushing from the compliment. More, she had reveled in it.

Men wanted to fuck her. They never saw her worth.

Colin had slowed and stopped her pace by placing a hand on her forearm. "Piper?"

She had frozen. "What?"

"You know every guy in this college wants to fuck you, right?"

Of course she'd known that. She had slept with at least thirty percent of them already.

She shrugged. "Sure, whatever. I want more than that, you know."

"You deserve more."

Everything inside her knew this was wrong and yet it was all she had ever wanted from a man. To be seen, adored, respected. He'd stepped closer, her eyes tilting to his. It had been hypnotic. When he'd taken her hand instead of kissing her, and changed direction, taking her back to his apartment, she had allowed him to lead her there.

Men back then were ripping her panties off and fucking her up against a tree. This man was taking her home.

She was worth something.

At least that was how she saw it.

For once in her life she wanted what Sage had. Perhaps not her father's acceptance and love, but one night where she felt like she was special.

Boy, had she been stupid. And wrong.

Turns out Colin was no different. He'd had buyer's regret about thirty seconds afterwards and made no effort to hide it.

"Oh Jesus, what have we done?"

"Gee, thanks."

"Oh, come on, Piper. You know this wasn't going to be anything more than a fuck. Don't make me feel guilty."

She had cleaned up and left.

The next day, Sage had overheard her on the phone when Colin had called, concerned she would tell her sister.

Idiot.

It was his phone call that had gotten them caught.

When she'd turned and seen the look on Sage's face, it had broken them both. Sage had moved out, and they had both finished college, barely speaking to one another.

After their parents found out, they had told the sisters to make up and then said little more. In front of Sage, at least.

Piper's experience had been quite different.

"I'm incredibly disappointed in you, Piper. Unsurprised, if I'm honest, but disappointed nevertheless," her father had said, after she had been called into his office. "Make up with your sister and I don't want to hear any more about this." He had sat down at his desk as if dismissing her but looked up at the last minute. "And start dressing a little more respectably. You look like a damn slut."

Piper had run up to her bedroom and cried for hours.

He never spoke to Sage like that. Okay, fine, her sister had dressed like a scientist even before she qualified, but Piper was hardly kitted out in fishnets and come-fuck-me boots.

She dressed just like every other girl in college.

Her parents were strict Christians, so his statement, while harsh, wasn't new. It was only ever directed her way.

Piper had woken up the next day, broken on the inside, but with a new determination. She was going to prove to her father she was just as smart as Sage.

She'd show her father *and* the damn world.

How?

She wasn't quite sure, but she knew she wanted to be an investigative reporter and so she knuckled down and focused on her studies.

Okay, fine, and continued to sleep with terrible men.

One thing at a time.

And she was on her way. She was a journalist at *The Seattle Times* and was just looking for a story to break that would get her noticed.

Piper fired up her laptop and put in her password.

She also wanted to heal the rift between her and Sage. But to do that, she had to find her sister. She was worried about her. Sage might not have forgiven her—even though she said she had—but Piper loved her sister.

Something about Sage's new boyfriend had rubbed her the wrong way and her journalistic instincts were nagging at her.

Disappearing for two weeks and no social media? No, that was weird even for Sage.

Where were they—the moon?

Even more strange, every time Piper tried to focus on what she knew about Ari, a pain shot through her eyes. She knew she'd met him, but the memories were rough and vague. The only thing she could recall was an address that Sage had visited that kept popping into her mind.

Was that Ari's house?

She'd overheard her sister giving the Uber driver the address and it had stood out as strange to her because the neighborhood was extremely expensive. Heck, Amazon's Jeff Bezos lived there.

So yeah, not the type of people her sister would be hanging out with.

Unless she really *had* changed the damn world with some scientific miracle.

Piper snorted.

"Something's not right." She muttered to herself, closing the laptop, and turning off her light. "And I'm going to find out what it is."

Flashes of disjointed memories tore through her mind while she lay staring at the shadows in her room. A face. An incredibly handsome face.

It was the same every night.

The man's blue eyes glared at her in anger and… desire. Her nipples pebbled.

No.

Not again.

Her body reacted every time she saw him in her mind. His broad shoulders, sharp jaw, solid thighs. She was sure she had never met him and was starting to wonder if she just had an overactive imagination. Yet, nearly every night for the past two weeks, as soon as she relaxed in the evenings the visions of him came flooding in.

And her body flared to life.

Warmth flooded her core and she twisted in the sheets, groaning. It was as if these visions took control of her body, and it was starting to become a concern. She moaned into the pillow and squeezed her eyes shut as her pussy wanted more.

It wanted touch.

She saw those eyes, full of fire, irritation, and something else. He hated her. But he wanted her body.

She let a hand slide down and slip under her boxers.

No, stop.

"Mmph," she moaned as her fingers felt the hot wet mess the visions of him had created. Piper was a highly sexual woman, but this was nuts.

It wasn't real.

For the first few days it had been kind of fun and naughty. Now, after trying to fight the impulse, she felt like she was losing control of her body.

"Fuck." She flung back the sheets and pulled out her vibrator.

There was no use. She needed release.

Brrrrr.

CHAPTER THREE

Oliver wiped a hand over his face and stifled a groan.
Fucking pain in the goddamn ass.
So why the hell was he here, then? What he should be doing was sitting with Travis, the team manager, and their tech guys at The Institute and prepping for the meeting later tonight.

Oh, no. Instead, he was here, on the balcony of Piper's apartment, watching her vibrator slide in and out of her wet pussy.

That's right, he was a fucking Peeping Tom.

Not for the first night either, and it was becoming obvious he was in big trouble. He should be keeping far away from her, not stalking the damn human.

He'd tried to justify his behavior by telling himself he was just making sure Sage's sister was not going to be a problem for them anymore. After all, she'd turned up at the mansion twice and that was a problem. They couldn't have humans sniffing around.

Especially not journalists.

Still, here he was, standing with his hand on his cock, proving that this was much more than a recon check on a roaming human. At least his hand was outside his jeans, though he was pressing the thing so hard he was going to push himself off the fucking balcony.

But, high-five, buddy for keeping away last night.

One damn night.

Every other night for the past two weeks, he'd watched her through the window—he was an assassin after all, so it was no big deal to get up there without being seen or heard.

And...

Fine, and he'd slipped the lock and stepped inside, watching her sleep post her vibrator sessions.

Jesus, one night he'd nearly pulled out his cock and jerked on her creamy skin as he stood, taking in her half-covered body and the purple device lying on the bed. She was still glowing from the orgasm she'd had. Her nightie had been shoved up her body and twisted, revealing a breast that was screaming for his mouth to suckle on, and the curve of her sexy ass dying for his fingers to dig into them and lift her so he could sink inside her.

But he'd stood there, knowing if she rolled over and parted her legs he'd be confronted with the swollen pink folds of flesh, likely still glistening with her need. God, he'd used all his willpower to walk away.

Now here they were again. Oliver licked his lips as he watched Piper direct the vibrator and pull the red cotton of her boxers to the side. He had to force his feet to stay the fuck where they were.

This was not okay.

He had fucked Sage—Piper's damn sister.

Sure, she was Ari's mate, but in no universe was it okay for him to be standing here intruding on this female's privacy or desiring her like this.

And yet, here he was.

In and out the device slid, and in time with it his hand rubbed painfully up and down his cock through the dark denim.

Piper tugged her straps down and a sizeable breast he was now familiar with appeared.

Need it in my mouth.

Need to pleasure her.

She pinched the nipple and let out a moan.

"Who are you?" she cried out.

Wait, what?

Oliver stilled.

He'd heard hints of this before as she slept, but now, she was speaking loud and clear.

Her hand slid down to her pussy and began to circle her clit while the other sped up its plunging of the purple vibrator.

Who? Who was who?

He leaned a hand on the window and groaned, so ready to put his hand inside the denim.

Creak.

The window. Shit.

Snap.

"Oh, my God!" Piper cried as the window burst open, and Oliver nearly crumpled inside the building.

Except, vampire.

He caught himself and leapt, landing on his feet.

Inside.

Her.

Fucking.

Bedroom.

"You!" Piper exclaimed. "It's you!"

Oliver's eyes were still on the purple device half inserted into her pussy. "Shit."

"Shit? Shit!" she repeated. "That's all you have to say?"

Why wasn't she removing the damn vibrator or covering up? Suddenly she did, and his mouth gaped as the device slid out all moist with her juices. Then she used it to point at him.

"Who are you?" she demanded. "Why am I seeing you in my memories?"

She was?

That was why she was pleasuring herself?

She shouldn't damn well remember him.

He'd wiped all memory of him from her. This was the second time she had recalled him when she shouldn't be able to. But it was the first time he'd understood her frantic orgasms were because of him.

He took a step closer.

"Stop," she said, getting to her knees on the bed. "Don't come any nearer."

"I'm not going to hurt you, Piper." Oliver said. "In fact, unfortunately, I want to do quite the opposite."

"How do you know my name?" she asked, and when he groaned, she scuttled up the bed against the headboard. He had so many thoughts on what he'd like to do to her against that surface. "Why do I know you?"

"I'm sorry. You shouldn't remember me."

Had he been human, Oliver would've been concerned about the situation in which he found himself, but he wasn't. This time he'd just wipe her memories fully, and she'd never remember him falling through her window with a giant erection.

Except, why hadn't the memory erasure worked the first two times?

First things first. He was a male and wanted to know more about why she was so aroused.

"You were thinking about me?" he asked when he reached the edge of the bed.

She opened her mouth and closed it again, but the blush on her cheeks told him everything he needed to know.

"You desire me?" A smile reached his lips.

"You need to leave. I have a panic button and I will push it," she growled, and he could hear the fear in her voice.

He shook himself out of his aroused state and planted his hands on his hips, lifting his brows. What was it about this female that got him irritated so quickly?

"Ah, no you don't. You also don't have an alarm system and that window is clearly a huge security risk." He turned, pointing. "Get the damn thing fixed and a system put in tomorrow. It's totally ridiculous that you live here alone in such a vulnerable state."

Her mouth dropped open.

"Says the man standing in my bedroom while I was trying to masturbate."

His cock twitched.

"Because the window broke!" he snapped. "And you weren't *trying*. You were doing a great job."

"Oh, I'm sorry. Were you just wanting to watch?" One brow arched, then she shook her head. "Creep."

Creep?

He was keeping her safe.

Goddamn pain in his ass.

"Listen, princess." Oliver leaned closer. "The reason you're wet right now is because of me. I'd love to do so much more than watch, and you know you want it too, but sorry. No can do. You're off-limits. So, get your damn security sorted and I'll leave you alone."

Her breath hitched.

"Who the hell are you?"

"Your worst nightmare." Then he smirked. "Or is it a wet dream?" He shook his head, smile fading. "Doesn't matter. You shouldn't remember me. So stop fucking remembering."

She frowned.

Oliver crossed his arms, recalling the first time he had taken her memories. She'd found her way back to The Institute and demanded to see Sage, who was in transition to becoming a vampire.

Now she was awake, and it was yet to be decided if she would remain in the human world or they'd announce she was dead.

"What do you mean, stop remembering?" Piper asked, dropping her sex toy and straightening her clothes. "And can you please get out of my house?"

He grinned. "Do you want me to leave or answer your question?" he asked. She twisted her boxers and the glimpse of pussy disappeared.

Shame.

"Both."

"Will you get an alarm put in and get that damn lock fixed?"

"Dude, you're the one who broke into my house and were watching me. Totally creepy," Piper said. "Now, how do I know you? Did you drug me one night or something?"

Oliver stared at her and shook his head.

Suddenly she tried to get off the bed. She nudged at his chest to get him to move but obviously he stayed right where he was. So, she went to climb around him but her feet got trapped in the sheets and her half-naked body came tumbling at him.

Women were always throwing themselves at him, so this wasn't new. He grinned at his own joke, caught her hips, lifted her, and placed her on her feet. Right in front of him.

God damn, she was as pretty as a peach.

Defiant eyes peered up at him then she swallowed. "Thanks."

"You're welcome, darlin'."

More swallowing.

"For a Peeping Tom you're —"

"Hot?"

"Less creepy—"

"Sexy?"

"Than I thought."

He smirked and she let out an annoyed moan, then tried to nudge him away again, but he had her trapped between the bed and his body.

Oliver didn't want to move. He wanted to run his fingers over her shoulders and push those little red straps all the way down.

He grabbed her wrist and those sexy eyes shot back up to meet his. A little hitch in her breath made his cock jerk.

"Don't hurt—"

"I won't," he grated out.

"Or touch me."

"I can't." He really couldn't. Piper Roberts and her sexy body was off-limits.

A tongue swept out to wet her lips and he gritted his teeth.

"Why not?" Her question surprised him, and by the shaking of her head, it appeared she was just as shocked she'd asked it.

Oliver searched for an answer, knowing he should get the fuck on with this and wipe her memory.

"Not that I want you to," she said. "I just wondered what a man like you is doing outside my window, worried about my security and saying he can't touch me. Unless you're here to tell me I'm adopted and actually the princess of some country called Andovia, or something."

"What?"

He frowned.

She shook her head. "Never mind. Can you let go of my hand?"

Crap. He released her wrist and drew a breath.

"No, I didn't drug you." He finally answered her question from minutes ago. For some reason, he didn't want her thinking that about him. No decent vampire male would dream of doing such a thing. In any case, they usually had no reason to. Human women were drawn to vampire power and masculinity, so it wasn't difficult to find a female voluntarily interested in carnal pleasures.

Yet here he was standing inside her bedroom with a hard-on that wouldn't go away, no matter how many times he jerked off, when he could go relieve himself with any number of women in one of the bars down the road.

He needed to do that.

Right fucking now.

Then get back to work.

Piper tried to push past him again, and he gripped her hips.

"Stop," he said, the flesh under his hands burning his.

Fuck.

Her gaze flew up to his, and he squeezed his eyes shut for a long moment. When he opened them, desire was pouring from her crystal blue eyes.

"Who are you, with all your southern accent and muscles and things?"

"Shit. Stop looking at me like that." His hands gripped her hips tighter.

"Tell me who you are."

Her lips. If he could just…

"Who are you?" Piper leaned closer.

Just one taste.

Her lips parted and her pink tongue slipped out, wetting them. Oliver pulled her against his body, a growl in the depths of his throat as he lowered toward her.

One kiss. One taste.

Oli. You heading back soon?

Fucking fuck.

He took a step back and wiped a hand over his face.

"Oh great. A cock-teasing Peeping Tom. Just my goddamn luck." Piper threw her hands up in the air.

Ben, fuck. Remind me to knee you in the gonads when I see you.

Bad timing? He heard the humor in his friend's voice.
Something like that. I'll be back in five.

Now he had to clean up this fucking mess he had literally fallen into. If he was going to prove himself to Ari, he needed to get his head out of his ass—and this female's pussy—and back on the job.

He wasn't making the same mistake he had when he was younger.

Not this time.

Ari might not be his father, but he was a father figure of sorts and had believed in him when no one else had.

He wasn't fucking it up.

Not for pussy.

Not again.

"Come here, female." Oliver reached for the back of her head.

"Female? What—"

He slammed his lips hard down on hers and fire flared between them. *Now, stop fucking remembering me, then we can both get back to our lives.*

Then, yet again, he wiped her damn memories.

CHAPTER FOUR

Oliver teleported back to his room in The Institute mansion and let out a curse.
Fuck.
He threw back his head and ran his hand through his hair.
What a fuckup.
Before he'd teleported away, he'd done a patch job on the window lock. Thank God the glass hadn't broken.
Piper had climbed back into bed and curled up, as he'd instructed her to. He'd stood over her for a moment taking in her dark long hair fanned out over her pillows, and now she wasn't able to speak, her beautiful face reflected peace. She nearly looked like a well-mannered member of society.
He knew differently.
She was a pain in the ass.
There was no way he could focus on work until he did something about the rod in his pants, so he ripped off his clothes and stepped into the shower in his bathroom. Soaping up his body, he closed his eyes and recalled the moments her legs widened, and she'd slipped the vibrator beneath her boxer shorts.
Oliver palmed his cock and slid his hand up and down tightly.

Skillfully, Piper had circled her purple device through her moisture and moaned into the night air. Then he'd heard her turn up the speed.

He cupped his balls and groaned, slamming his other hand on the shower wall.

Bit by bit she'd pressed it inside and her body had arched into it, eager for more. Eager for him.

That was when he'd fallen inside.

Time to change the ending. At least in his head.

He imagined himself flying over to her bed and ripping off the little red shorts. She would gasp as he tied her wrists and kept them up and away so he could taste her as he pleased.

Making his way down her body, his mouth suckling her nipples, she would cry out. Then his hands would spread her wider, his breath hot at her core as she begged for his mouth.

Fuck.

Jerk.

He was close.

He needed to see the rest. To see her come. His tongue would lengthen to taste her wet, glistening pussy as her hips lifted.

And... he came all over his hand.

Oliver groaned almost painfully as he stroked the last of it out. Every goddamn day he'd been doing this.

It had to end.

Thinking about Ari's mate's sister was not going to end well. Piper was a distraction, and they had a lot going on right now.

He wasn't going to disappoint Ari.

"You are a disappointment, boy." Oliver recalled the moment he heard those words from his father. They were some of the last.

He wouldn't make that mistake again.

Not for a female.

Not one that wasn't his mate, and neither Piper nor Angela Glass were his mate. Angela had been nothing more than a neighbor. Her husband had worked with his father. Most of the humans in the hood thought Oliver was his father's brother, visiting from New York because of the age. He was in his early twenties by that point and his father a mature vampire. None of them ever looked older than thirty so most just told humans they were siblings.

It was the year 1959, and their street looked like something out of Pleasantville. His father worked the nightshift with Angela's husband, Bobby, at the Ford manufacturing plant.

They often got together for barbeques and after one fourth of July party it had been clear that Angela was not happy in her marriage. Her eyes on Oli's biceps was one big giveaway but when her gaze had drifted south, he'd been sure.

Their eyes had met, and then she'd bitten her lip.

It hadn't taken much from there.

His father had gone to work and his mother to a book club group, when a quiet knock on the door had interrupted him reading a book. When he opened the door and saw her standing on the doorstep in a pretty Sunday-type dress, neither of them had said a word. He'd just opened the door wider, and she'd come inside.

"You shouldn't be here, Angela, darlin'," Oliver had said.

"I know."

He'd stepped forward, frowning, and lifted her arm. The short-sleeved dress had revealed the bruising he'd spotted on her before. "He do this to you?"

She nodded.

Oliver had shaken his head, furious.

"You need to leave him." Even he knew it wasn't that simple.

"Please, I just want—"

"I know what you want."

Fast-forward thirty minutes and she was lying underneath him, panting as she came down from her second orgasm.

Twelve hours later and his father was yelling at him.

"She's a married woman. To Bobby, for God's sake. What were you thinking? I'm ashamed to call you my son."

"He's fucking *beating* her," Oliver had yelled back.

"So, you fuck her?" his father had retorted. "How is that going to help her? So selfish."

"What in the Sam Hill is going on here? Please, both of you. Stop." His mother had tried to break up the fight.

"You aren't human. She's not your mate. You cannot disappear with her and solve all her problems." His father continued with his judgments.

"Fine. I'll kill the bastard," Oliver said.

"Jesus F. Christ." His father had looked at his mother. "Can you hear this kid? Who raised him?"

Oliver had shaken his head. "I am not a goddamn kid. I am twenty-three years old."

"A baby vamp."

His fangs had crept out and his father had shaken his head.

"You're a disappointment, Oliver. A man does not fuck around with another man's wife," he'd said. "I'm going to bed."

A man doesn't lift a hand to a female. That had been his last thought as his father walked away.

That night, he'd woken to the sound of his mother wailing. The cops were on the doorstep. His father had been the victim of a gunshot wound, right in the goddamn heart. Anywhere else and he would have healed himself.

Not in the heart. Knife, sword, bullet. It was all the same.

Damage that organ and a vampire was dead.

He'd never gotten the opportunity to prove to his father that he was a good male.

A worthy male.

He'd stayed to take care of his mother, but within two years she had taken her life, as mates did.

They couldn't survive long without the other.

Oliver had packed up and moved to Las Vegas, where he'd filled his life with drinking, fucking, gambling, and fighting.

He'd even tried to numb the pain with human drugs, but they did nothing but make him feel nauseous. Still, the drugs had connected him with some bad-ass guys and even hotter women.

The city was the perfect place for a vampire. During the day while he slept, most people thought he was sleeping off the effects of the wild nights.

And they weren't wrong.

Still, his life was going nowhere.

He fought drunken idiots working as a bouncer at the Golden Nugget casino and sunk his cock into fast women. The gig was filling his pockets nicely but doing nothing to prove he was any better than his father had said he was.

Until Ari.

Ari Moretti had turned up one day, dressed top to toe in Pierre Cardin that Oliver knew cost more than he'd make in a year.

He'd instantly recognized him as a vampire and a powerful one. The male had gone about his business, checking into the hotel, and attending meetings. For two nights, he watched the powerful vampire meet with influential casino bosses and other dangerous people.

And he knew the male was watching him back.

One night he'd been out on the strip just hanging with some guys, keeping an eye on a group of local girls—who were trashed—when some out-of-state cars had rolled in.

His body had stiffened, sensing something instinctively, and he'd nudged his pal.

They both turned as Ari and two of the local mob bosses walked out of the casino. Suddenly he'd heard the windows in the vehicles being wound down and the slide of gun barrels being pulled back.

Semi's.

Think fast.

Take out the gunman or save the people around him?

His eyes darted to Ari's, and the male nodded at him and then the cars.

Got it.

Oliver had turned back to the still-moving vehicles and found the gunmen.

Plural.

He pushed his pal to the ground and moved. Fucking fast. He couldn't stop the vehicles or get the humans, but he could get to the metal.

In one, two and three, he whipped the weapons out of their hands and sped down the alleyway, dropping them into the dumpster.

Job done.

Everyone around him was confused and stunned. He'd put on the same act and played along.

Later that night, Ari had sought him out and drew him into the shadows. "Not many males can move like that."

Oliver had smirked, enjoying the praise.

"Oh great, another fucking smart-ass." Ari had rolled his eyes.

Oli's eyes had narrowed. "Excuse me?"

"I have a proposal for you," Ari had said, ignoring the question. "But you'll need to clean your act right up. I can change your life if you want it."

Fortunately, he'd been smart enough to do just that.

Now he'd been given the incredible opportunity to not just be an assassin at The Institute, but the head assassin. A job he'd been promoted to because Ben had resigned.

The title was not yet earned, but Oliver was determined to prove himself.

And he would.

Piper and her sweet, damn pussy needed to just get out of his goddamn mind. He wasn't going to fuck this up. He would prove to Ari he was worthy of this job if it was the last thing he ever did.

And yeah, fucking Ari's sister-in-law was definitely not on his to-do list.

CHAPTER FIVE

Oliver walked down the hallway and slowed when he saw Ari step out of his quarters.

"Hey."

"Oli," Ari replied.

"How is she?" Oli asked, referring to the newest vampire on the block. Sage.

Ari nodded and a small smile formed on his lips. "Good. I'm forgiven."

Oliver slapped him on the back. "I'm happy. For you and Sage. So, will y'all be joining us tonight?"

Ari began to walk off. "Later. Continue with the plan and I'll drop by in a few hours."

Oliver nodded and carried on down to the Operations Office where he knew the team were already working away. He pressed his thumb on the panel and the door opened to a bunch of noise.

"No, fuck, go back," Jason said, punching his finger on the screen. He was one of the senior assassins.

Oliver shut the door and plunged his hands in his pockets, taking in the scene around him. "What's going on?"

"We've got some footage of Callan," Jason said.

"No, we fucking haven't. It's just some homeless guy." Darren, the head tech, spoke. "We don't even know what he looks like. Not really."

Sage had helped them do a rough sketch the night before she'd gone in, but at that point, she'd only seen Callan once, so it was useless as fuck.

Jason was obsessed with finding the guy.

The Moretti's had held back on putting anything out on *VampNet* because the last thing anyone wanted was an entire population of vampires freaking out about humans being able to overpower them.

While it appeared they could, Ari and his team didn't yet know how.

It was a fine line between warning people and scaring them.

Scared people did stupid things.

"Visual aside, what drew your attention?" he asked Jason as the door opened behind him.

In walked three large vampires: Ben, now a senior lieutenant commander—or SLC—Craig, commander, and Brayden Moretti, captain of the royal army. Brayden was also the Moretti prince. His family was collaborating with The Institute in bringing down the pharmaceutical company who had kidnapped and experimented on vampires.

They all did the head-tilt-hello thing, then found sitting and leaning places.

"No, Ari?" Brayden asked.

"He'll join us in a few hours. He's with Sage."

"No details, thanks," Craig said. "I'm back on rations."

"It's been six hours," Brayden said, rolling his eyes.

It was the first time in three weeks they were grouping again after the Moretti's had returned to the royal castle in Maine. The three senior vampires had arrived back overnight.

"That's three hundred and sixty minutes, my friend," Craig replied, shrugging and putting his feet up on a spare chair.

Oliver grinned at Ben, who was shaking his head.

"Dude, you wait. I give you twenty-four hours before you're having video sex with Anna." Craig pointed at him.

"Who said I haven't already?" Ben shrugged.

Darren snorted.

"What's up, Jace?" Ben asked, picking up on the guy's angst. He'd only recently resigned from the head assassin position, so it didn't surprise Oliver his friend was still in tune with the team.

"We were just getting to that," Oliver said.

"Sorry, you're in charge." Ben waved his hand.

"Okay, if you two are finished kissing and shit, can we get focused?" Craig asked, leaning back in his chair.

"Feeling left out?" Ben asked, and landed on his ass when Craig kicked the chair out from under him.

Brayden grinned and gave Oli a nod—a clear direction to carry on and ignore the two idiots.

"Play the footage again, Darren," Oliver instructed. "Jason thinks this might be Callan, but I've not seen the video yet."

Craig and Ben suddenly became all business and leaned forward. The video played, and they all watched as a large man climbed out of the water and up the embankment of Lake Washington near Chism Beach Park.

"I mean, it might be fifty degrees out there right now, but it's hardly swimming weather. Even for a vampire." Jason shrugged.

"Could be a homeless guy," Craig said.

"Or it's Callan," Jason said.

"It's been two weeks. He's probably miles away by now," Brayden said.

"Or he could be hiding nearby... look, fuck, I don't know. I just want to find the poor bastard." Jason shook his head.

Craig glanced at Oliver, and he realized the commander had picked up on Jason's stress. He appreciated the senior vampire had directed his concern to Oli as head assassin.

What had happened to those vampires was weighing heavily on all of them. It was their job as enforcers to stop this. The situation with Callan was even harder. The guy had been held prisoner for over six months, from what they'd been able to ascertain.

He made his way around the room and slapped Jason on the back.

"We may or may not find him." Oliver sat at the end of the table. "We have no idea what condition he was in after he left Sage. He was strong enough to get them both out and then, depending on what the fuckers did to him, he may have made it or not."

The silence in the room was thick.

"Mother fuckers," Craig muttered.

"Oliver is right," Brayden finally said. He'd been wondering if the prince would speak up on the topic. "I'll speak to the king again about whether we put anything on *Vamp-Net*, but we still think the risk high, versus the chance of us gaining anything."

The last thing they wanted to do was panic the entire race with this information. Less was more sometimes, and they had to weigh the pros against the cons.

"Bri said without a surname or a decent photo, it's unlikely anyone will engage with a post," Craig said, referring to his mate, Brianna, who was now leading communications and public relations for the Moretti royal family.

"She's right. The noise online when the vampires started going missing a few months ago was enough to rattle people's cages. We really have nothing to go on. It's like looking for a needle in a haystack," Darren said.

Oliver stared at the screen, which played the same reel on repeat. Darren was right. They were throwing darts in the dark right now.

Travis, the team manager, walked in munching on an apple. "What's up?"

"When do Alex, Logan and Elijah return?" Oliver asked.

The other senior assassins were out on jobs. Ari had given the go-ahead to pick up other client work while they were regrouping after they had successfully—or unsuccessfully, depending on how you looked at it—freed Callan from BioZen.

"Tomorrow. Next day at the latest." Travis plonked down on a seat.

Oliver glanced at the prince and quickly at Craig. It might be his show while Ari was otherwise detained, but Brayden was the most senior person present, and this was a joint effort. Plus, no matter how often they'd seen them recently, the damn prince was alpha as fuck and pretty intimidating for any vampire no matter how badass.

"How about we go through the intel we got while Sage was inside BioZen, then we can divide and conquer," Oliver said.

"Do it," Craig agreed, as Brayden nodded.

"Why don't I head out to Chism Beach and take a look around? See what I find? Just so we can be sure," Ben offered.

Oliver glanced at Jason, then nodded.

"Okay. The three of us will go after this." Oliver nodded at Darren. "Start from the top."

"Oh, joy," the tech manager said.

CHAPTER SIX

Piper parked her car in the underground carpark and stepped into the elevator. She glanced at her phone, then put it in her pocket. Then pulled it out again.
What was she looking for again?
She rubbed her forehead.
What the hell did I drink last night?
She felt like she had a hangover, but not like a hangover. It was as if she was walking around in a fog. It was the third time she'd felt like this recently. Maybe she needed to go to the doctor.
"Hey," she said to a few colleagues as everyone made their way to their desks with coffees and miserable-looking faces.
Because, Monday.
Sitting down at her desk she mumbled her own hello to her neighbors.
"Hard weekend?" Jeremy asked, smirking.
Was it?
"Ahh," she began, then frowned.
"Jesus, girl, was it that good?" Then he frowned. "Or bad?"

Despite herself, Piper grinned. "Why does your voice go twice as camp when you even *think* about sex?"

Jeremy tilted his head. "Hmm, it's the penis factor."

"I know I'm going to regret asking this, but what is the penis factor?"

"It's like when you see that handbag you really want on sale."

Piper blinked. "I'm lost."

"I know, honey."

Jesus.

She couldn't handle Jeremy on a Monday morning. Or Wednesday afternoon.

And where the hell was Kara?

"Okay, well no, I didn't have a hard night. I guess I just had a bad sleep. It's a double-coffee morning." She fired up her laptop.

"Speaking of... double caramel latte," Kara said, plonking the reusable coffee cup in front of her.

"Oh, thank God." Piper hugged it like it was life.

Because in truth, it was.

Kara sat down at her desk and frowned. "You okay, Pips?"

Piper nodded.

The photo on her desk caught her attention, which was weird because it was the same one she'd stared at for two years. It was of her and Sage at a college football game, grinning like idiots. It was taken just weeks after she started, and they were both so happy to be rooming together at Brown.

Being born twelve months apart meant her last year in high school had been spent separated from Sage. She'd been a popular student and Kara had been there, but she hated being so far away from her sister.

They were polar opposites—Sage the nerdy science student and Piper the cheerleader—and yet, at the time, she'd thought nothing and no one could get between them.

Sage.

That's right. Where the hell was her sister? Piper sent off another text and scrolled through those she'd already sent.

Fifteen days' worth.

Even Sage wouldn't ignore her for that long.

"Still no word?" Kara asked, glancing at the photo she'd been staring at.

Piper shook her head.

"I mean, I know she hasn't fully forgiven me, but she's never ignored me for two whole weeks. Something's wrong."

Kara nodded slowly. "She hasn't posted on socials either."

"I know, right?"

"She hasn't?" Jeremy asked, his voice way too pitchy. "You need to call the police."

"But your mom said she knew where she was, right?" Kara asked.

"Kind of. She's super-vague in her answers," Piper answered, opening her emails. "I'll call her again at lunchtime. She was supposed to be home yesterday."

"That's not like her," Kara said, and Piper nodded slowly.

It was very weird.

She'd thought many times she got her powers of interrogation from her mother. That woman asked more questions than the FBI.

A few hours later she pressed call and when her mother answered, she dived straight into it.

"Have you heard from Sage?"

"She's in the tropics with Ari, darling," her mother replied.

Right. She knew that.

Didn't she?

"Has she messaged you?"

"No. Well, yes. I'm not sure. But she's fine. She'll be back soon."

Piper narrowed her eyes. Her mother was never that relaxed about hearing from either of her daughters. Something wasn't right.

"Which island is she staying on?"

"Not sure, darling. Now, are you coming for dinner one night this week?"

"Mom!" Piper snapped. "Where is Sage?"

"I told you. Chicken, or would you rather have fish? I can never keep up with what you girls will eat. Are you doing gluten or dairy-free this month?"

Piper shared a look with Kara, who was listening to the conversation on speaker. They were sitting across the road in the park catching some of the midday sunshine.

Weird, Kara mouthed.

I know, she mouthed back.

Something wasn't right and she was going to get to the bottom of it.

"Gluten-free. I'll let you know which night I can come. Gotta go."

"Bye darling," her mom said.

"Okay, which aliens abducted your mother?" Kara asked, and bit into her sandwich. "That's downright creepy."

"I told you about her boyfriend, right?"

Kara nodded. "The big hot guy?"

"Yes. I think he's got something to do with all this." Piper ignored her lunch. She had lost her appetite. "I don't know how, but I'm going to find out."

"Like he's kidnapped her?"

Piper shrugged. "She's been weird since she met him. Faking a migraine, hanging up on me—okay, fine, maybe that's not so unusual—but she quit her job, which she loved. And now disappearing to the islands when she's more into skiing."

"I mean, people can decide to like a tropical island holiday suddenly. That's not really grounds for a police investigation," Kara said. "Don't glare at me. I don't want you getting into a confrontation with the police again."

"That was one time."

Kara stared at her.

"Fine, two... three times. But that's not what we're focusing on right now."

Kara snorted.

"My point is... okay, this is going to sound weird, but every time I focus on her boyfriend I get a piercing headache, right here." She pointed to her temple.

"So this Ari guy is causing headaches in both you and Sage? I'm not following."

Piper let out a sigh. "Plus, I've been having dreams about a friend of his. Sexual. I think it's his friend. God, honestly, I feel like I'm going insane."

"Sexy dreams about some hottie doesn't sound horrible to me, nor does it sound insane. Girl, maybe you just need to shag this guy?"

Piper lowered her head into her hands. "I don't know who he is."

When her friend didn't respond, she tilted her head and opened one eye to look at her. Kara was staring at her, confused. "Trust me, I have no idea either. It's like he's haunting me."

"I'm not sure whether that's completely romantic or creepy," Kara said. "Maybe you should speak to a doctor?"

Great, now her best friend thought she was insane.

After work, Piper drove to Sage's house and parked outside. She sat in her car for over ten minutes, just watching. The sun began to set and when she was sure her sister or her roommate, Tony, wasn't home, she got out and crossed the road.

Reaching up on the top of the door, she felt for the hole and the sticky tack.

Bingo.

Same as she'd done in college.

Piper pulled the key out and let herself in.

Whoa, the place was spotless. Sage wasn't a messy person, but it looked like the place was ready for an open home. She continued walking through and found Tony's room empty.

When had he moved out?

Sage's room looked odd. It was too tidy and looked unlived in, even for someone on holiday.

Piper opened the wardrobe doors and found the space completely bare.

What the hell?

She ripped open a few drawers and they were also empty. Aside from a few random t-shirts and things, there were no personal belongings anywhere in her sister's room.

Piper stood looking around the room, her brain whirling.

Think.

Think.

Think.

She moved to the bed and reached down, slightly lifting the mattress.

Gotcha.

She sat on the bed and opened her sister's diary.

Twenty minutes later Piper stared, open-mouthed, at her sister's bedroom wall.

Holy shit. *Two* men?

Sage had a threesome.

With Ari and—she glanced back at the diary—no name was given for the second man.

Ari? An image of a man flashed before her.

"Argh." A piercing pain sliced through her head. She pressed her hand against her eyes. "Shit."

She flicked back a few more weeks and kept reading.

Pain.

So much pain.

"Fuck it." She couldn't focus with the pain. Piper tucked the diary under her arm and made her way down to the car. She needed to get home, if she was getting a migraine, to take some drugs. She hadn't had one in years, but this felt like a doozy.

The pain seemed to be subsiding by the time she walked in her front door, but she knew if she took the drugs now it was less likely to get any worse. She took off her makeup and got ready for bed, then grabbed her pills and a large glass of water.

Tucked up under her covers, she swallowed down the meds and then began to scroll through Sage's diary.

*Date with Ari…*blah blah.

Promotion at work… hope I get it…

Had lunch with Carl… God, how many guys did her sister have in her life?

She flipped a few more pages, going back a number of weeks, and felt the drugs begin to kick in. She slid down the bed further and turned onto her side.

Applied for the promotion… got an interview. Angry at Piper… yeah, yeah. Although it made her sad to read, she tried to skip past it. Piper hated that she was invading her sister's privacy, but Sage was missing. There was no denying it after Piper had seen her apartment.

Her eyes begin to droop.

Overheard scientists talking about vampires. They're real. I'm sure of it.

What the hell?

Vampires… Her eyes closed even as her brain fought to process what she'd just read.

CHAPTER SEVEN

"So, how's mated life?" Oliver asked as they walked down an overgrown path to the waterline where the potential sighting of Callan had been.

"It's good." Ben grinned. "Amazing."

"How long are you staying in Seattle?"

Ben shrugged. "Not sure. I guess as long as necessary, but I know Craig and Bray won't want to stay away from their mates for long. So we'll see."

Oliver glanced at his longtime friend. "Can't imagine feeling hamstrung like that. Don't you hate it?"

Ben let out a small laugh. "Do you hate desiring sex?"

"No."

"But you need sex."

Oliver shrugged. "Sure, but I can sort that out myself if I'm hankering for some action."

"It's not the same though, right?"

"I don't know, man. Y'all look like you're losing your goddamn minds without your mates." He laughed.

Ben rubbed his face. "It's been nearly two days without Anna and the first time we've been apart. Ask me again in three days."

"Yeah, see. Fuck that."

"One day you'll understand. There's no way I can explain it. She's literally as important as the air I breathe."

Wow.

Oliver didn't know if that sounded romantic as fuck or completely terrifying.

Oli.

Jason? You joining us?

Job just came in. Ari's sending me to NY. You need another body there?

No. Ben and I can take this.

"It's just us. Like the good old days." Oli grinned.

"You good being the head now?" Ben asked, referring to his promotion to head assassin.

"Hell yes. I was pretty honored when Ari offered it to me. And shocked." He kicked at some black cloth on the ground. They both stopped and stared at it for a long moment, assessing. Then moved on.

No words were needed. They'd worked together for a long time and knew how the other thought and functioned. It had taken zero-point-five seconds to rule out the cloth as an object of interest.

"Why? You were the obvious choice."

"Yeah?" Oliver asked, trying not to sound like an insecure dick.

"I mean, you're not as awesome as me, but you'll do." Ben playfully dodged the right hander Oliver aimed at his gut. "Dude."

Oliver laughed.

"Well, I intend to show Ari he made the right decision." Ben began to say something, but Oliver interrupted him. "Check this out."

Using a stick, he lifted a large white t-shirt from the ground. They both knew it was a stab in the dark. Callan had been wearing one similar when he left BioZen, and it was about his size, but it was hardly solid evidence. It wasn't like they had his DNA to match.

About an hour later, Ben stopped.

"Let's wrap this up and go for a beer," he said, shaking his head. "I don't think we're going to find anything else. If he came through here, he's long gone."

Maybe.

They returned to the mansion around one in the morning for the next meeting. When they walked into the room, both Ari and Sage were there.

"Hey, darlin'." He smiled at her.

"Hey, Oli," she replied, with the sweetest blush. Sage had stayed in Ari's quarters for the past two weeks as she adjusted to being a vampire and forgave him for taking her humanity. Oli had seen her once or twice when she'd done the sketch for them, but it had been brief. She looked well. Bright-eyed and glowing as all new vampires were.

"It's amazing, right?" he asked.

She shrugged and nodded.

"Too soon, Oli," Ari said, his voice the dark protective one he used whenever it came to his mate.

Oli winked at her and took a seat.

"Do that again and you lose the eye." Ari growled.

Oliver stifled a smile.

"This is Ben. He used to do my job and now works for the Moretti's," Oliver said, introducing them as the others all entered the room. "And you know Brayden and Craig."

"Sage," Brayden said, walking over to her. "Welcome to the family. How do you feel?"

Oh, right.

Sage was a Moretti vampire now. Not just because she was Ari's mate, but because they all were.

"Good. Weird," she said.

"When you're feeling ready, I'd love you to come to *Casa Moretti* in Maine and learn more." The prince added, his Italian accent roaring to life as he spoke his native tongue. "Willow would love to see you."

"And Bri," Craig said, referring to his beautiful red-headed mate that nearly every male in the race was in love with.

Not that anyone told the enormous vampire. That would be a death wish.

"We'll visit soon," Ari said, reaching out his hand and squeezing Sage with an affectionate smile. "Now, I have asked Sage to join us so we can go through her transcripts and see what we might have missed. We need a lead and right now we have zip."

Muttered *yups* and *yeah, fuck's,* filled the room.

"I'll do my best," Sage said.

"Pull them up on the screen," Oliver said, glancing at Darren who was in his usual spot.

As they went through, page by page, reading the transcripts of the conversations that took place while Sage was inside BioZen and in the experimental laboratories, Craig glanced up. "Do you have any friends still working there?"

"We haven't decided if Sage will keep her human life, or we'll declare her deceased and all that," Ari said.

"Like Bri did," Craig said nodding. "It's complicated. But if this is the only option available, we should consider it seriously. This is the protection of the race we're talking about."

Ari drew in a slow, even breath, and the air sizzled around him. Oliver watched all the powerful vampires navigate their dominance. In any normal circumstances, things would be more challenging, but they were all working hard to keep their alpha selves in check for the greater good.

For the good of the vampire race.

"Let's table it as an option," Ari said, and left it at that.

Craig nodded, but shot Brayden a look. The prince didn't respond.

They all knew how important this was. BioZen were experimenting on vampires for God knows what reason, but one thing they all knew—it wasn't fucking good.

They'd held Callan for what appeared to be nearly half a year. The data and research BioZen would have obtained during that time was pretty thorough. Sage had only seen a very small sample of the data when she was promoted into the program and then, when she helped him escape, the vampire had fled.

Oliver didn't blame him. He'd been tortured and used as a lab rat without mercy.

Sage had been unable to stomach what they were doing and shocked at the discovery that vampires were real—and that she was sleeping with one.

Well, technically two, if she counted Oli as well, but he wasn't sure she did. Not openly.

He looked up and Ari was watching him.

Shit.

Don't think about Sage.

Don't think about Piper.

Except he *was* thinking about Piper. He wanted to know if she'd fixed that window.

Do not go back.

Darren continued reading out the transcripts until suddenly, Sage let out a little noise. "That. Go back."

Darren scrolled up the page.

"There."

They all read it. Once. Twice.

"Good morning, everybody. Sorry to rush you, but we need to get the induction started as I'm flying out this afternoon," Dr. Phillips said. *"This is Brian. He's the lead*

scientist in the Callan lab. We'll be showing you around this morning. Please follow all his instructions."

"We'll need you all in PPE gear after you've scrubbed."

Oliver turned to Sage, wondering what she was seeing that they didn't.

"Sage?" Ari finally asked.

The new vampire was chewing her lip. "Could be nothing. It's just something I thought was odd at the time and then with everything that happened, I forgot about it."

"No idea is stupid in this room," Ben said. "Just tell us what you're thinking."

"Debatable," Craig said. Ben gave him the bird.

"Ignore the incredible hulk," Ben said. "Go ahead."

"Well, Dr. Phillips never travels. I don't know him well, but he's always at work. You know the guy who never goes home and never takes holidays?"

A bunch of heads nodded.

"So, where was he going?" Craig asked, tapping his pen on his enormous shoe which was resting on his knee.

Sage shrugged.

"No idea. I think we should look into it. He heads up that department, so unless he's going to Disneyland or the Bahamas, I think it could give us a lead," Sage said.

"Good work, baby," Ari said. "I want every fucking airport and airfield checked, and all air traffic control conversations scanned over that period."

"On it," Darren said.

"And fast. Get your entire team on this now," Ari added.

He watched Darren pull up his message app and begin to instruct his team.

Brayden stepped away from the wall he'd been leaning on, and Craig glanced at him. The two were as in-sync as Oli was with Ben. "Get our team doing the same. More eyes and ears, and all that."

Craig pulled out his phone.

Oliver looked over at Ari, waiting on his instructions. "Prepare a team to move at any moment. When we get a location, I want wheels up in thirty," Ari said.

"Got it." Oliver nodded, glancing around the room which was empty of senior assassins, except for Travis who was more desk-bound these days. "Can we call anyone back?"

Travis frowned and tapped his tablet. "Alex in... twenty hours. Elijah in twenty-five."

"Ben, you up—" Craig started.

"I'm in." The former vampire assassin answered before he could finish. "I need some action."

"Yeah, well, none of us are getting any action right now. Again." Craig groaned.

"That's why it pays to be single," Oliver said, and realized he totally had the wrong audience as multiple sets of eyes glared at him.

"True that," Travis nodded, without lifting his head from his tablet.

Thank you, Travis.

Darren shot him a smirk.

Ari stood, pulling Sage's chair out for her. "Keep me posted. We're going for a drive."

Oliver checked his watch. It was four in the morning.

"Meet you in the training room in two hours. I have something I need to do," Oliver told Ben, then found himself a short time later back on a certain female's balcony.

CHAPTER EIGHT

"Do I look different to you?" Sage asked Ari. "Now I'm a vampire."

This felt like a trick question. One of those, *does my ass look big in these jeans,* type of question. Ari wasn't going to fall for it. He was old and wise, and God help him, he hoped those traits would serve him well in this relationship. Ari was confident of pleasing women in every physical way, but on a day-to-day basis when it came to an actual romantic partnership, he had zero experience.

Sage was his mate, but that didn't mean he'd be any good at this stuff.

"No," he said, going to her and dropping a kiss on her lips. "You were a beautiful human, and you're still beautiful now."

"Thanks, Romeo. What I mean is, has my body changed or my eyes? I see things differently now, so everything is enhanced. My skin looks flawless to me. Is it?"

Ah, that.

"You're right. Your body is still undergoing minor changes as it heals and pushes out disease and toxins which humans are unable to do. Any impurities will disappear and often that shows in the skin. So yes, you are enhancing. Your muscles will become stronger and more defined, as will your tastebuds and sight."

"My eyesight, hearing and taste are already different. It's so…" Sage's voice faded. "Never mind."

Ari pressed his lips together. He knew what was going on and didn't want Sage to feel guilty. She was a scientist, and it was natural for her to be curious and want to understand more. He'd never had an issue with that—it was what she might choose when she discovered what BioZen were doing that had been his greatest fear.

"*Mia, stellina*, you can study vampires if it is what you choose. There is nothing to be ashamed about. Perhaps it would be wise for us to take the lead on that piece of work, and not humans."

Sage chewed her lip. "I don't know. It feels wrong after what I saw."

Ari smiled down at her. God, he loved her. How could he have ever questioned her morals and ethics? To be fair he'd only just met her, but it still seemed unthinkable now that she would partake in any experiments on anyone without their permission.

"You have forever to reconsider."

She pulled out of his arms and walked to the fridge taking out a flask of plasma, then poured herself a small glass. Ari slipped his hands into his pockets and watched her. A small smile hit his lips as she grimaced.

"This, I don't know if I can get used to." She shivered and rinsed the glass. "I crave it, and yet it makes me feel sick knowing what it is."

Ari walked to the table and sat. "I felt the same. In the early days."

"You did?"

He nodded.

"Except Gio and I had to hunt for blood. We didn't get nice little packets of it delivered to our doorstep." He winked.

"Hunt. So, kill?"

"Yes," he laughed. "That is what the word means."

"Humans?"

He didn't want to go into detail and freak her out, but she was his mate and he'd waited a lifetime to share his life with someone.

"Yes. Sometimes. Mostly animals," he replied. "Those first few weeks and months were very confusing for us as we came to terms with what we were and how we could survive. There was no handbook. When the first craving for blood arrived, we took human lives, unable to control or understand what was happening."

"How horrible."

Yes, it had been terrifying, confusing and they had felt like outcasts. Like animals.

"The guilt was terrible but because we had each other to talk to, we soon worked out that animal blood was just as sufficient. And over time we learned that plasma was richer in minerals. We could hunt and consume less."

Sage sat down next to him, and they turned to one another. "I'm glad I don't have to hunt."

He took her chin. "You should learn. If our lives suddenly changed for whatever reason, it is a good skill to have."

"No, Ari."

"One step at a time, darlin'. For now, we need to decide if you should remain in contact with your family and friends, or we tell them you are deceased."

It had been just over two weeks since he had changed her. Her family would be expecting her back from their fake holiday and time was running out for a decision.

Not that he couldn't buy them more time, but he'd seen enough humans changed to know this part of the process was important for them to move on with their lives.

"It will be temporary. Ten. Fifteen years at most. You won't age and questions will begin to be asked, so eventually it will have to happen. Or you can decide to do it now."

Sage nodded, and her eyes darted around the room, replicating the obviously busy state of her mind.

He appreciated it was a huge decision.

"It's not like they can come here for Sunday dinner," Sage said. "Perhaps it would be best if I died."

Ari watched her for a long moment.

"We can control things, *mia stellina*. I can plant memories of a big house we live in and let them think they've been recently."

More chewing of the lip.

"Can we still get married?"

"Of course." He took her hand and lifted it to his lips. "I know what it is to be human. To want those things, and I promised you I would give you everything."

"So we can have a wedding and invite my parents and sister."

"Yes. If that is what you desire." Ari nodded.

Sage's face lit up. "It is."

"Then that's what we will do. I'm sure a few of the females in our extended family would love a human wedding event." Ari laughed.

Sage grinned and nodded.

"I guess I better propose to you one day, then," Ari said, smirking.

"We're mated," Sage said, frowning.

"I know. But I am going to do it just as if we are humans. So, come with me." Ari rose from his seat.

Sage let out a nervous laugh. "Where?"

Had he been prepared for this conversation? Yes.

Was he nervous? Also, yes.

As ridiculous as that sounded. He hadn't been human for over fifteen hundred years and yet… he was suffering from nerves.

"What are we doing?" Sage giggled.

Ari pulled her close, wrapping his arms around her lower back, and whispered. "Close your eyes."

She did and he teleported them right to the top of the Space Needle in downtown Seattle.

"Oh, my God!" she gasped, as the wind flapped her hair around. "Ari."

He dropped to one knee, keeping a hold of one of her hands, and gazed up at his one true mate.

"Sage, *mia stellina*." He squeezed her hand to capture her attention, as her eyes were darting all around.

"Ari, we are going to die up here."

He laughed. "Vampires, remember?"

"Still," she said, stepping closer to him.

"I've got you, baby." He waited until she finally dropped her gaze and felt her connect with him. Out of his pocket he pulled a gold ring with a five-carat oval diamond and baguettes on the side.

At least, that was how the man in the jewelry shop had explained the design.

"Holy shit," she exclaimed, her free hand flying to her mouth.

"Sage Roberts, will you be my wife? My mate, my partner for all the rest of the days we're alive?" Ari asked, and felt his entire body buzz with the intensity of the moment.

He had dreamed of this for so damn long.

Soooo fucking long.

"Oh, Ari." Sage threw herself into his arms. He caught her with an *oomph* and wrapped his arms around her.

"You have to say yes, sweetheart. That's the next bit."

She pulled back and began nodding with a stupid grin on her face.

"Say it, for God's sake, woman."

"Yesyesyesyesyesyesyes."

"Thank fuck." He pushed the ring onto her finger.

Sage held out her hand and gaped at the ring for a few seconds, then her eyes returned to his. "Kiss me and get me the hell off of this thing."

Ari burst out laughing, then pulled her into his arms, kissing the hell out of her, before teleporting them back to the mansion. This time he chose the garden, where the night was calm and the sky was full of stars.

Sage patted down her hair and then stared at her ring some more. "It's so beautiful. And huge."

"You deserve everything."

"I *have* everything. I have you. That's all I truly want." Her voice was thick with emotion.

"Well, you're getting more than that." He was going to give her the world and more. No one alive could truly understand what he had been through to get to this point in life. His life had been one long experience and while he valued every moment, loneliness was one of the most difficult things anyone could experience. Especially when it was as endless as his.

Fifteen hundred long years.

He didn't feel like his life had just begun now that Sage was in it, but it felt enhanced. Complete.

"So, I'll tell my family we got engaged on holiday," Sage said. "And we're getting married at Christmas."

"Sure. A winter wedding."

"Can we wait a few more days? I need to get my head around this. Prepare responses to all their questions. Prepare to lie to everyone."

"Take as long as you like," Ari said.

He had already given her new bank cards and explained her mortgage was paid. She wasn't going back to BioZen after being drugged by them. And, you know, experimenting on his race.

"There's a lot to adjust to," Sage said, looping her arm through his as they walked back to the mansion.

"I know. Let's just take it day by day. We're creating our life together, sweetheart. There is no rush. I'm just happy to have you in my arms and to have your forgiveness."

Sage turned to him, and he cupped her face. "There really was no choice. I love you more than life, Ari. You are the only one for me."

"That is all your family will want to see. Show them that and they will ignore any other oddities their human minds pick up."

They continued walking, his heart bursting with joy.

"I'm going to be a bride!" Sage yelled to the sky, and he grinned as wide as the moon.

CHAPTER NINE

Xander sipped his coffee and watched his wife's lips flapping from across the dining room table.

Blah, blah, blah.

"… because we have the gala dinner in November, so we need to be back there to help with the organizing. Well I have to help. You'll be working of course," Suzanna said. "*Plus*, I'll need to be fitted for my dress. These things take time, Xander."

God help him.

"Can't you just buy something online?" he asked, not really giving a fuck.

She gasped as if he'd asked her to do something illegal. He wished she'd do something illegal with that mouth of hers. Apparently, it was too good to suck cock. Well, more than once a year. She thought it was a nice Christmas or birthday treat for him.

Frankly she was terrible at it, so whatever.

Lately he'd been thinking a lot about Elizabeth—his finance manager who was based in Italy. It had been too long since he'd been buried inside her. Their weekly video calls were just teasing him.

"My point is, we need to head to Seattle. We're always there this time of year. *Xander*. Are you listening to me?"

Unfortunately, yes, he was.

And unfortunately, they had to stay in Baltimore where it was safe. No one—meaning the vampires—knew where he was. They'd been watching him for a long time and made their move only hours after they had left Italy. He'd been lucky. But after Ari Moretti's recent verbal threat over the phone he wasn't taking any risks.

"My business is nearly complete here, but until then, we will need to remain here, *cara moglie*," he said, even though his wife wasn't his darling.

She did have one thing right. They needed to attend the gala, so he had to organize some tighter security or a way to move around the country, and the globe, undetected.

His new investor may be the perfect contact, but he wasn't about to ask for any favors just yet. With men as dangerous as the investor, it was about taking your time and waiting for an opportunity to arise.

His phone rang.

"Enjoy your day. I will be in my office," Xander said, standing then walking out of the room. When his office door closed, he answered.

"*Buongiorno*, Nikolay."

"English, Tomassi. It's hard enough for me to translate with your accent," the man replied firmly.

Well, good fucking morning to you, too.

Except he'd never actually say that to Nikolay Mikhailov. The guy was the head of the Bratva—the Russian mob—and was one of the most dangerous men on the planet.

Wanted by the FBI, and rumored to be aligned with the Russian president as well as other world leaders, Nikolay was known to be a ruthless and cold enemy. When his father and former mob boss, Boris Mikhailov, was assassinated, there was no second-guessing who had done it.

Or so the story went.

Whether it was true or not was beside the point.

Mikhailov was dangerous.

And Xander's new investor.

How he'd known BioZen was involved with the experiments on vampires, Xander had no idea, and he'd been wise enough not to ask. Still, he recalled their first conversation, which had been chilling.

"Mr. Tomassi," a powerful and dark Russian-accented voice had asked when he'd answered his phone.

"Yes. This is he."

"I hear you have a vampire product I could be interested in."

He'd stilled, but thought fast.

"Are you? Interested in vampire products."

"Yes," the man said. "And I want my order to be prioritized."

Xander's brows had risen, but he was smart enough to know it wasn't a request, but an order.

"How many units are we talking?" Xander had asked, sitting down abruptly in his office chair.

"Two hundred, immediately. Then I'm talking thousands," the Russian voice said. "My name is Nikolay Mikhailov. Consider me your new partner, Mr. Tomassi."

Xander had rubbed his lips nervously.

He had been looking for an investor, so the timing was right. But he knew exactly who Nikolay was. A quick Google as they were talking removed any doubts.

He was a dangerous, wealthy, and powerful man. Tall, broad, chestnut-brown hair with silver-blue eyes that made you look twice to ensure he was human.

Ironically.

He had no doubt this man drew women to him like a moth to a flame. Men like Mikhailov had an aura about them that melted panties and parted lips. Women lusted after power.

Perhaps he was too powerful for Xander. He didn't like that. However, the vampires were a powerful enemy, so it wasn't a bad thing to partner with the mob.

Now they had an agreement and Xander had to deliver. They were on a timeline and Mikhailov wanted everything yesterday.

"When will I get my first shipment?" he demanded.

Jesus.

They hadn't begun producing the product yet.

He slipped his finger under the collar of his shirt and tugged. "Few more months, we think. I will have solid delivery dates in the next few days."

He heard a grunt.

"Don't make me wait, Xander."

Did the guy think creating a new species of humans with vampire DNA happened overnight? They weren't making flavored fucking popcorn.

"You'll get the first batch of the hybrid soldier. You have my promise," he said.

And he would, because Xander knew you didn't fuck with Nikolay Mikhailov.

CHAPTER TEN

Oliver tightened the last of the screws in the window and tucked the screwdriver in his back pocket.

Travis, I'm texting you tomorrow. Send one of our human security teams to the address. Needs a full set up.

On it.

Oliver slid his phone back into his pocket and let out a sigh.

One nudge of the window and it had nearly flown open again, so Oliver had flashed back to The Institute, grabbed some tools, then returned to repair it properly.

He wondered if Sage would announce her death or if Piper would be in his world by proxy of his relationship with Ari. Either way, his body needed to get over its infatuation with her. She was off-limits.

He closed the window and locked it.

With him on the inside.

So, clearly, he was not paying attention to his own advice.

He turned to watch her sleep. She was very still, more still than usual. He'd become a Piper sleep expert over the past two weeks.

Embarrassing.

Oliver walked to the bed and found a notebook had slipped out of her hands.
Don't read it.
He picked it up.
Do not *read it.*
He opened it and flicked through. Neat writing filled the pages. A few words caught his attention.
Wait a minute.
He checked the front and back cover for information, but the thing was covered in *live, love, laugh,* telling him nothing. He opened it again and went back to the words which had caught his attention. Words which described having sex with *him.*
He knew exactly who owned this notebook, because he had done those sexual things.
This was Sage's diary.
How in the Sam Hill did Piper have her sister's diary?
He narrowed his eyes and stared down at the female. One glance at her bedside table and he spotted some pills.
Was she sick?
He Googled the drug on his phone and discovered they were for migraines.
"Fuck, what am I doing?" Oliver mumbled to himself. Then he froze as Piper began to twist and turn and throw back the covers as if she were having a bad dream.
Shit.
Her nightie lifted, and staring right back at him was a pretty pink nipple. His cock pressed painfully against his zipper, and he cursed, adjusting himself. His tongue swept across his lips with the need to taste her.
No. She's off-limits.
He could have any woman he wanted, but not this one.
Clearly, she missed her sister and was worried about her. Why else would she have her diary? It wasn't like he could tell Sage. Then he'd have to admit he'd been in Piper's

bedroom and there was no fucking way he was telling anyone that.

When he left tonight, it would be for the last time.

He had a job to do, and it looked like they'd be on the move soon.

Whatever Sage and Ari decided would determine if Piper was to be a part of their lives. *Their* lives. Not his. Mostly.

Her back arched and she let out a little noise.

Was she dreaming?

Of him?

When her nipples hardened, and her body wriggled some more, Oliver let out a quiet curse.

Just one taste.

He stood watching her, wishing he could reach out and brush his thumb gently across her taut nipple.

A small moan escaped her lips.

God.

He should leave.

If only he could place his mouth around her pink bud, giving her the pleasure he believed she wanted.

Needed.

As if knowing what he was thinking, her body gently arched some more, and his cock jerked against his jeans painfully.

Was she wet?

Did she need his touch as much as he desired to touch her?

Oliver let out a quiet curse. This was wrong. He shouldn't be here watching Piper in her personal space. Yet he felt a primal need to protect her for some insane reason. That, and her body called to him.

What would she do if she opened her eyes and saw him? Would she desire him? There would be no finding out. He had to walk away. Oliver wiped his hand over his mouth and face. Twice.

Fucking hell.

This was utter torture.

"Goodbye, Piper. You sassy minx. I wish I could lick every damn inch of you and fuck you until you scream," he said quietly. "But you're just going to have to remain my little wet dream."

Dammit.

Oliver took one last look at the dark-haired beauty.

Look after yourself, you damn pain in the ass.

Then he turned and teleported back to the mansion and headed to the training center to meet Ben and prepare the teams.

CHAPTER ELEVEN

"Come in, Piper." Roger Stevens, the editor of *The Seattle Times*, waved when he spotted her hovering in the doorway.

"Mr. Stevens, hi," she said to her boss.

"Sit. I have five minutes. What have you got for me today?"

She heard the touch of impatience in his voice. It was true, she was in there weekly with a pitch for some story or another, but she was driven.

She planted herself in the chair in front of his desk and opened her laptop. "This is going to sound crazy—"

"No less than last week's, I imagine." He laughed.

"Okay, fine. The idea of a global pandemic that locks down the entire human population wasn't my best work and is highly unrealistic, but this is different." When he stared at her, she cleared her throat and tapped a few keys.

"So, my sister works, or maybe worked for BioZen—"

"The large pharmaceutical company?"

"Yes, and she recently got a promotion to a top-secret division called Project Callan," Piper explained. "I've been doing some research today and made a few calls. No one has heard of it."

Roger leaned back in his large black corporate chair and shrugged. "Nothing new there. They're known for their tight security, and they pay well enough to keep lips closed."

Piper nodded.

"Right. Except my sister has been missing for two weeks. And in one of her recent diary entries she mentions the existence of vampires."

Roger's eyes widened and then he laughed.

"You're joking, right?"

"No."

"You want to do a story about vampires?"

"I mean, there was that thing a few months ago," she said with her brows raised.

"Which was a bunch of conspiracy theorists out of their pot-smoked minds," Roger said, shaking his head.

"Was it, though?"

"You think your sister has been kidnapped by vampires?"

"Well, no…"

"Have you filed a missing person's report?"

"No, my mother says they're on holiday."

"They?" Roger asked.

"Sage and… well, her new boyfriend."

"So she has a new boyfriend, and he takes her on holiday, and she doesn't contact her family. But you think vampires are involved?"

Piper clenched her teeth.

"No. Yes. Please, let me explain." Piper held up a hand. "Sage is a scientist. I read through her diary, and it appears she overheard some of her colleagues talking about vampires. She believes they're right. Then a few weeks later she meets these two, well, anyway, this man, and he's suddenly in her life."

Roger stared back at her.

"You met him."

"I, yes, I think so. I mean, it's foggy."

"Foggy."

"I think... shit, I know I sound crazy, but I think someone is messing with my memories."

Roger's brows slowly rose.

"Let me finish. So she gets this job in the new secret department and suddenly she disappears. The day she apparently went on holiday, I spoke to her. She was in an Uber heading to her boyfriend's house. Then boom, she's gone for over two weeks."

"Boom," Roger repeated.

"I went to her apartment and her belongings were gone. Today I contacted her bank to find out if there has been any activity on her account and the last one was about ten days ago. A final payment on her entire mortgage."

"Someone paid her mortgage?"

Piper nodded.

"Did you find out who?" Roger asked.

"No, but I have some contacts, so I'm going to keep digging."

"You should call the police."

"The first thing they'll do is call my parents, who insist Sage is on holiday with her boyfriend. But trying to get the details from them on where she's holidaying is weird. It's like talking to a machine. My mother does not compute."

"Weird," Roger said, leaning forward.

Gotcha.

Piper knew he was interested, even if the story was odd.

"So what's the angle? Because *vampires stole my sister* is not going to cut it. We're not that kind of tabloid."

Piper nodded. "No. I think there's a bigger story here. I want to investigate BioZen. I think they're doing some vampire research. *Or,* did they create vampires? Heck, stranger things have happened."

Roger let out a rough laugh. "Fuck, have they?"

Good point.

"I think there are enough questions here to go digging, at least. If my sister isn't back in forty-eight hours, I will call the police, but meanwhile I'll tap into all my sources and with your permission, speak to BioZen."

Roger frowned.

Yeah, that was why she was here.

If it was any other company, she would have just fired ahead. But the pharma industry was powerful and influential. She had enough experience under her belt already to know which toes to step on without permission, and it was not these ones.

"Shit, Roberts. Couldn't you have chosen POTUS instead or something?"

She grinned.

"At least if we find something, it'll be the biggest story we've ever had." As well as finding her sister, which was exactly what Piper was hoping for. Then Daddy dearest would have to acknowledge just how fucking amazing she was.

Sage could cure cancer for all she cared—and she hoped her sister did—but if Piper exposed the existence of vampires to the world, not only would it be the most shocking discovery for the human race, she would be the most awarded journalist in history.

"Don't get too excited, and tread carefully. I want you to keep me updated regularly and… don't piss anyone off."

She only just stopped herself from racing around the desk and hugging the older man.

"Thank you, sir." Piper stood and hugged her laptop to her chest. "I'll do my best."

Roger groaned as she almost danced out of his office.

"I'm going to regret this; I just know it," Piper heard him mumble, then he called her back.

She swiveled and stepped back into the doorway. "Set up in Marlene's old office. I don't want anyone overhearing your calls. Keep this between us."

Woohoo. Her own office. Things were looking up.

"Yes, sir."

Piper headed back to her desk to pack up.

"You get fired?" Kara asked with raised brows.

"Ha-ha. No, I'm working on a secret project, so Roger has given me Marlene's office."

"That's awesome. So jealous," Kara said.

"The office with the great view? We are so having lunch in there from now on," Jeremy declared.

"Deal." She grinned.

"Also, spill." He stood and leaned his elbows on the partition wall. "What's the secret project?"

Piper filled a box with all her things and dropped her pot plant on top. "No can do. Not this time." This was way too important. She was now a serious investigative journalist.

Technically. And one day soon it would be her real title. And hopefully she'd have her sister back.

"Help me move this stuff," she said, and while Kara jumped up to help, Jeremy flopped back down into his chair.

"Honey, these muscles are to impress the boys, not for a career in furniture removal."

Piper laughed.

A few hours later, Piper's grin had faded to a frown. Not that she'd expected BioZen to open the doors and send her case files, but she'd hit brick wall after brick wall.

All her contacts had responded, saying they'd never heard of Project Callan. They also weren't interested in digging further. So, she decided to take matters into her own hands.

Literally.

Well, tomorrow at least.

Right now, she had a little problem to take care of. One she'd been ignoring since she woke up and needed some serious relief before she exploded. One that would need to wait until she got home and pulled out her now-overused vibrator.

Piper woke up the next morning and the first thing she did was check her phone.

No messages from Sage.

She texted her mom.

I'll see you tonight for dinner. Chicken. No gluten. Any word from Sage?

Okay, darling. No, she's on holiday with her boyfriend. You know that.

Jesus.

Two weeks and two days.

Why was she the only one concerned about this? Usually, her mother was a total control freak about these things. Had her mother met Ari—

Pain sliced through her head.

Oh God. Not another migraine.

See you at seven.

She climbed out of bed and spotted her vibrator on the bedside cabinet. Ugh. Her batteries were going to die soon with the workout it was getting. Night after night she dreamed of the man with brilliant blue eyes who set her body on fire.

All day yesterday she'd felt as if she'd been left unsatisfied by a lover. Her nipples had burned to be touched, and it felt like she'd been wet all day. Sitting in her office she had constantly squeezed her thighs together wondering whether

she needed some sex toys to put inside herself to keep the horniness at bay.
Did people actually do that during work?
Wasn't it more to play than deal with arousal?
Maybe she was ill.
When she got home, she had come twice. By herself.
"I need to get laid," she muttered and hit the shower, getting ready for another day of vampire research.

An hour later she was standing in the lobby of BioZen.

She refused to be intimidated by the clinical feel of the enormous space. Around her, aside from people making their way to their offices, there was white everything. White tiles, white walls, and white escalators which were only accessible if you were staff.

On the large three-story wall behind the long reception desk was a huge BioZen logo. She stood staring at it, waiting for assistance.

"Yes, can I help you?" One of the three receptionists finally spoke to her. She was standing, not seated, with an earpiece she had pressed, which Piper assumed connected her to the phones.

Clearly, she was well paid by the looks of the designer clothing on display. Piper knew her sister had received a healthy salary. She was able to purchase a home of her own while Piper still rented.

Something their father regularly reminded her of.

"Yes, hi. I'm here to see Sage Roberts," she said, and then lied. "I have an appointment."

The woman, of similar age to Piper, frowned and tapped on a keyboard.

"Sage Roberts?"

"Yes."

"Sorry, we don't have an employee of that name working here." The woman glanced behind her as if she was about to be dismissed for admitting such a thing.

"What? There has to be a mistake." Piper raised her voice a little and got the wide-eyed response she was hoping for.

Nobody liked a scene.

"Perhaps you have the wrong company?"

How could they have zero record of her sister who had worked here for years? Wait, had Sage left? Pain sliced through her mind. Did she know that?

"Then I need to speak to a manager. Sage worked here for years," Piper said, pressing her fingers to her temples.

The woman's eyes darted to the side as she clicked a few keys, looking irritated and a little stressed.

Good.

"Darlene, hey, it's Maggie. Is Rebecca available?" she said. "No, I have someone here asking for Sage Roberts."

Silence.

"Oh. Yes. No. Dr. Phillips. No, I mean yes." Maggie's nervous eyes darted back and forth.

Piper took note of the name, recalling it from Sage's diary. The woman tapped her earpiece and her eyes returned to Piper.

"Sorry, it looks like Sandy is also unavailable," Maggie said.

"Also? So Sage did work here?" she asked, immediately picking up on the nuance.

The woman swallowed.

"No. I mean, she's unavailable and so is Dr. Phillips, the head of the department," she stumbled.

"Are they on holiday or just unavailable today?"

"Dr. Phillips is currently working in another location," Maggie answered.

"I can go there. Where is it?" Piper pushed.

"No, he's in California so… why don't you leave your number, and I will get someone to call you." The woman handed her a notepad and pen. She clearly just wanted Piper gone and out of the building.

California? She could totally go there and continue her research if this Dr. Phillips was a key person. BioZen had offices in locations all around the United States and the world.

She scribbled down her name and number, then dropped the pen. "Thank you, Maggie, you have been very helpful."

"Piper Roberts? You're related?"

She nodded.

"Yes. You can tell your employers that I want to know where my sister is. And I will not stop looking until I find her."

Maggie swallowed again.

"It might be of interest that I am a journalist. Or not." She lifted a shoulder. "I look forward to their call."

She smiled and walked out of the building.

Looks like she was heading to sunny California.

CHAPTER TWELVE

Duck.
Boof.
Oomph.
"Dude, you're getting soft." Ben laughed as he pitched another gloved punch into Oliver's gut. Oli threw a counter-punch, which was a total decoy as his leg kicked out, and Ben went down.
He dropped on top of Ben.
"What was that?" Oli grinned.
As Ben thrust his body around, he knew he had about zero-point-three seconds before the powerful vampire was up again, so he launched to his feet first. They were far too well-matched to ever beat each other.
Frustrating as hell, but a lot of fun.
He needed the physical challenge right now to take the edge off his constant need to fuck Piper.
Out of the corner of his eye, he spotted Ari walking toward them with purpose. The vampire stopped at the edge of the ring. Without a word, both Ben and Oliver walked to meet him, their bodies alert.
"We have a location," the ancient vampire said. "Prep for a flight to California in an hour."

Oliver nodded.

"Briefing in twenty," Ari added, and as he walked away, they undid their gloves and climbed under the ropes.

"Feels like the good old days." Ben grinned as they made their way to the showers.

Oliver grinned back, then cast his friend a look. "Wish we had more of the senior crew here. Not that you're not strong and stuff, but I feel like we may be walking into a shit storm after Italy."

Ben nodded, ignoring the jibe. "I agree. Let me speak to Craig."

After their showers and a quick pack of the bags, they all met back in the Operations Room.

Craig, Ari, Travis, and Darren were seated around the table.

Ari looked up as he and Ben joined them.

"Okay, so we have two possible options. Either Dr. Evil flew into a private airfield in Los Angeles or Pennsylvania," Darren said.

Oliver noticed the prince was missing and Craig must have noticed him looking around.

"Brayden is heading back to Maine, so I'm meeting Lance in Pennsylvania to have a sniff around. Alex is going to meet us there as he's close by. Travis tells us he'll be finished his job by the time we fly in," Craig said.

"Makes sense." Oliver nodded, glancing at the data on the screen.

"We need more muscle. After what we saw in Italy, if we come up against that again, we could lose time." Ben glanced at the commander.

Ari shook his head. "Shouldn't have taken those fucking jobs. I wasn't expecting any leads. Not like this."

"Shit happens," Craig said. "I can send Kurt your way. We have enough SLC's back home now Brayden is on his way."

Ben glanced at Oliver, who nodded.

"Get him to meet us in LA." He turned to Travis. "You booking accommodation?"

"Adding another room," Travis said, tapping away.

All eyes turned to Ari.

"Let us know what you need, Commander. The rest of you, BAU check-ins." He referred to their *Business as Usual* protocol. "Wheel's up in twenty."

Craig stood and pulled on his Moretti black jacket; the same one Ben was wearing. There was a lot of pride in that uniform for all vampires, whether they donned one or not.

Oliver had always been happy in his unmarked black gear while working for Ari. No assassin put a logo on their clothing.

"If you can send the data to my team so they have all the latest intel, that would be great," Craig said, shaking Ari's hand. "And thanks for having us all recently. It's great combining our knowledge and collaborating."

"Ditto. I'm looking forward to seeing the Maine castle when we visit soon."

Oliver shot a glance at Ben who was watching his old boss. He knew the two were incredibly close and wondered what his friend thought of Ari visiting the royal family once again.

"Yeah, it's a little fancier than Italy so I think you'll be impressed." Craig grinned. "Brianna will be pleased to hear Sage is visiting."

"In the meantime, let's see if we can catch these evil fuckers." Ari glanced around the room.

"I'll call Kurt on the way to the plane," Craig said to Ben as he began walking out the door. "Stay the fuck out of trouble."

Ben grinned.

"Jesus," Craig muttered, and disappeared around the corner.

"He secretly loves me."

Ari and Oliver shared a knowing smile and shook their heads.

"Let's go, lover boy." Oliver laughed and the two of them grabbed their bags and began to walk out.

"Oli," Ari called.

He turned.

"Sage has chosen to remain in her family's life for now. Remind me how you left things with Piper?"

Oliver froze.

"Left things?" he asked, his voice a little too high.

Ari's eyes narrowed.

Fuck.

"When you wiped her memory," Ari clarified.

Shit, shit, shit.

"Yeah, just dropped her home and removed what I could while leaving some of you in there, so she didn't question too much. You know, while Sage was transitioning."

Ari nodded. "She hasn't come snooping again?" Ari asked.

"No."

The ancient vampire nodded again while continuing to hold Oli's stare. "Check in once you arrive."

"Yup."

Oliver turned and followed Ben out the door and down the hall. When they were near the front door at the other end of the mansion, Ben finally turned to him.

"What the hell was that about?"

"Nothing."

Oliver ran his hand over his hair. Ben opened the door, and they stepped out into the cool night air.

"Seriously, man. Ari knew you were lying through your teeth. You need to start talking."

Fuck.

CHAPTER THIRTEEN

Piper hung her coat and a couple of dresses in her hotel room wardrobe, then glanced around. She'd booked a basic room with a queen-sized bed and a view of the building next door.
That was as far as *The Seattle Times* budget stretched.
It wasn't like she was going to spend much time in it.
Her stomach grumbled.
She needed something to eat and to stretch her legs after the flight to Los Angeles. It was nice being in a warmer climate, so she chose a short-sleeved red dress and some black heels, freshened up her makeup and hair, then slipped her cross-body handbag over her head and went downstairs.
The night air was thick with the sounds of tourists and traffic. She wandered past a number of restaurants before deciding on a steak house. Sitting at the bar, she ordered a glass of rosé, a medium rare steak and salad.
Her mom hadn't been happy when she'd cancelled, but for once Piper had been pleased by her over-the-top reaction. And yet when she'd asked about Sage again, she got the same robotic answer; she's on holiday.
Jesus.
Kara was right. It was like she was inside some sci-fi movie and aliens had abducted her mother and returned

some fake copy. Which got her thinking. While Piper didn't read all those romance novels her sister did—okay, fine, she'd read one or two—she knew enough about vampire fiction and their myths that they could mess around with the mind.

What if it was true?

What if she was the victim of brainwashing, or whatever they called it?

She dug into her steak, and ordered a second glass of wine, feeling relaxed for the first time in days. She was excited to see what she could find out in Los Angeles even if she was looking for a needle in a haystack.

As a journalist, that's where you always started.

Maybe Sage was here at BioZen and the holiday was just a cover, because she was working on a top-secret project.

The fact she had left her diary behind seemed odd. Not to mention clearing out her belongings.

And why would she lie about being on holiday?

Piper tapped her finger on the stem of her glass. One question at a time. That was her motto.

Behind every question there was either an answer, or another question which would eventually lead to the answer.

It just might not be the answer she wanted.

Oliver dropped his bag on the ground and glanced around the lobby of the hotel.

"Either you've really pissed Ari off, or there have been budget costs." Ben laughed.

Yeah, it wasn't their usual flash hotel, but there were enough stars that they'd be comfortable. It wasn't exactly a dive.

"It's fine. You've just been living it up with the Moretti's," Oliver teased.

"Hey assholes," Kurt said, walking in behind them. Speaking of.

"You just get in?" Ben asked him as they fist-pumped each other.

The Moretti SLC nodded. "Bumpy fucking flight."

"Thanks for coming out," Oliver said, shaking his hand.

"No problem. We all want to bust apart and destroy whatever these assholes have planned. It's dodgy as hell."

They all shook their heads at the thought of what those in their race had already been through at the hands of BioZen scientists. The problem was, they didn't know what BioZen was doing with the information.

But it wouldn't be good.

Good for the company's profit margins, but not for the vampires. Or likely humanity.

"Let's talk upstairs. The king has been progressing conversations with his contacts, so this doesn't completely fall on our shoulders," Kurt said. "But let's see what we can find out."

It was a reminder that, while The Institute was taking the lead on this mission, the royal family was the one in charge. Sure, Ari lived by his own rules, and as a Moretti he could to some degree. But the head of the vampire race was still, and always would be, Vincent Moretti.

This wasn't a time for politics, though. They all wanted the same thing; to live their lives in peace alongside the human race. They'd done it for over fifteen hundred years and could continue to do it as long as their existence remained hidden.

Which was becoming harder and harder with technology and people's need to know the truth. The human quest for knowledge was understandable. It was how they had progressed and evolved in such a short period of time. Relatively speaking.

It was the people who used that knowledge for nefarious purposes that fucked it up for everyone. Broken people.

Those who needed control because, deep down, they were fearful.

Of what?

Who the fuck cared? They were dangerous, whatever the reason behind it.

This wasn't a therapy session.

"I'll go check us in," Ben said, and Oliver gave him a short nod. They had worked together so long, including traveling all over the globe, that this just felt like another day at the office.

"Ah, shit. Apparently, they need my ID. I'll come with." Kurt stared at his phone then shoved it in his pocket. "Back in a minute."

Oliver widened his stance, kicked his bag between his legs and pulled out his phone. He scrolled through the data Darren's team had sent through and began considering their first steps for this mission.

Around him people came and went, and the elevators dinged open and closed.

"Let's go," Ben said when he and Kurt returned a few minutes later. All three of them, dressed top to toe in black and no doubt looking nothing like local Californian guys, walked to the bank of elevators.

Oliver pressed the button.

Ding.

One of them opened and two elderly holiday makers stepped in first. Ben and Kurt went next and then Oliver followed, turning and pressing the number for their floor.

"Hold the elevator! Hold it," a voice called out.

His eyebrows shot up.

For the love of God?

"You have to be fucking kidding me," he muttered.

"Problem?" Kurt asked.

Oliver groaned, shook his head, and muttered *no,* thinking what a lie it was, then placed his hand on the door frame to keep it open.

Piper fucking Roberts ran into the elevator car, panting. "Thank you, floor nineteen, please."

She stood way too close to him as he leaned down and pressed the button. She hadn't made eye contact with him, so Oliver stood frozen, trying to ignore the fresh smell of spring blossoms that had become a familiar aphrodisiac in his life.

Her scent.

Ding.

"Excuse us. This is our floor, William. Come along," the elderly lady said.

"I know, Doris. I booked it," William replied defensively.

Jesus.

The older couple tried to squeeze past the three huge vampires. "Excuse me," Doris said. "Excuse, oh, I'm sorry."

Oliver muttered a curse and stared at Piper's much smaller-framed body. He cleared his throat while attempting to move out of the car.

There was no way he was touching her.

"Oh," Piper said, twisting and turning at the commotion.

Ben let out a small laugh.

"Thank you. Aren't you such big boys?" Doris said, giving them all a wink when she got out.

"Spinach." Kurt winked back.

"Oh, my God." Piper laughed as they all stepped back in, and the doors closed. Oliver wasn't laughing. He stared straight ahead, trying not to engage with her at all, but could feel her gaze on him. His eyes drifted down to her just as her smile faded and recognition kicked in.

"You," she said, drawing in a sharp breath, and took a step back, bumping into Kurt.

"Whoa, darling," the big vampire said.
Oliver grabbed her arms and then abruptly let her go.
"Okay, this is interesting."
Ben frowned.
"Are you following me?" Piper accused.
"Oli, what's going on?" Ben asked.
"Oliver!" Piper said, pointing at him. "That's, oh my God. My dreams!"
Her fingers pressed to the sides of her head and he could see she was in pain.
Damn it.
How did she keep remembering him? This was becoming a huge problem.
"Well, as much as we'd all like details of this dream, I think someone better start talking." Kurt crossed his arms.
"This is Sage's sister. Piper," Oliver said in a low, dark voice.
"Oh, shit." Ben and Kurt both cursed.

"Who the hell are you?" Piper asked, trying to take a step away, but she was stuck in an elevator surrounded by three huge men who looked like they belonged inside a paranormal military movie.
Maybe they were actors?
Was that why she kept dreaming about this one particular guy?
Had she seen him in a movie?
No. They weren't actors. Even though they were all incredibly gorgeous, they gave off an extremely dangerous vibe. And yeah, they *were* gorgeous. Good lord, their bodies were bulging with muscles. Their biceps, arms, chests, and thighs.

She was completely flustered by their raw masculine power.

All three of them were wearing black everything with tattoos poking out underneath their t-shirts like total badass dudes. She bet there was ink in other sexy places, too.

Holy hell.

She knew she should run like hell, but she needed to know who this Oliver was and why he seemed so familiar. More importantly why—aside from the obvious—her body craved him like he was a shot of heroin.

Her cheeks heated.

"Oh, boy," the one behind her said.

"Well, princess, the thing is, I'm trying to *stop* you from remembering me. For your fucking protection," Oliver ground out, leaning into her face.

He looked completely pissed. At her. How could he be? She'd never met him before. He said he was trying to stop her from remembering him. That made no sense.

She narrowed her eyes. "Do we know each other?"

"Yes. But you shouldn't know me and frankly, it's causing problems."

"She keeps breaking through the blocks?" One of the muscly hunks spoke.

"Three fucking times," Oliver said, glaring at her.

Blocks?

"What blocks? What are you talking about? Why are you in my—"

"Dreams. I know. Trust me, darlin'. I *know.*" He closed his eyes for a moment as if she were the bane of his existence.

A hot shiver ran through her as his bright blue eyes flipped open and scanned her body. She turned and pushed the number nineteen button a million times to hurry up the journey.

Suddenly, Piper felt she was in danger. She wanted answers, but not that much.

"Just FYI, I have mace and there are cameras everywhere, so think twice before making a move." Piper stared at them in what she hoped was a brave manner.

Two of the three guys smirked in response, which, fair call, she was only five foot five and they looked like they could snap her neck in two seconds and laugh about it over a beer.

Oliver wasn't smirking, though. His eyes were deadly serious. He still looked pissed and a little like he wanted to… kiss her angrily. The scary thing was, she wanted him to do it and that was why she needed this elevator to open *now*!

"You never answered my question. What are you doing here in Los Angeles?" Oliver growled.

The doors opened.

"Visiting family." She took a tentative step backwards out of the car. "So you have a good holiday or whatever."

She hit the wall opposite with her back and the doors began to close.

Oliver glared at her.

Close.

Please fucking close.

Two inches.

One inch.

She drew in a breath and…

CHAPTER FOURTEEN

Oliver stared at the metal as the gap began to disappear, then with vamp speed, his hand slid between the doors and they opened.

Piper gasped, still flat against the wall.

He knew he was scaring her.

You going to tidy this up?

He handed Ben his bag, nodding in answer to the telepathic message. "I'll be up in ten."

"I'll scream," Piper said, fear lacing her words.

"No, darlin'. You won't." Oliver took her arm and walked her down the hallway, then swiped into her hotel room. He leaned against a wall and crossed his arms, while she dropped her handbag on a table and began to tidy up a few things.

"Sit down," he said quietly but firmly.

"Why am I doing what you tell me to do?" she growled as she sat on the sofa. Then pressed her fingers to her temples once more. "Shit, I need my pills."

Oliver frowned, hating that he was the cause of her pain.

"Stop trying to remember so hard and it will stop."

Slowly, she lifted her head and stared at him. "Why did that work? Have you done something to my mind? To my memories?"

"Answer my question first and I will answer one of yours."

She chewed her lip, thinking for a moment, and then nodded.

"Why are you in LA?"

Oliver ran his eyes over her body. She was dressed for the warmer weather and her sexy red dress showed off her toned thighs and arms. Her body shouldn't be so familiar to him, but it was.

He knew she was attracted to him just by looking at the blush on her cheeks and the gloss of her eyes. Human females were drawn to a vampire's strong testosterone and alpha nature. It wouldn't take much for him to have her if he wanted.

But she was off-limits, and he had to remember that.

He was here to do one thing: wipe her memory effectively.

Then he could report back to Ari and not lie this time.

First, he wanted to know why she was here.

"I'm looking for my sister," she answered. "She's gone missing."

Oh.

Why did she think Sage was in LA?

"I see," he replied, and they stared at each other a long moment.

"It's my turn to ask a question." When he nodded, she continued. "Have you done something to my memories?"

His eyes widened.

That was an interesting conclusion for a human to come to.

"Why would you ask that?" He pushed away from the wall and walked to the coffee table, kicking it back so he could sit in front of her, but not crowd her.

She flinched back from him anyway, and he hated that.

Night after night he'd spent with her, feeling a forbidden intimacy building between them, and she remembered nothing of that. Only his face.

A desire to reach out and run his fingers down her arm while she melted into him suddenly came over him. He clenched his hands into fists.

"Have you?"

"Yes," he answered honestly.

"Have we—" she began to ask, her eyes dropping to his cock.

"What?"

"Fucked?"

His cock pressed against his jeans, wanting to be released and get inside the female who was now only inches from him.

"That's your question? After learning I've messed around with your memories." He let out a small laugh.

Piper pulled up her legs and crossed them under her. In doing so, she flashed her panties momentarily and he gritted his teeth.

Shit.

"Well, I doubt you're going to tell me how you do it, so the next best question is why. So, did we? And why is it so important I forget?"

Oliver spread his legs wider and leaned his elbows on his thighs. "The question is why you keep damn well remembering, Piper. I can't tell you why, but it's important you stop."

"Does it have to do with Sage?"

He stilled.

"It does! Where is she? You know where she is," she cried, dropping her feet back on the floor.

Fuck.

"Ari is a friend of mine. She is with him. On holiday," he lied.

"Like fuck they are," she mumbled. Defiant eyes lifted to his. "I'm going to find her. Wipe my memory as much as you damn want, but I *will* find my sister."

Oliver tilted his head. It still didn't explain why she was in LA.

"Why do you think she's in California? Is this a holiday spot she likes?"

Piper let out a small laugh. "We both know she's not on a damn holiday, Oliver."

"So you just flew across the country to search for her in a random place?"

"No, I'm also here on business. I'm a journalist. I… never mind."

"Explain."

Piper stared at him for a long moment. "I'm doing a top-secret story on the company she worked for. Is that why you're here? Are you looking for your friend, Ari? Have they both gone missing?"

Jesus, she was like a dog with a bone.

"Piper, you need to stay far away from BioZen. This is way too dangerous."

Her mouth fell open. "They have, haven't they? Just tell me."

Oliver held up a hand. "No. Stop."

She climbed off the sofa, and he stood, grabbing her arms.

"Please. Stop your witch hunt. Sage will be home soon, but it's not safe for you here. You need to go back to Seattle."

She tried to shrug him off, but he held her tight.

"You're going to do it again, aren't you?"

"Yes, darlin'," he said, their eyes locked.

"Before you do. Did we…" Her eyes burned with the desire she'd been trying to hide.

"No."

"But we want to," she said. "*You* want to."

"Yes." Fuck it, but he couldn't lie about that. His body wanted her so damn much it was vibrating. He wanted to tell her he'd watched her, almost had his mouth on her breast, and stroked himself off so many times to thoughts of her and her moans.

"Then why not let me remember that?"

Heat flooded his body. "I can't. This. Us. It's not possible."

"I keep dreaming of you. It's… becoming painful." She shook her head. "Did you do that to me?"

Desire overwhelmed him.

Oliver wanted to throw her on the bed and fuck her till she shook from the dozen or so orgasms he'd give her.

"No. I don't know why that's happening," he replied honestly. "I'm sorry. It's the same for me."

Her eyes flew open.

"My body wants to fuck you more than any man I've ever met. This is so fucked up. Half the time I can't remember and it's all fuzzy."

God, he needed her to stop talking and yet he couldn't let go of her.

He let out a groan.

"Let me go," she said, and he saw her nipples were hard under the fabric of her dress.

"Tell me your panties are not wet, and I'll let you go."

"You know they are."

Fuck.

"Tell me not to touch you," he growled.

She released a small moan and beneath his hands, he felt her body weaken. He gripped her arms tighter.

"Piper," he said.

"What is wrong with me?" Another moan escaped. "You need to go."

He did, but he couldn't walk away now. He had to touch her, taste her, and hear her sounds of pleasure because of his body. Maybe if they fucked just once, this need would disappear.

"Tell me you want this," he ground out.

"I need this. God damn you."

Fuck, so did he. So fucking bad he could barely breathe.

Oliver pulled her against his chest and slammed his lips down on hers. Their mouths opened to one another, and his brain exploded with a million senses. She was all sweetness and forbidden lust, and he knew this was wrong, but he wasn't stopping. They pulled at each other's clothing and fabric flew everywhere. The control he had on his vampire strength was only just kept at bay.

Lifting her, he carried her to the edge of the bed and kneeled between her legs, tugging her panties aside. "Fuck, I've been dying to do this for so long."

He stared at the wet pink flesh before him and licked his lips. Piper arched, palming her hands on the mattress behind her, and pressed her pussy into his face. "Yes, my God. Lick me please."

Oh, he was going to do way more than that.

He slid her panties down and lifted her legs onto his shoulders, then tugged her hips to his face and sucked her entire pussy into his mouth.

"Godddd," she cried out.

Fuck, she tasted like sweet naughtiness if that could ever be a flavor. He lapped and licked, sucking on her clit while reaching for one of her breasts. Leaning up, he took one in his mouth, his fingers circling her nub as she panted and moaned.

"Oliver."

He looked up at her. "Do you want my cock first or do you want to come on my face?"

"Everything. All of it."

He sucked the other nipple, pressing two fingers into her. "Oh, God."

In and out, his fingers glided, his suction increasing on her nipple. His thumb found her clit and pressed, circling it as their eyes remained connected.

Pop.

Her nipple left his mouth and his tongue teased it. "You're close, aren't you?"

"Mmphhhf."

He grinned, lowered back to her pussy, and pushed her down on the bed. He lifted her ass off the bed and spread her legs wide.

"Good girl. Open up and show me all of you."

"Jesus Christ." She cried out as her body trembled under his touch.

All the pent-up desire for him was right at his fingertips, and he was going to make sure she was pleasured before he left.

"I want you to come on my fingers as I taste all this gorgeous juice." Oliver fucked her with his fingers, watching her pussy pulsing. When his thumb nudged at her rear and his tongue lapped at her clit, she screamed out her first orgasm.

He stood and unzipped his pants.

When she sat, he gripped her jaw. "I want to see my cock in your mouth."

She immediately parted her lips, and he pressed inside. He threw his head back and loudly cursed.

Oh, yes.

His hand took over, and he reached down, palming a breast. "Touch yourself."

"Where?" She spoke around his flesh.

"Touch your pussy as you suck me." When she did, he nearly came in her mouth. Watching her fingers spread through her pussy as her other hand slid up and down his shaft with her mouth following was pure pleasure.

He pulled out moments later, wanting to last until he got inside her.

"This is where you get to say no." He lay her back on the bed. He planted a hand on the sheet beside her head and waited.

"Yes or no. Ten seconds." She wrapped her legs around his hips and his cock pressed against the heat of her wet and open pussy. She was primed and ready for him to slip inside.

He waited for her words. But they didn't come. Instead she smiled hazily at him, and arched, taking his head inside her cunt.

Fuck. He hissed, feeling the roar of heat around his cock.

"Piper," he growled. He had to get her consent.

"Yes, Oliver, fuck me."

He cursed and thrust into her inch by inch, as her hot channel wrapped around his cock and her fingers dug into his arms. It was more than he had imagined. So much damn more.

"God, you are so fucking tight and hot." He pulled back and then pressed in deeper each time. When he was completely buried inside her, their eyes locked.

"Oliver." She gasped suddenly.

"You okay?" he asked, slowing.

"No."

He froze.

"What?" He lifted up a little higher on his arms.

"This feels…" Her hands dug into his shoulders. "Different."

"Sore different?"

She shook her head. He had no idea what was wrong.

"What? Fucking talk to me." He pressed her. "Do you want me to stop?"

Please don't say stop. Though he would, if that's what she wanted.

"No. Move. I need…. just keep going," Piper pleaded.

Keep going?

Her eyes filled, and he began to wonder if he'd broken her mind more than he realized. As his hips moved again, a fire spread up his spine, and desire burned so hot he thought he'd come right there and then.

Piper clenched around him while her hands roamed over his skin, driving him to the edge. When her mouth met his again, Oliver let go. His brain switched off and he became aware only of the delicious pleasure they were creating with their bodies.

Her hands, her mouth, her tongue. Her pussy. He felt her all.

Oliver lifted her on top of him, giving her free rein to ride him. She tossed her head around, rubbing her own clit, gasping when he took hold of her sizeable breasts.

She was a goddess.

Oliver thrust up into her, taking hold of her hips. He had an overwhelming need to pleasure this female like no other.

He wanted her screaming, panting, and then jelly in his arms, but still begging and wanting more.

Her eyes met his, and he grinned.

"So fucking sexy," he said. "Shall we take this up a notch?"

Her mouth gaped as he sat up, tugged her knees up, and then cupped her ass.

"Lean back," he instructed and, when she did, her back hit his knees. Then he began to lift her up and down his cock while his fingers pressed against her rear entrance.

"Oh, fuck," she cried. Their faces were so close he could breathe in her gasps.

"Let go baby, let go and feel it all."

And fucked if his cock wasn't on fire as their bodies slapped noisily together. Up and down, he moved her over his swollen and thick cock.

"Oh, God, Oliver," Piper screamed. Her body clenched around him, her eyes losing focus as his orgasm struck like a goddamn Mack truck.

"Piper, fuck!"

Jeeeesus.

He dropped his legs and her knees fell open, then she collapsed on his chest.

It was then Oliver realized his plan hadn't worked.

He wanted more of her.

So much more.

And yeah, he wasn't wiping these memories. Not for all the money in the world.

CHAPTER FIFTEEN

Piper's eyes flickered open, and she found the sun streaming into her hotel room. She went to lift her head and moaned.
What the hell?
Oh!
Oliver.
She sat up suddenly, recalling the hours of incredible sex, moaning further as she began to feel all the aches from her head to her toes. Yes, even her toes. But oh, God, it had been worth it.
And surprisingly, she remembered it.
Or did she?
Ugh.
She was mildly grateful Oliver had confessed to messing with her memories, but in the haze of lust he'd spun she ironically forgot to ask him exactly *how* he was able to make her forget.
He made me forget my own name at one point last night, but I doubt that was how he was doing it.
Damn it.
After they'd collapsed, she had felt his lips on hers and heard soft instructions to sleep. And she had. It was hard to know if it was delicious exhaustion or manipulation.

Piper flopped back down onto her pillows. "Holy shit."

Oliver had been everything she'd dreamed of and more. She'd expected a man his size to be big, but usually they arrogantly thought the girth was enough and got lazy or didn't know what to do with it.

Oliver did.

He knew exactly what to do with his cock.

And his mouth, his fingers, his everything.

It had become clear, very quickly, her pleasure was important to him. And what a pleasant surprise that was. Certainly a first in her world.

Piper reached for the glass of water and noticed a piece of paper under it.

Go home, Piper. Please trust me on this. I will visit you when I return and explain everything. Oli x

She let out a sigh. It wasn't the romantic love note she'd been expecting. Not that what they'd done was make love. Far from it. Trying to get rid of her wasn't exactly the welcome she was hoping for after what they'd shared.

Well, too bad.

She wasn't leaving—she had a job to do, a story to break and a Pulitzer to win.

Piper decided it was best to carry on with her plans and find out what she could about Oliver and his friends and any other leads she came across. She would have to keep her wits about her, and not let that cock of his distract her.

She stretched her deliciously sore limbs.

Somehow, they were all linked. Sage, Ari, Oliver and BioZen. She just didn't know how.

Yet.

But she would.

After a long hot shower, Piper grabbed a bagel from the breakfast buffet and climbed into an Uber.

First, she visited two of the largest BioZen facilities, asking for both Sage and Dr. Phillips. She was told the same thing: Sage no longer worked there. Dr. Phillips was not located at that venue, and they couldn't give out his number.

Whatever.

She left her card again and sniffed around until the security people began making their way toward her.

She stopped for lunch at a café nearby and sat watching employees and eventually opened her laptop.

Sipping her ridiculously hot coffee, she scrolled through thread after thread of vampire conspiracy theories. Many of them started months ago when the news first broke about their existence.

It had been shocking at the time and for days the world was in a spin. Then the media machines had quickly worked overtime to report the news as fake. While most people had believed it was all a conspiracy—and wanted to believe that—there was a small group who thought there truly was another race of intelligent beings living amongst them.

Piper quickly noticed a couple of regular commenters stirring up trouble. She immediately picked it for what it was. Counterterrorism. People hired to post and comment with the intent to shift beliefs.

Fake news spammers in other words.

Or… were they *truth* news spammers?

Who knew?

It was what marketers did every day through advertising and news media.

In a world where data and knowledge was king, you had to step away from listening to those claiming to be an expert—or worse, the one source of truth—and trust your intuition.

And Piper did.

She didn't rely on other people telling her what the truth was. She did her own research and used her intuition. She hoped it would make her a phenomenally successful journalist one day soon.

With a few more clicks she traced more credible posters who looked like they had something tangible to share.

She clicked on contact and sent several of them a message.

Now she'd wait.

CHAPTER SIXTEEN

Oliver finished typing out the message to Darren, asking for the updated intel, then threw his phone on the sofa behind him and lifted the lid on his laptop.

"Stop fucking staring at me," he growled at Ben.

"Why? I'm studying the anatomy of an idiot," Ben replied.

Kurt shook his head and kept scrolling on his smartphone.

"I fucked her. That's all. Get over it."

He was being a dick and knew it, but he wasn't ready to be lectured about Piper. And it wasn't Ben's place to do it. Sure, Ben was trying to be a friend and keep him from making a poor decision, but it was a little late for that.

"Didn't Ari tell you she was off-limits?" Ben asked, raising his brows.

"Oh, you mean like that time he said the Moretti royal family were off-limits?" Ben's brows dropped. "Yeah, thought so. Fuck off, Ben."

The two of them had been friends for decades.

Best friends.

This wasn't their first debate, nor would it be their last. The Institute was full of alpha testosterone and, despite their training, at times fists and words could fly. Sometimes you just had to punch an asshole in the face.

And Ben was being an asshole.

Even though he was right. Oli should have stayed the fuck away from Piper Roberts, except he didn't regret a single damn moment of it.

His cock twitched.

Sorry, false alarm, buddy.

"Slightly different, Oliver Cammbiaaaaghi," Ben said, over-emphasizing his full name and giving him the bird. "Anyway, Anna was my mate."

Kurt let out a long sigh, stood and pulled his black Moretti sweatpants up, giving the waistband a snap. "Okay, ladies. Put your cocks away and let's get back to work. Do we have the intel from The Institute yet?"

Oliver shook his head and placed the laptop on the sofa beside him. "Should be through in the next few minutes."

He got up and walked to the glass doors, pulling the thick drapes aside. The sun was setting fast. None of them liked staying in hotels that weren't vampire protected, but hopefully they were only here for a few days. Meanwhile, the heavy drapes were sufficient to keep out the bright light.

Oliver hoped Piper had seen his message and decided to fly home, though the chances of that happening were close to zero.

It was worth a try.

Plus, he hadn't wanted to just disappear without leaving a note. What he'd really wanted to say was: *your pussy was the sweetest thing I've ever tasted, and I want to please you all over again.*

Or: w*atching your face as I slid you up and down my cock was the hottest thing I've ever fucking seen.*

Just thinking about it had his cock hardening.

Shit.

Ben was right. He had to forget about Piper. He had lied to Ari yesterday—or at the very least he'd omitted a really important piece of information.

Thing was, he had it handled. He'd convince her to go home now he'd fucked her, and wipe her memories. Then they could all go back to their lives and carry on.

"Why was she able to remember you?" Ben asked, like a dog with a fucking bone.

Oli turned.

"I don't fucking know. She's magic or something."

She has a magic pussy, I know that.

"That's weird." Kurt said, crossing his arms and leaning on a doorframe. "You ever had that happen before?"

Oliver looked from Ben to Kurt, then shook his head.

"Never."

"This is going out on a limb here, but you don't think BioZen have done anything to her that's impacting our abilities, do you?"

He frowned at the SLC for a long moment. "I know she's related to Sage, but she only found out about the program after Ari and I met her. There's no connection. Unless it's completely coincidental."

Ben nodded thoughtfully.

"You said she's a journalist?" Oliver nodded at Ben. "Then it's doubtful. The last thing they're going to do is get media involved with unethical experimentations. The media would blow that story up in a millisecond."

There was heavy silence as they suddenly realized what they were saying. Eyeballs bulged and brows shot up.

"Fuck me." Kurt pushed away from the wall.

"Jesus. Is that what they're doing?" Oliver ran a hand through his hair. They better not have harmed Piper, or he'd fucking rip their heads off on the spot.

Whoa.

Where they hell had that thought come from?

"They're making little super-soldiers. Fuck me," Ben said, shooting to his feet.

"Ring Ari. I'll call the prince," Kurt ordered. "We need to find these pricks, and fast."

As Kurt burst out of the room with his phone in his hand, the door slowly closed behind him, as hotel room doors did. The quiet click didn't seem to fit the mood and would have been comical if the situation wasn't so damn serious.

Ben stood and slipped his hands in his pockets. "I doubt very much that's why Piper remembers you." He calmly walked to the door. "You need to tell Ari everything."

"I can't."

"Dude, she's hot. He'll understand. It's not like you to keep it in your pants, anyway."

Oli shook his head. "You don't—"

"I know she's Sage's sister. That's more reason to tell him."

Oliver felt the tension in his neck spread through his body. Jesus, he'd fucked up.

"He'll get it," Ben pressed. "But you need to wipe—"

"I fucked Sage," Oliver spit out.

Ben froze, then his mouth fell open.

"Twice. Well, once. Technically. Two separate times." He couldn't stop talking. "Once with my cock. That was the second time. The first time I only licked... Jesus. It doesn't matter."

Ben wiped his hand over his face. "Ari knows?"

"Of course he knows. He was there. Well, he was there for the first time. And listening the second."

"Listening?" Ben asked, his brows raised. Then he let out a short laugh. "Okay, I know we've all done some interesting stuff with females, but he's always been more of an action guy."

Oliver scowled.

"Right. Missed the point. You fucked his mate." Ben nodded repeatedly. "And lived to tell the story. So… now you're fucking his mate's sister."

"No. Last night was the first time."

"Really? Because it sounded like—"

"It was the first time. And the last," Oliver said firmly, because it had to be. "It's out of my system. Forbidden fruit and all that."

Ben nodded, looking completely unconvinced.

"She's here looking into the same people we are. She just doesn't know that. I've told her to leave, but she's as stubborn as a mule. We need to keep an eye on her. If only to keep Ari's new sister-in-law alive."

He then shared what he'd learned from Piper the night before. He was right to be concerned about her getting close to dangerous people and looking into things she had no idea about. Eventually she'd hit a brick wall—BioZen weren't exactly going to tell her anything—and go home.

But when?

Damn the sunlight. Oliver had barely slept lying there wondering what she was up to while he couldn't follow or keep an eye on her.

This path she was on wasn't a safe one.

He knew this was what journalists did, but this was a whole new ball game. If BioZen learned what she was trying to do…

Shit.

"So she's writing a story? That isn't good," Ben said. "Tell Ari that Sage needs to get in touch with her sister and ask her to come home."

Oliver ran a hand over his short hair. "Yeah, that could do it."

After Ben left, Oliver pressed the green button on his phone and waited for Ari to answer.

"*Ciao*, Oliver," Ari said in greeting.

"Hey," replied, waiting for the video to load properly. When it did, he saw the familiar bookcase on the wall behind the director. Good, he was in his office, but he wanted to be sure before he launched into it. "We need to speak privately."

"*Si*, I'm alone. What's going on, Oliver?"

Oliver knew the ancient vampire well enough, that when his Italian accent got thick, the male was in a serious mood. And it was thick.

"We believe the humans have already begun human experimentation. It's likely why Dr. Phillips is in California. He's led the science of this program so it makes sense Tomassi would appoint him as the lead on the execution phase."

"Especially while Xander Tomassi remains hidden," Ari replied.

Oliver nodded. "Kurt is updating the royal family as we speak."

"Do we have proof yet?" Ari asked.

Oliver shook his head. "No, but I suspect we will find it. Although Ben—"

He stopped short of sharing his friend's thoughts on why Oli's memory wipe had failed on Piper.

"Ben?"

"No, nothing important. We are heading out in a few minutes, so will you update the team, or should I brief Travis?"

Ari stared at him for a long moment and Oliver felt a chill run through him. Damn it, he needed to get his shit together. He wanted to prove he was worthy of this job and his desire for Piper was fucking that up.

"One other thing," he said, and Ari's eyes locked on his as if he'd been waiting for him to share something else. "Piper Roberts is here."

Those ancient eyes darkened. "Why?"

Why? That felt all kinds of accusatory, but he couldn't blame his boss. Ari was too old and experienced to accept a lie as truth. He'd know Ben hadn't told the full truth.

The last thing Oliver wanted was the trust between them broken. He had to fix this.

"She's here on business. She's a journalist, if you recall, and she's doing a story," Oliver replied.

"You spoke to her?"

Fuck.

"Yes."

"Does she remember you?"

Shit.

"Yes."

"I think it's time you told me what's going on, Oliver. All of it," Ari said sternly.

Oliver let out a long sigh and moved to sit on the couch. "Wiping her memory isn't working. I've tried twice, three times. Maybe more."

"More? How many fucking times have you seen her?" Ari's voice rose. "Wait. Are you—"

"Yes," he replied, running a hand over his head. "Last night. I fucked her, okay?"

Ari groaned. "Christ. This makes things complicated. We're about to send Sage back into her family's life and my goddamn head assassin is fucking her sister."

Oliver rubbed the back of his neck.

He felt like he should apologize, but he wasn't going to. He hardly wanted to admit this to himself, but last night had been... kind of incredible. She'd never hear him say it, but apologizing for what they shared felt disrespectful and he wouldn't do that.

"Sage needs to ring Piper tonight and tell her she's alive and kicking," Oliver said. "Piper is here looking for you both and thinks BioZen is mixed up in your disappearance."

Ari cursed.

"I wiped her memory, Ari. I swear it. She keeps remembering. That's why she arrived at the mansion the night you turned Sage."

"How?"

"I don't know." He replied honestly. "It partly worked. It's jumbled her memories more than anything. She knows you and I are friends. She remembers that I know Sage. That's appears to be all."

He let that sink in, then added. "Ari, she's smart and brave, but naïve enough to get herself into trouble here. If BioZen work out what she's looking into, I'm pretty sure they'll hurt her. And we can't protect her during the day."

More cursing.

"Keep an eye on her. And try to keep your cock inside your pants," Ari said, and Oliver tried not to cringe. "Sage will phone her. I just don't know when. That will be up to her."

Oli nodded.

"Oliver."

He raised a brow.

"I selected you as my head assassin for a reason. Don't lie to me again."

"I won't, sir."

"You never have before, so I gave you time to rectify it. And you have. If… fuck, I can't believe I'm about to say this, but *if* Piper is your mate, then you need to tell me," Ari said.

Mate? Oliver blanched. "No. Fuck no."

"Okay."

"She's just... some females... you know how it is. She pushed my buttons and I had to fuck her. Yes, I'm an asshole. Wrong female to get horny over. I get it."

"Especially because of Sage," Ari said.

"I know. Shit. God, don't tell her."

Sage had a special place in his heart. Not because of what the three of them had done. She wasn't the first or the last female he'd had a threesome with. Nights like that were common in his life.

Perhaps it was because she was Ari's mate, or that she had helped Callan escape? Deep down, he knew it wasn't that. Vampires might only have one mate, but just like humans, they got along with some people better than others.

When he'd been playing sexually with Sage, a connection had formed that didn't happen often. He cared for her, and he liked that she saw the goodness in him. His job saw him do some dark stuff, and it was like Sage chased away the bad.

Piper, on the other hand, made him want to be a really bad boy. With her. And he loved it. He could be all of himself and her body reacted so fucking beautifully.

But no more.

She was off-limits.

"I won't lie to my mate," Ari said. "But I won't offer the information unless she asks me directly."

Oliver bunched his lips together and nodded. Sage would ask. He knew it. So, clearly, did Ari. Both the sisters were smart and intuitive.

"Okay." Oliver walked to the counter, picking up his handgun and tucking it into the back of his jeans. He lifted one of two medium length blades, flicked it around in his hands and then slid it into his ankle holster. Then repeated it with the second, which went into a wrist strap.

A beep on his phone alerted him the information had come through from Darren.

"Keep me updated," Ari ordered.

"Roger that," he said, and ended the call.

Oliver shoved his phone into his front jeans pocket and slid on his black jacket. He grabbed a bottle of water out of the fridge and then walked out the door.

Time to go hunting.

For evil little scientists.

And hot, sexy little journalists.

CHAPTER SEVENTEEN

Vincent leaned back in his large chair and stared at Brayden. "This isn't good."

"Nope."

"If it's true, they've progressed much faster than we thought."

Brayden tapped his ankle up and down on his knee. This was the worst-case fucking scenario. Or close to it.

"So none of your pals on the team have seen or heard anything?"

Vincent frowned at him.

"It's called Operation Daylight. It's not a goddamn *softball* team, Brayden," the king said. "And no. Every single member would have a vested interest in speaking up if they discovered a new species of soldier was being created by BioZen."

Brayden shook his head. "I don't trust any of them. Show me a world leader in history that's been completely honest and trustworthy, and I'll eat my shoe."

"Gandhi," Vincent said.

"Pfft. Debatable."

"The Pope, one through whatever number we're up to now."

Brayden laughed. "Nice try but no cigar."

Wasn't the church even more corrupt than politicians? They had both seen far too many things over their long lives, and had information long forgotten by humans passed down from their father and grandfather. Ari's brother.

Vincent let out a sigh and reached for a pen which he started tapping on the desk pad in front of him. The king was a scribbler and there were notes and wiggles all over the paper.

Brayden knew Vincent thought as he scribbled. He just didn't see a way to strategize out of this. He wanted to take action.

Sure there was a time to be patient, but if they waited much longer, God knows what these scientists could let out into the world.

"I'll speak to POTUS, and we might call an urgent video meeting on this with the Operation Daylight team. It might be hearsay but if they are moving into execution phase then this could be happening globally. They have the funds to act quickly."

Yeah, and that was a fucking terrifying thought. For all they knew, the entire globe could be covered in little human-vampire soldiers within months.

"I'll call Ari in a moment unless you want to," Brayden said.

"No, you go ahead. I'll call him if things escalate."

"Okay." Brayden nodded, pleased the king was leaving this to him. "Kurt is with Ben and Oliver in Los Angeles still, so if they find any proof, we'll know when they know."

Vincent tapped his pen on the pad. "Good. Stay in close contact with them. I know you do anyway, but I just need to say it."

Brayden gave him a nod.

"I get it. This is a nightmare."

"Do we need to send more of our teams?" Vincent asked.

Brayden shook his head.

"Not yet. Craig is with Alex in Portland, so they can mobilize if they need more bodies on the ground. We're running completely blind right now. Once we have some intel, I'll be dispersing more teams. This is too fucking important to sit back."

The king grunted.

"We can't let them replicate our strength and abilities into humans, Vincent. You know that," Brayden said. "We have to destroy them."

Humans roaming the globe with the type of power the average vampire had—even half of it – would be incredibly dangerous for all living creatures.

They had to be stopped.

And fast.

"I can't just act aggressively and without consultation. We are in this treaty with the world leaders. It will be of great benefit to us long term. But it comes at a cost," Vincent said. "It's how the world works right now."

"And that cost is letting a third unknown and uncontrollable species be created? By humans with a history of war and destruction?"

"Fuck!" Vincent stood and thrust his hand through his thick dark hair. "I know."

Brayden shook his head and stood.

"Think on it. I understand your situation, but I'm telling you there isn't time for boardroom chit-chat."

Vincent nodded and stared at the painting of their parents on the wall. Both of them were happy to be back in the Maine castle, which had been their home for over a century.

Brayden turned to leave.

"What are your plans?" Vincent asked.

"I'm not going into the field. I need to stay in the castle," Brayden replied, knowing it would raise questions. It was

highly unlike him to sit things out, but nothing, not even this, would make him leave his mate's side right now.
Absolutely nothing.
Well, unless the king's life was being threatened.

CHAPTER EIGHTEEN

"What do we have?" Kurt asked as they stood outside the hotel, waiting for their rental car to be brought around.

Sure, they could have teleported here and there, but this was Los Angeles, and they didn't really know where they were going. Plus, appearing out of nowhere in crowded places wasn't a good idea.

Instead, they'd rented a black SUV and were going to drive around the damn city looking for a needle in a haystack. Should be as effective as throwing darts into the wind.

But that was the recon life. You started at zero.

Oliver pulled out his phone and began scrolling through the intel that Darren had sent through earlier.

"We're headed to a couple of BioZen's properties. The team found documentation online about a newly rented spot. It wasn't immediately obvious as it went through several changes in ownership including some offshore accounts before they traced it back to the pharma company. Dodgy assholes," Oliver said, as Ben took the phone from him.

"Looks residential. Could be Phillips' house," Ben said.

"Well, we're not out to scare wives and kids if he has them, so let's just observe and see what we find," Kurt said, rubbing the scruff on his face.

"Agreed." Oliver nodded.

"Yeah man. We're not the monsters here," Ben added.

Kurt snorted. "Shame humans don't realize."

"The ladies don't mind us biting." Oliver smirked.

"No they don't." Kurt grinned. "And I don't mind providing the service."

"You ever go to one of the prince's infamous orgies?" Oliver asked, his curiosity getting the better of him.

Kurt grinned wider. "God, I miss those nights. Talk about Uber Eats."

They all burst out laughing as their rental SUV pulled up alongside them.

A young man in a hotel uniform handed him the keys, and Oliver tipped him a few dollars while Ben and Kurt loaded it with a couple of bags he knew contained their tools of the trade—aka weapons and shit.

He went around to the driver's door and got comfortable adjusting mirrors and the seat. When he pulled away from the curb, Ben handed him a pouch of plasma with the seal ripped open.

Oliver squeezed it into his mouth and moaned.

Two hours later, they'd scoped out the two large BioZen properties and, as expected, the security was tight. However, they'd been able to get close enough to assess there were no new constructions at either place.

"It's still an assumption," Ben said. "They could be utilizing current facilities that we don't have eyes on."

"Not for something like this," Kurt said. "They'd have super tight security like we saw in Seattle, to keep it away from most of their employees' eyes. It'll be a pretty big operation, I'd say, and hard to hide. I've got my money on it being in a different, undisclosed location."

Oliver nodded as he leaned on the steering wheel. He agreed with the Moretti soldier. He stared into the rear parking lot of the pharmaceutical company and tried to put himself in Tomassi's shoes.

Think like the enemy.

"Let's go look at this other address and see if it is Phillips' home and then work out a plan," he said.

They drove a few miles away and slowed as they entered the quiet residential area. He turned off the headlights and let the vehicle slide to a stop.

"Two Joes up ahead." He spoke quietly.

"SUV across the road," Kurt added, as they all scanned the environment and quickly identified the private security surrounding the scientist's house.

"Do we think it's him?" Oliver asked.

"Yeah. Let's drop the tracer and get out of here. We want to be as covert as possible on this," Ben replied, referring to the plan they'd agreed on during the drive.

They didn't want to draw attention to the fact they were in California and this way they could have some visibility on what was happening during the day if it was the scientist's car. Hopefully, he'd lead them directly to the new location. Unless they were all completely off track. If so, they would have to reset.

They still had no idea where Xander Tomassi was, so *if* they were right, this was their chance to get a step ahead for a change.

"Who's going in? Shall we toss a coin, or should I do it while you two paint your nails?" Kurt asked.

Ben grinned.

"I'll go, you idiots," Oliver said. He held out his hand and Kurt dropped the magnetic device in it. "Don't fall asleep."

He heard their sniggers as he teleported out of the vehicle, then tele-jumped, as he called it, to get a little closer.

Once he was near the house he glanced around. Two security men, dressed just like him in head-to-toe black, stood near the driveway. Oliver stood silently in the shadows watching them for a moment until he was sure they were human.

His eyes slid to the SUV across the road where two sizable human men sat quietly sipping shitty coffee out of a flask.

At least he imagined it was shitty, and they had donuts in the console to match.

Once he was sure he hadn't drawn anyone's attention, he turned his focus on the house. It was a large four-bedroom home by the look of the structure. Nothing fancy. The landscaping was pretty simple and one of those lock-up-and-leave type homes.

Not that he was Mr. Nine to Five and knew these things from direct experience. Like all the assassins at The Institute, they were trained to assess everything fast, even if the situation wasn't one they were familiar with.

He took a step out of the shadows and further down the drive. Bingo. A brand-new silver Lexus sedan. He teleported beside the vehicle and crouched.

Then waited.

Silence.

Did they invite you in for a midnight snack or are you just slow these days?

Fuck off, Ben. Oliver grinned.

He slipped his hand under the vehicle and waited for the magnet to connect.

Tap.

If any of the security guys had seen or heard him and ended up pointing a gun at his head in the next thirty seconds, it would be fine. He had back-up, but he'd still prefer to do this unnoticed.

He stood and looked around, confident he hadn't been seen, and teleported back to the seat inside the SUV.

"Jesus, give me a flipping heart attack," Ben said, slamming himself against the passenger door.

Oliver grinned, turning on the engine. "I'm sorry, do you have a swear jar at home now you've mated?"

"Fuck off."

"It's all starting to make sense now." Kurt shook his head. "How did you two ever get anything done working together?"

Oliver shot Ben a grin, then quietly moved the vehicle out of the road, flicked on the headlights and they sped back to the hotel.

Oliver threw the keys to the valet as Kurt grabbed the bags and they all walked back into the lobby.

They got a few looks, but that wasn't unusual. Three huge vampires dressed all in black looking like a bunch of, well, assassins, were likely to get noticed. If the humans had any idea the level of metal Oli and his colleagues were carrying, they would scatter like mice.

If the humans knew they were vampires, they'd scream.

Oliver let slip a half smirk.

Still, it wasn't funny. It was their job to ensure humans didn't find out about them. For as long as possible. He couldn't imagine a time when humans could be trusted.

"Beer?" Ben asked, nodding to the bar.

"Yeah, there's nothing we can do until morning, when Phillips leaves for work. Shower, then I'll meet you both down here," Kurt said.

Every part of Oliver's body was screaming to go to Piper's room. He wanted to know if she was still here.

Liar. You want to taste her again.

Ari *had* said keep an eye on her, so perhaps he'd pop by for a visit.

CHAPTER NINETEEN

"So, what did you find?" Piper asked the man sitting opposite her. George McMasters was on his second IPA craft beer and making it very clear he found her attractive.

Sure, he was a good-looking guy. Tall, nice bod, shaggy blond Californian hair, but that's not why she was having a drink with him.

George believed in vampires.

Like, he was absolutely convinced they were real.

"Nothing yet. At least nothing we can take to the bank, you know."

Dammit.

"Would you be willing to share your contacts with us? I mean, if this article gets published, then I'll put your name in it, of course. This kind of exposure would be huge for your blog."

George nodded slowly. "I want to say yes. *The Seattle Times* obviously has some clout, but these people are very private. I can't just hand their details over."

Piper uncrossed and re-crossed her legs. George watched them as he took a swig of his beer. It wasn't the first time she'd used her sexuality to encourage a man to spill his secrets. She never slept with them—okay fine, she'd slept with one or two but only because she wanted to. But she didn't do it to get the information. If they didn't share, then she walked.

George finally realized he was staring at her legs and caught himself.

"Start from the top and let's see if we can find a way to work together because one way or another, after what I've learned today, I am not walking away from this story." Piper smiled and took a sip of her wine.

"Shit. Then we're going to need more drinks."

Piper indicated to the barman for another round. She'd heard back from all the bloggers she reached out to, and they were eager to share what they knew. Most of them wanted fame and to go viral.

Like George, the others had a ton of theories, but what made him stand out was his claim to know someone who had seen a vampire.

"So you haven't met him or her?" Piper asked.

"Not yet."

"But you could arrange it? Could I be there?" she asked, pressing. George's eyes dropped to her bare legs. Maybe sitting at the bar had not been the best idea. He literally wasn't paying attention.

"Let me talk to my contacts," George said. "First, let's get to know each other. You know, so I can trust you. Are you single or—"

"Hello, darling. Miss me?" a voice asked as a set of lips found hers.

Piper froze.

Large warm hands landed on her back and thigh, and when his lips left hers, the bluest eyes burned into hers.

"Well, I guess that answers that question." George laughed, then held out a hand. "George McMasters."

"Oliver Cambiaghi."

The two men shook hands while she recovered from the shock of his kiss.

"What are you doing here, *darling*? I told you I was in a business meeting," she ground out, after clearing her throat.

Oliver wrapped his arm around her lower body possessively and let out a light laugh. "Oh, honey, its after ten. You know you work far too much."

George stared at the two of them, lifting his beer to his mouth. "So what do you think about this story she's doing then? Are you a believer?"

"In?" Oliver asked.

Oh crap.

"Vampires."

Shit.

What in the actual fuck?

Oliver stiffened.

Vampires? She was doing a fucking story on vampires?

Of course, she fucking was. Of all the goddamn people on the planet, Piper fucking Roberts was the journalist pursuing this story.

"I believe my pretty wife has worked enough for tonight," Oliver said firmly in response.

"Wi—"

His hand slid between her thighs and he took joy in her little gasp. He turned his back on George, blocking him out.

"Can I whisk you away for some naughty fun, darlin'? We've only been married a short time, and as you can see, I can barely keep my hands off her," Oliver said over his shoulder.

"Gotcha man." George dropped his beer on the bar. "Give me a bell tomorrow, Piper. I'll talk to my contacts and see what I can set up."

"Thanks, George. Sorry..." Piper tried to peek over his shoulder, giving Oliver a dark look.

George laughed. "Hey, have fun, you two lovebirds."

Oliver watched the man walk away, then his eyes dropped to Piper's. The fire in them shot straight to his cock.

"Wife? Really?" she growled.

"Consummated just last night." He grinned.

"Over my dead body."

"Preferably not. I'm into kinky things, but that's going too far, even for me, darlin'."

Piper swallowed.

"Don't worry. I think I know your limits." He smirked. "However, I'm not opposed to pushing them."

"You know nothing about me," she snapped, trying to get off the stool. "Take your hands off me and stop with all that southern accent of yours. You think it will let you get away with anything."

He barely had much of an accent left after living in Seattle for decades, but he let out a snort and let her jump down from the stool. Then took her arm and led her over to a table. His eyes tracked to the entrance as Kurt and Ben walked in.

Grab us both a beer and come join us, he told Ben telepathically.

I thought you were keeping away from her?

Ari told me to keep an eye on her. So I am. She just met with a man to discuss vampires.

The fuck?

He sat Piper down on the cushioned bench and dropped down next to her, then casually laid his hand along the bench top behind her.

"Vampires?" he asked, raising his brows in question.

"You can't just push me around like this," she said, ignoring him, but Oliver could tell she was affected being this close to him.

Just as he was affected by her presence.

He leaned down into her hair. "My two friends are joining us in a moment, so before they do, tell me how wet you are right now."

Her head snapped around and she hissed at him. "Stop it."

Before he could stop himself, his hand was on one of her thighs, nudging them apart. Her groan shot straight to his cock, and he had to shift as the hardness pressed against his zipper.

Because, commando.

Two beers landed in front of them, drawing his attention.

"We meet again," Kurt said, dropping into a seat. Ben followed.

"I'm Ben. You're Sage's sister?"

"Yes." She nodded.

"I'm Kurt."

"Hey."

"Piper was just telling me about vampires," Oliver said.

She groaned and tried to push his hand off her thigh, but he wasn't moving. "No, I wasn't."

Oliver knew Ben noticed the scuffle and was taking notes. Too bad. His body was all up in flames being next to her like this. So much for it only being one night. He wanted to throw her on the table, spread her wide and slam into her.

Fuck the public.

Fuck the rules.

"You believe in vampires?" Ben asked, taking a sip of his lager.

She shrugged.

"I'm just working on a story. I don't know what I believe. What do you think?" Piper asked, digging her nails deep into his skin in an attempt to get him to move his hand.

That's my little tiger.

"Seems unlikely. You know, with technology and shit," Ben answered, shaking his head.

"Don't they drink blood? Wouldn't we all have teeth marks if they were just walking around biting people?" Kurt asked, and dropped his beer on the table with a smirk.

Oliver ran a hand over his mouth to hide his smile.

Piper's hand flew to her neck unconsciously, and he suddenly wanted to sink his damn fangs into her. God, she would taste delicious if her pussy was anything to go by.

Shit.

"What about you?" she asked him. "Seeing as *you* wanted to talk about it."

He cleared his throat.

"What I want is for you to get your sexy ass on a plane and go home. You're dabbling in dangerous stuff, darlin'. Let me arrange a jet to take you home."

She narrowed her eyes at him. "No."

He shook his head.

"And that's the second time you've refused to answer the question," she pointed out, as he lifted his beer to his lips.

"Oh my God, you're a believer!" she exclaimed, and he nearly spat his beer across the table. "I can see it in your eyes. Tell me what you know."

"Oh, boy." Kurt turned away, glancing around the bar.

"What I know is that you need to go home. Now, do I need to fly you home myself or will you get on the damn jet?" He growled.

She stared at him and began to grin.

What the fuck?

"You believe," she said, still smiling, and took a big sip of her beer. Across from him, Ben and Kurt were smirking.

"What are y'all smiling at?"

And the assholes just kept smiling at him. It was like being surrounded by a bunch of fucking circus clowns.

"Well, husband, I need my beauty sleep, so I am going to love and leave you. Thank you for this enlightening conversation." She patted his leg.

Kurt choked on his beer.

Ben's brows shot to his hairline.

Husband?

Oliver shook his head, then Piper moved her hands up his thigh, close to his cock, and squeezed. "Let me pass or I will scream."

Oliver raised a brow. "God, you're a smoking hot pain in the ass. Did you know that?"

"Good to know," she said, patting his leg as if to placate him, and then stood when he moved out of her way.

"Gentlemen," she said with a wave, and then she swaggered out of the bar with a wiggle of her hips.

Oliver rubbed his jaw, his eyes never leaving her. When she turned the corner and disappeared, he cursed.

"Go," Kurt said. "You're no good to anyone in this state. Well, except her."

Ben laughed.

CHAPTER TWENTY

"Piper's in LA?" Sage asked, her eyes widening. "Looking for me?"

Ari nodded.

"Oliver is keeping an eye on her, but she's, and I quote, *like a dog with a bone.*" He failed to hide his smirk.

Sage pressed her lips together.

"Hmm, she's like that at times. But I thought you'd dealt with my family."

So did I.

"Some people don't respond well to having their memory wiped."

Which wasn't true. If it were, half the planet would know about vampires, but he didn't want to worry his new mate. He trusted Oliver would deal with the situation one way or another. It didn't sound like he was taking his eyes off her.

It was unlike his new head assassin to let his cock lead his thinking, and that's why he had asked if Piper was Oliver's mate. The two of them had clashed from the moment they met. He'd witnessed it himself the night he teleported to Piper's apartment.

Initially, he thought it was a fair and reasonable reaction to the sassy human. Now? He was beginning to wonder if there was a deeper pull between them.

He wasn't completely lying to Sage about the memory wiping being ineffective. Ari had seen it from time to time over his long life. The difference was, it wasn't the human that was the issue. It was the vampire.

For some reason, Oliver didn't want Piper to forget.

Sure, he could ask Ben to step in, but Ari had learned enough in his life to let things play out and not interfere unless necessary. Piper wasn't a huge threat, and with his team and the Moretti warriors there, she was protected enough for the moment.

"How typical that my stubborn sister is one of them." Sage shook her head. "So you want me to ring her?"

Ari nodded.

"She's sniffing around BioZen, and I don't need to tell you why that's a bad idea."

He saw the concern on Sage's face.

"Sage," he said, stepping closer and cupping her face. "I know Piper hurt you years ago, but now you're immortal and have a long life ahead of you. Consider forgiving her."

"I have."

He held her eyes.

"Okay fine, I haven't completely." She lowered her eyes. "I don't know how to. There's no forgiveness manual."

He smiled sadly at her. "No. There's not."

Those beautiful eyes lifted to his again. "So, how do you forgive?"

"You choose it, sweetheart. That's it. By making the decision, life will show you the rest." He kissed her nose and turned to leave. "I'll be in my office if you need me. Stick to our agreed story when you speak to Piper, the one we'll tell your parents, and everything will be okay."

"Got it. Lie to my entire family." Sage nodded. "No problem."

Ari felt a pang of guilt for a split second then pushed it away. Sage was still adjusting to her new life and working out who and what she was now. And how she fit into her former human world. In one hundred years her family would be a blip in her memory bank.

He was her mate and future.

They could be the Adam and Eve to their own bloodline of Moretti's if they were blessed with children. He had to be patient and allow her to work through these massive changes in her life.

If he'd had his way, Sage would step fully into her new vampire life right now, but he knew the importance of family and wouldn't take away what few years she had left with them.

But when the time came and they created their own family, it would change everything for the race. Ari was ready to outline what that meant to everyone, including the royal family.

Sage tried for a third time and then decided to leave a message.

"Piper, it's me. Sage." *Obviously.* She rolled her eyes. "We're back from our holiday in the Caribbean. Wondered if you wanted to catch up. Call me back. I have… *news!*"

She hung up.

News? Boy, did she ever. *Hey! I'm a vampire.* But that wasn't what she was going to tell her sister.

She was Captain Obvious today.

She was going to break the news that Ari had asked her to marry him. On top of the damn Space Needle, risking her life.

Something she'd leave out.

Not that she could die anymore. Mostly. God, it was so confusing.

Becoming a vampire was not at all what she thought it would be. Not that she'd had much time to dwell on it in the twenty-four hours she'd known about vampires before Ari changed her. But the scientist in her was curious to understand more. Even before she knew vamps were real, she'd never imagined, while reading her sexy paranormal romance books, that it would feel like *this*.

Firstly, the emotions were a surprise. She grieved her human state. She couldn't go out in daylight ever again. She would never grow old, get gray hair, or wrinkles, and she'd never get sick.

Aside from never actually having a tropical holiday, despite their cover story, none of those things appeared to be anything to cry over. Hell, who didn't want to stay young and healthy forever? Yet, it felt completely unnatural and defied what she had always known—especially as a scientist—as normal.

Everyone was telling her she'd adjust.

Brianna and Willow had sat with her during her transition, but because she'd been in a state of shock and rage at Ari for turning her without permission, she'd barely acknowledged them, let alone taken the opportunity to ask questions.

Nevertheless, they had shared their thoughts, and she'd tried to recall as many of them as possible.

At the time, Ari had been her focus. She had been fighting an overwhelming love for him, which day by day dampened her anger. As a human, it had been powerful, but now it was all-encompassing.

She breathed every day simply so she could love him.

And she knew he did the same.

Then, to her surprise, she learned Ari was not just any old (literally) vampire—he was the remaining original vampire. His twin brother, Gio, had passed away over a thousand years ago.

She was only beginning to understand what that meant, but it was clear Ari wanted a family. A line of his own. From what she understood, it could take decades for that to happen.

Sage didn't know how she felt about that.

While she'd been happy to put her career first for a while, she'd never planned to wait a hundred years to be a mother. Plus, how did one fit into society with a vampire baby?

God, she had so many questions.

Ari appeared to be forthcoming with answers, but she knew he was drip-feeding facts so as not to overwhelm her. She loved him for it, but she was a scientist. Knowledge was power, and she wasn't going to sit around and be wrapped in bubble wrap by her ridiculously sexy mate.

She texted Willow.

Hey, thanks for plugging in your number. Can we do a video chat one night? I'm spiraling. Just like you said I might. Sage.

...

Absolutely. And Brianna?

Yes! Sorry, I was rude while you were in Seattle.

Girl. Do not apologize. Losing your humanity is a big damn deal. But it's going to be okay, and we're here for you.

Thanks Willow.

Send me the time and date, and we'll see your gorgeous face then.

Sage flopped onto the sofa and let out a long sigh.

In her other life, she probably wouldn't have been friends with Willow. The Moretti princess was cool and full of life. Sage was a scientist who wore sensible shoes and glasses. But she'd liked the female immediately.

Brianna was simply adorable, and despite Sage's state, she hadn't missed the dynamics and bantering between the two female vampires. It was like watching a sitcom.

Ari had talked about going to the Moretti castle in Maine in the coming months, so Sage was excited to get to know them better. After all, Willow was technically her great-great-great niece or something really damn weird like that.

Brianna was a token member of the Moretti family through her mate Craig and her friendship with the princess.

She wished the women were based in Seattle. It may have only been a few weeks but already she was overwhelmed with all the males in the mansion. A few girlfriends would be nice.

It wasn't like he could call Tina for a catch up or pop in for lunch at the BioZen café. She wasn't the first person to leave behind a work friend and never touch base again. It happened, and Sage had too many other things to focus on. But she did miss their little chats.

She let out a sigh.

Most women would be thrilled to be surrounded by so many gorgeous muscly men who walked around shirtless. It wasn't horrible, that was for sure. She loved Ari, but still appreciated the testosterone wallpaper.

Not that she'd ever say that out loud.

It would just be nice to have some girl-vampire friends.

Words she never thought she'd say.

She let out a long breath and called her mom.

"Hello," her mom answered.

"Hey, Mom."

"Sage! Oh Sage. Darling, you're home," Maryanne Roberts said. "How was your holiday? Tell me all about it."

Tears sprang to her eyes. If only she knew her daughter had died. The human baby she gave birth to no longer lived. Now she was a different species.

It was wrong, and yet such a gift.

"It was good. We completely unplugged and had a great rest. Lots of cocktails and lazy walks on the beach."

Stick to the script.

"Sounds amazing. I keep telling your father we should go to the Caribbean."

"You should, Mom." Sage drew in a nervous breath. "So I have some news to share with you. Can we pop around one night?"

Silence.

"Oh?"

"Tomorrow night?"

"I think your father is at the club. What about lunch?"

Shit.

This is where it was going to be tricky. They couldn't go for lunch. Not today, not tomorrow, not next week or next year.

"Sorry, days are difficult for Ari. How's the night after that or can Dad skip the club for once?" she asked.

She heard her mother umming and ahhing.

"I'll speak to him. You didn't lose your job, did you? Piper said something… oh, maybe I dreamed it."

Sage frowned.

"Piper said something about my job?" she asked.

So she had been snooping around BioZen.

It was nice to know her sister cared so much, but Sage knew there must be more to it. Why had she gone to LA looking for her? It seemed an odd coincidence that the vampires were there digging into BioZen and now Piper was there.

And Sage didn't believe in coincidences.

More importantly she knew her sister was, as Ari put it, like a dog with a bone, when she wanted to know something. She had to get hold of her before she upset the wrong people.

If she hadn't already.

At least Oliver was there. She trusted him.

"Ignore me. I can't remember," her mother said. "Okay, I'll text you when I've spoken to your father. It's late. I better get to bed. Goodnight, darling."

"Night, Mom."

Sage ended the call and stared out the large glass windows into the dark night.

It was going to take a little while to adjust to this new life. She'd take it one day at a time. Ari had told her to take her time deciding what she wanted to do, and she was fortunate there was no financial pressure on them.

For now, she had a wedding to plan and was going to do some redecorating. Ari had some lovely and interesting things in his living quarters—many priceless antiques—but this was her home now, too, and while it wasn't quite a bachelor pad, she wanted some of her things in here and to give it a more feminine feel.

So that would keep her busy for now.

That, and getting her sister home from LA and whatever trouble she was getting into.

Poor Oliver.

CHAPTER TWENTY-ONE

Piper felt his presence before she saw him. Her card was poised ready to slide through the device on her hotel room door when his hand covered hers and slid it down.

Then those fingers ran up her arm and before she knew what she was doing, she leaned back into him. He pulled her hair away from her neck and his mouth was on her.

"You want to fuck a vampire, Piper?" Oliver asked.

She closed her eyes and moaned.

"You want me to bite you? Sink my fangs into you. Make you come as your blood runs down my throat?"

Fucking hell.

Her pussy clenched and her nipples hardened as her already aroused body ached for him to do all of those things. Regardless of how crazy they sounded.

Oliver pushed the door open and somehow her body disconnected from his and her feet took a couple of steps inside. When she turned, he was right there, his startling eyes dark and fully aroused as they roamed over her body.

"Why do you want me to leave?" she asked. He began to unbutton the top she was wearing.

"Don't wear shit like this around other men," Oliver replied, blatantly ignoring her.

She blinked.

"He was lucky I took a humorous approach tonight, *wife*. I wanted to tear out his throat for looking at you the way he did."

She frowned despite the heat for this dominating man pulsing at her core.

"It was a business meeting. Wait, why the fuck am I explaining myself? I'm a single woman. I can do what I want." She pushed at him.

"Piper," he growled.

"No. Stop with all this growly man stuff. I want answers. You need to stop." She waved her hand around in the air. "Stop with all this sexy stuff, and talk to me."

He smirked, but his eyes were still full of need.

"Ughhh," she stomped further into the room and pulled her phone out of her pocket and dropped that, and the room key, on the table.

"You think I'm sexy?"

"I think you're frustrating."

Oliver sat on the edge of her bed and pulled off his top. "Come here."

Fucking God on a stick. He was gorgeous.

Layers of tanned muscles—an eight-pack at least—tempted her while she searched for one little word.

No.

Say no.

Demand answers.

She swallowed slowly as her eyes lowered to the little dusting of hair leading to… paradise. She knew it was that, because she'd already experienced his thick, long cock.

He undid the top button of his jeans.

Damn him.

"Oliver, please answer my… questions." Piper tried to glance away. It was getting hard to think.

He unzipped and pulled out his swollen cock. She swallowed again, not able to take her eyes off it, even when he kicked his jeans off.

"I'll answer your questions afterwards. Right now, I want you on your knees and your mouth around me." He stroked himself. "Now, Piper."

Like a moth to a flame, she was across the room and Oliver pulled her down to his mouth, cupping her face.

"I hate you."

"Channel that hate, baby." He tore open her top, then pulled it from her and tossed it across the room. Piper gasped, but he was already doing the same to her skirt.

"You're an animal."

"More of a predator. Let me show you." He winked. "On your knees."

Piper's body trembled as he guided her down and onto his cock. His words were dark, but his touch was nearly tender. Dominant but not dangerous.

The contradiction sent a thrill through her she'd never felt before and she wanted more.

A lot more.

She lapped his swollen head and then took all of him into her mouth. Her eyes stayed on his as his mouth opened in complete pleasure.

"Yes, shit. God, Piper."

He lifted his hips to sink into her mouth deeper, his hand on her neck, reminding her that he was in control and there was no question about it.

She licked and rolled her lips up and down him until he pressed in deeper, and she gagged. She'd never been one for deep-throating.

"Fuck, you're so damn gorgeous."

Her eyes lifted to his and the raw lust radiating from him sent need plummeting to her core. Suddenly he grabbed the base of his cock and pulled out of her mouth.

"What?"

Had he not liked it? She'd never had any complaints before, and it went without saying she'd had plenty of practice.

"I'm going to be inside your pussy when I come," Oliver said, gripping her hips and pulling her onto his lap. "Damn panties."

"Don't rip them," she cried. "I don't have all that many with me."

Her hands flew to his, but he lifted her with complete ease and slid them off.

"Good. Because you're going home."

She rolled her eyes and undid her bra before he tried to destroy that. When she wiggled, trying to widen her legs around his enormous frame, Oliver noticed and simply lifted her up at her hips and she stretched out her legs behind him.

God, he was strong.

"You eat a lot of spinach?" He might have been buff, but she wasn't a size zero.

"Something like that."

His fingers slid between her legs and they both groaned as he found her hot, wet flesh.

"Have you been wet all day wanting me?" he asked, his fingers sliding through the delicately aroused parts of her that needed so much more.

She bit her lips.

"Answer me."

She nodded. God damn, she was supposed to be on guard and getting answers from him, not turning to putty in his hands. And fingers.

He pressed inside and she arched.

"Good girl."

In and out, his fingers fucked her, slipping down to her ass, tempting those sensitive spots before circling around her clit. The man knew his way around a pussy.

"Watch me," he said. "Look at me as you come."

Piper's heart thumped with desire and fear and a complete feeling of being overwhelmed by this powerful man underneath her. She wanted to look away, but his eyes owned her. He had control of her body and, despite her mental resistance, every inch of her was having a party.

Traitor.

When his other hand flicked her nipple, she began to lose all control.

"Shit."

"Let go. Scream for me," he said. "Then you can have my dick inside you."

Oh, Jesus. The compliance continued as her walls contracted and pleasure filled her core. She screamed, digging her hands into his bulging biceps, then flopped onto his chest.

Oliver gripped her head and pulled her back to look at him, then wiped her juices on her lower lip and slammed his mouth down on her.

She was going to die.

Right now. In this moment. Full of utter pleasure.

Then he lifted her and walked to the window. He dropped her to her feet and spun her.

"Legs wide and hands up."

As she did as he said—again—he ran one hand down the side of her body and the other across her breasts. Pinching. She cried out.

"I can't wait to get back inside you." He tilted her ass out. She felt his swollen head at her entrance. "Are you ready to be fucked again, darlin'?"

She needed his cock in her more than another breath of air. She pressed back, trying to take him.

"Say please."

"No."

She needed some damn pride after this.

His mouth was at her neck, his breath hot and then something a little sharp. She turned, drawing in a breath. Surely, he wasn't going to bite her.

"Say please."

Her pussy throbbed with need.

"God damn you, Oliver. Fucking *please*."

All she heard was a dark growl as he thrust inside her, his hands firmly gripping her hips. He went deep, hard, and fast.

"Fuck me," he cried. "You. Feel. Too. Fucking. Good."

Her breasts pressed against the cold glass of the window as her fingers clawed and slid while Oliver slammed into her. The act was aggressive, dominant, and absolutely perfect.

She felt him swell and come moments before her next orgasm hit.

They both screamed out their pleasure and when he tugged her head back and took her lips, his eyes burning with pleasure, she knew they were far from being done.

Oliver stepped into the shower and turned, reaching out to the female he'd spent the last two hours pleasuring.

Piper took his hand, followed him inside, and melted against him. Her legs could barely hold her up, but she'd told him to stop carrying her everywhere.

He'd let her have control back, the predator in him satisfied after dominating her so completely. He had been surprised she hadn't put up more resistance, but he sensed her powerful desire for him.

She wasn't alone.

His need to fuck her seemed to be unending. It was only because she was human and exhausted that he was stopping.

He wrapped his arms around her and let the water flow over them. Pouring soap on the sponge, he ran it over her body, kissing her when she lifted her face from his chest.

Then he did his own.

"How do you stay in such incredible shape?"

I'm a vampire.

"I train a lot."

"You look like an athlete," she mumbled, running her hands over his shoulders, chest, and biceps. Oliver pushed her wet hair from her face and waited for her eyes to meet his.

"This is the only time you don't fight me," he said, his thumb running over her cheekbones. "Is this what I need to do? Fuck the fire out of you."

"You like my fire."

Yeah, he did.

"I also like you alive," he growled quietly. "You need to go home, Piper."

She shook her head and frowned at him.

He wanted to shake her. Oliver couldn't tell her anything to make her see reason, but it didn't mean he wasn't frustrated. A woman like Piper was too independent and stubborn.

She was vulnerable right now, and he didn't like it.

"You don't understand. I have to break this story. I have to… I have to *be* someone, Oliver."

What the hell was she talking about?

"You *are* someone. You don't have to prove yourself to anyone. You are perfect just as you are."

Wow. He'd had no idea he felt like that.

"I mean, you're still a pain in the ass," he clarified, "but you are not nobody."

She nudged him and laughed. Then sobered. "You don't understand."

"Then tell me."

She shook her head, turned in his arms, and ran her head under the water. When she emerged, she wiped her face with her hands and let out a long sigh.

"Have you ever felt like a failure?" she asked.

Ah, yes. He knew all about that.

"Like, for no reason. You just weren't good enough? And for some inexplicable reason you do something really stupid just to prove them right. And then you're stuck trying to redeem yourself forever."

Oliver wrapped his arms around her and pulled her back against him.

"Piper, you're perfect. Trust me. Whatever happened, just let it go and move on. Don't put your life in danger to prove something to someone who doesn't matter."

She glanced away.

"I'm not perfect. If you really knew me—"

"Who hurt you and said these bullshit things?" Oliver growled as unreasonable anger rose within him. Whoever it was, he wanted to kill them with his bare hands.

This female... he needed to protect her.

And that kind of scared him.

He wrapped his arms around Piper, who was now in a white hotel robe, and they stood staring out the window at the night lights.

Memories of the disappointment on his father's face came flooding back. Here he was telling Piper to ignore her abuser, but after all this time, he still craved his father's respect. He'd never get it because the vampire was dead. Now he'd transferred his need for acceptance and praise to Ari.

And he was fucking that up completely.

His focus and mind should be on the job and yet he was in Ari's sister-in-law's room, fucking.

Not just fucking her, but embracing her.

Worse, he wanted to know who had been filling her head with these thoughts that she wasn't good enough.

"Who said those things to you?"

"It doesn't matter, Oli. You just need to understand that I can't and won't leave," she said. "I'm breaking this story and proving to *him,* and the world, that I'm not a failure."

Then it hit him.

It was her father. A young woman with daddy issues was hardly new. Hell, everyone had issues from their childhood.

Even vampires.

"Nothing is going to stop me." She turned.

Fuck it.

He understood the driving force behind her motivation and a part of him respected her passion for proving she was worthy—even if she already was. Unfortunately, Piper had chosen a story he could never let see the light of day. He didn't doubt she was capable of finding the truth. Hell, she was standing right next to a damn vampire.

This wasn't the answer to her problems. She could end up dead, or worse, and Oliver wasn't going to let that happen.

"The story. It's about vampires?" he asked, playing dumb.

"Yes," she nodded. "Please don't tell anyone."

That he could pinky-swear.

"Is that why George is going to call you tomorrow?" Oliver asked.

She went to pull away, but he grabbed her hand and stared down into her glowing wild, beautiful blue eyes that matched his.

"Oliver, stop. My leads are confidential and private. I'm not telling you anything more."

"Piper, you need to go back to Seattle. This is dangerous."

She narrowed her eyes, and they were full of questions, but she didn't ask them.

"No," she finally said.

God damn it.

Yes, Ari had told him to keep an eye on her and keep her safe. But this was more than a job. He was getting far too attached to this female.

Oliver knew the desire to prove someone wrong. He knew that the actions he'd have to take soon would destroy her plans and ensure she hated him.

And he didn't know if he was okay with that.

Despite everything.

CHAPTER TWENTY-TWO

Oliver lay awake for hours while Piper slept peacefully tucked up against him.

It had been days since he'd had a good amount of sleep and while vampires needed far less than humans, he was pushing it. So he turned on his side, pulled Piper closer and her heat lulled him into a deep slumber.

A warm glow woke him. Also known as the fucking sun.

Fortunately it was just a peek through the curtains, but he had to get the fuck out of there. If she tried to open them and he couldn't wipe her memory, that would be bad.

Very bad.

"Oli?"

Shit.

"Yeah, babe?" He began to untangle their bodies. "I have to go, but I'll see you tonight. Stay in the hotel today, okay."

She opened her eyes and began blinking away the sleep.

"I've got an early start." He leaned down and kissed her, then began to dress as he eyeballed the blinds.

Shiiiit.

"Where's your phone, darlin'?" he asked quickly. She waved at the table across the room. He scooped it up and sat on the bed beside her. "Unlock it."

Piper sleepily reached out her hand and he shook his head humorously as he pressed her thumb against the button. Then he programmed his number in and rang his phone.

"I want you to text me when you wake."

"I am awake." She yawned.

He rolled his eyes. "Then when you *stay in the hotel* for breakfast, lunch, and dinner. Text me."

"You don't even believe in vampires. What are you worried about?"

He was nearly out of time. And he couldn't answer that question. It was then he saw the missed calls on her phone. He opened the app.

Sage.

Thank fuck.

He turned the phone. "Your sister has been calling you."

Piper sat up so fast she nearly headbutted him. She snatched the phone from his hand while he took in her bare breasts.

He might have spent hours with them last night, but he was still a male.

"Oh, my God. What time is it? Five a.m. Is it too early to call?"

It wasn't.

Sage was a vampire and likely to be awake.

"Call her. If she's awake, she'll answer."

Yesterday, Oliver thought this one phone conversation between the sisters would solve all his problems. Now he knew differently. Even if Piper returned to Seattle and was safe, his desire for her would still be there.

How he was going to get her out of his system, he didn't know.

But she wasn't just here looking for Sage. She'd stumbled onto a story about *vam-fucking-pires.*

He didn't know why she was in Los Angeles, and it was unlikely she would share more information with him. For now, if they could stop her going near BioZen, especially if she was asking about vampires, it would keep her safe before he could finish what they were doing and take her home himself.

It was possible she'd read something in Sage's diary. Had she written something in it during those last days she was at BioZen?

Shit.

She was never going to drop this story unless he found a way to cut her off at every point. Or get Ben to wipe her memories. But he didn't want her to forget him.

It just wasn't something he could allow right now.

He craved this female.

"Ring her," Oliver said. "If you want to fly home, text me and I'll have you on a plane within the hour."

Piper rubbed her eyes. "Last night you said something about a private jet."

"Yup. You can have the entire damn thing to yourself. Just go home."

"What exactly do you do to afford a private jet?"

He didn't have time for any of this right now.

"I have friends in high places. That's all you need to know." He pressed his lips to hers as she groaned.

"Another unanswered question. You do know I'm a journalist, right?"

How could he forget?

"Getting answers out of people is my forte and you're making me look really bad."

He took her chin. "Darlin', fly home for me and I will give you all the answers you could ever want. And my cock as a bonus."

It was an empty promise, well except the sex, but he wasn't above lying and manipulating to keep her safe.

"Nope. But I'll take a raincheck on your cock." She grinned.

Oliver sighed, kissed her once more, and then glanced at the drapes. He was out of time.

"I'll see you tonight." He walked to the door, out of her sight, and teleported to his room.

Ben sat on the sofa, his laptop on the coffee table and was sipping a cup of coffee when Oliver teleported in. He felt Ben's eyes on him as he poured himself a cup and flopped down on the sofa.

"If that female is your mate, you need to tell Ari."

Oliver pressed back into the sofa in reaction.

"Fuck off, man."

Ben shrugged.

"Look, she's hot and I just don't want to see her get killed digging into a story about our race. Nor do I want her doing the damn story, for obvious reasons."

Ben stared at him for a long moment. "Fine. But you need to consider it's a possibility."

"No. I'm not mating anyone."

Kurt walked in through one of the adjoining doors and nodded at them. He was freshly showered and had the look of a man well pleasured.

Probably similar to his own.

"Morning ladies."

The guy was a smartass. He was lucky he was so damn huge. Oliver wasn't sure how old Kurt was, but as a Moretti SLC, even Oli wouldn't want to challenge the guy.

"See, this is the downside of being mated," Ben said, slugging down the last of his coffee. "I'm the only one who didn't get laid last night."

Kurt dropped into an armchair. "Cry me a river. I have to put up with all the smooching when your mates are around."

Oliver smirked.

"You can wipe the smile off your dial. Looks like you're next," Kurt said, pointedly.

What the hell?

"Jesus, I shag the same female twice and everyone loses their goddamn mind." He rolled his eyes. "She's hot and..."

Oliver stopped from saying anything more. He'd been about to launch into some locker room description about how delicious her pussy was.

Hell no. He wasn't talking about Piper's body with these males. Or anyone.

It felt wrong. Disloyal.

"... stuff."

Kurt and Ben stared at him for a couple of seconds, then burst into laughter.

"Assholes," he mumbled. "I'm going for a shower."

An hour later, the three of them stood staring at a screen as the car that was presumably Dr. Phillips', began to move out of his driveway.

Or at least, the tracker did, and they had to hope it hadn't been found by his security team and they were being taken on a joy ride.

Back in Seattle, Ari and the team were watching the same little red dot move on the Operation Room screens.

"Looks to be headed to the San Gabriel Valley area," Ari said, rubbing his jaw.

"I reckon they would've crushed the tracker if they'd found it," Travis said.

"Unless they're fucking with us," Kurt said.

"These guys are pros. I don't think they'd bother," Ben said.

"Watching a scientist must be boring as fuck. They could be looking for some fun." Darren spoke up.

Jesus, it was like a running commentary.

"They better buckle up. The fun is about to come to an end." Ari growled.

Oliver and Ben shared a look. They both knew Ari well and it was clear the ancient vampire was running out of patience with BioZen.

Good.

The sooner they cleaned this shit up, the better.

Finally, twenty minutes later, the red dot stopped. Darren traced the location.

"Gotcha. It used to be leased by a manufacturing company. Natural health. Supplements, I guess," Darren said. "The name on the lease… wait… ugh, the fuck?"

"Let me—" Travis said, and their voices dropped out.

"Okay, while we dig into the ownership, you three get some rest and prepare to go for a little look-see when the sun goes down," Ari said.

Kurt stood and stretched.

"I'm off to call Anna," Ben said, and walked through the adjoining door.

Oliver turned back to the screen where Ari was leaning back in his chair. "Sage called her sister. Have you seen her again?"

Kurt crossed his arms, looking all tough guy, and refused to look at Oliver.

"Yes, we bumped into her last night at the bar." Oliver nodded. "She's investigating a story on…"

Fuck, why did he feel like he was betraying her?

"On?"

"Vampires," he finished.

Ari cursed.

"Yep," Kurt said. "I'd like to know how she picked up this trail."

Oliver had his suspicions, but he was staying quiet.

"Christ, what is with the Roberts sisters?" Ari said, rubbing his fingers through his hair. "Hopefully, Sage has encouraged her to return home."

"I'm not sure it will work," Oliver said. "Darren, can you look into a George Ames? She met with him last night to discuss vampires. No idea who he is, but at a guess the guy is some kind of conspiracy theorist. Or he knows someone at BioZen who's talked. Highly unlikely, but he's a young guy, so it could've been a drunken slip by a mate."

"We need to contain this." Kurt shot him a look which reminded him the SLC reported to the Moretti prince and that Piper now posed a risk to the race. They may have humored her last night, but the reality was, she couldn't be allowed to continue.

"Agreed," Ari said. "Do what you need to keep my sister-in-law safe. And quiet."

Oliver let out a snort. Keep Piper quiet? He wasn't a fucking miracle worker.

CHAPTER TWENTY-THREE

Xander walked into his office and shut the door. He was going stir crazy being locked up in this house with Suzanne and his toy soldiers. His wife was still going on about returning to Seattle, and that damn gala.

There was nothing toy-like about these former SEALs and Marines. He was paying top dollar for them, so he knew they were some of the best.

After Ari Moretti's threatening phone call, he wasn't about to let them go, either.

Xander had found very little about Moretti in his research.

He found a social security number for the vampire, and assuming it was legit, that was it. The guy had no digital footprint. No social media accounts, no email, no webpage, or business details. Not a single photo anywhere.

Unsurprising, but he'd expected to find something. Maybe even some bullshit cover, but absolutely nothing? That was weird.

Even weirder was the fact that Stefano Russo had never mentioned him. *Loose lips* Russo had told them everything. They had pages and pages of names, roles, and information on all the royal family and many of the senior members of their army. Along with other prominent members of the vampire race.

Ari Moretti?

Not a thing.

It was as if he didn't exist.

Xander wasn't an expert in the vampire royal structure, but he had assumed anyone with the Moretti surname was a member of the family.

Perhaps not.

But his gut said he was. There had been power in his voice and his threat. Immense power.

Xander thrived on power and could recognize it anywhere.

So, without any information on the vamp, Xander had decided to remain in Baltimore where it appeared he was safe and untraceable.

He sat at his desk just as the notification popped up that his meeting was starting. Xander clicked the join button and watched as Dr Phillips' face appeared.

"Mr. Tomassi."

"Good morning, Douglas. How's the house and are the family settled in?" he asked, even though he didn't care.

Although that wasn't completely true. Douglas Phillips was his most important employee and he wanted the man to be happy, so he would continue to thrive and complete this important work.

"Pretty good, thanks. The excitement has worn off after a week and the kids are grumpy, complaining about everything, but we'll work through that," Douglas replied. "Promises of Disneyland are helping."

Xander gave him a quick smile. "Good. How are the renovations going?"

He'd relocated Dr. Phillips and his family to California to oversee the setup of the new facility where they would begin human trials. They were moving fast on this and, given the fact the vampires were now on their tail, it was more important than ever to get up and running quickly.

"They're doing the final touches this week. We should be ready to begin the trials next week. Hopefully. There were some supply issues with the Tungsten and, as you know, that's vital to protect our people and production inside."

Tungsten, the strongest steel on earth, was the only material resistant to the strength of the vampires. Thanks to good old Stefano Russo for helping them on that one, or they'd never be where they were today.

"We have the project teams working on it back in Seattle," Douglas continued, "Some of the team have been recruited over and will be moving out to California. The other roles are currently being recruited externally."

Xander felt a chill run through him. "Don't make another mistake like we did with the Roberts girl."

Dr. Phillips stared at him for a moment and the hairs on the back of Xander's neck rose.

"What is it?"

"Her sister has been asking for her." The man rubbed his cheek awkwardly.

"Sage Roberts' sister?" Xander asked.

"Yes. Piper Roberts. She visited the Seattle office and was sent away. Now she's here in LA and has been to three of our offices asking for me. I don't know how she got my name or what she knows."

Fucking hell.

"This is a problem." Xander growled. "When were you going to tell me about this? *Fuck*, Douglas."

The blond-haired scientist lifted his cup of coffee to his lips and drank. "Honestly, I thought she was just looking for her sister. I figured she'd go to the police and take the usual routes, but…"

"But?"

"She's a journalist."

"Oh, Jesus fucking Christ." Xander slammed back into his corporate leather chair and ran a hand through his hair. His eyes darted to the two security men standing guard outside the glass doors in his office.

"Who for?"

"*The Seattle Times.*"

So not the *New York Times*, but big enough.

"Where is she staying? Do we know how to find her?"

"I have her phone number," Douglas replied, lifting his phone to search for the details.

"Send it through and leave it with me. She won't be a problem anymore."

"Don't—"

"Leave it with me." He spoke firmly.

Dr. Phillips nodded, then wiped his hand over his mouth. "What about Callan? Have you been able to find him?"

"No. Not a single sighting anywhere in the United States." He had men out tracking the vampire. They'd been told he was human, but they'd found nothing. It was likely the royal family had retrieved Callan, but he wasn't going into that with Douglas who needed to remain focused on the science. Xander told him what he needed to know and not a word more.

"Mr. Tomassi… Xander… I don't need to tell you how concerning this is. We altered Callan's DNA. We were still observing his cells and gathering data. We have no idea how it will manifest or change him."

Xander lifted his coffee to his lips. "Well, best we get the trials started as it looks like we're going to need these powerful altered humans, aren't we?"

Was he worried? Yes and no.

The world was undergoing a major change—led by him. It was just that most people weren't yet aware of that fact.

They'd thank him for it one day soon.

Vampires had been walking the earth capable of crushing human necks with little thought. The work they were doing was just balancing out the playing field.

"So, let's go through your project timeline." Xander was keen to understand the exact timeline, so he had an answer for Nikolay Mikhailov when he next called.

He didn't know exactly what the man was intending to do with the end product, but he had an idea. It didn't take much brain power to put two and two together with the line of work the man was in.

If you could call it work.

After the call ended, he walked across the office to the glass doors and plunged his hands into his suit pants pockets.

So he had another little problem to sort out. A curly one. Sage was obviously under the protection of Ari Moretti, and it was likely that protection extended to her sister. Still, he couldn't allow a journalist to sniff around looking for his head scientist. Not with the human trials about to begin.

His employees were under strict employment and confidentiality contracts and were paid well to stay silent. Still, people were greedy and stupid. All it would take was one wagging tongue and billions of dollars could be at risk.

If Piper Roberts knew about vampires, and Sage had shared what they were doing at BioZen, he had a feeling the sister would try to blow the entire story open.

He would if he was in her shoes.

Unfortunately for Piper Roberts, she had chosen the wrong path.

Ari Moretti and the royal family might be powerful, but there were many billions, potentially trillions, of dollars at stake here long term. He couldn't allow news of vampires to hit the global airwaves.

Not yet.

It was time to make a call and start removing the threat to their plans once and for all.

Xander was done playing nice.

CHAPTER TWENTY-FOUR

"Where? Tell me the address and I'll meet you there," Piper replied, excited.

"I'll text you the details," George said. "No recording devices, etcetera. They just want to meet you and see if you're trustworthy."

"Sure, fine. No problem. I'll see you in about an hour," Piper said, hanging up and doing a little dance.

Today was going well. She'd had a little sleep in after her gymnastic-level sex evening with Oliver and then spoken to her sister.

Finally.

Now she was heading to meet up with a handful of bloggers who had information about vampires. This was the break she'd been looking for. She was confident she'd gain their trust.

Her phone pinged with an address, and she smiled.

BioZen had been one big brick wall, so she needed these guys. If they failed to come through, then she'd find out where the pharmaceutical employees went for Friday after-work drinks. Drunk lips were loose lips.

She tracked the address and pinned it on her map and then reflected on her conversation with Sage. While she was relieved to hear her sister was safe, the chat had raised even more questions.

Her holiday details were vague as fuck.

"Where did you stay in the Caribbean?"

"A hotel. It was nice. Flash. Super-hot," Sage had replied, describing *every* five-star hotel on *every* tropical island.

"So, like the Marriott?" Piper asked.

Silence.

"Um, you know, I can't remember. I think so."

Liar. There was no Marriott in the Caribbean.

"So you just turned off your phone for two whole weeks? I don't think I could do that," Piper had said.

"It was great. You know, it's easy to do when you're away with a sexy man."

Now that was the truth.

Although, two weeks and no TikTok or Instagram? That might be a push. Then she imagined a week in the tropics with Oliver and knew if anyone could distract her, *he* could.

"So things are going well with Ari?"

"Yup," Sage had replied. "Are you around next week? Mom is having us over for dinner. I'd love for you to join us."

Piper's eyes had widened. "Since when did you like family dinners?"

"I just thought, after being away, and now Ari is in my life… we have news."

"Oh my God, you're pregnant!" she'd gasped.

"I'm not pregnant." Sage had groaned.

"You eloped. Shit, tell me you didn't marry him."

"Piper. Stop. Are you coming for dinner or not?" Sage had snapped.

The thing with being a journalist, maybe not all but many, was you could generally smell a rat anywhere. Right now, her nose was twitching. Piper could barely remember

Ari and she knew it had to do with Oliver messing with her memories. It was like a bunch of jigsaw pieces she was trying to piece together.

She didn't know if he was dangerous to her sister or family, but she knew she didn't trust him.

She should feel the same way about Oliver. Yet, whenever he was near, it was like watching an enormous tiger stalking you and all you could do was admire its beauty, knowing it was going to eat you.

And God damn, he did that well.

But she did trust him for some strange reason. He seemed to want her out of LA and back in Seattle to keep her safe. He wouldn't elaborate and there was so much they weren't telling each other.

In some ways, it felt like she was sleeping with the enemy, and yet she couldn't stop.

"Sage, I would, but I'm in Los Angeles," she replied. "For work. I'm on an assignment."

Silence.

"Sage?"

"Oh, that's great. What story are you working on?" Sage asked, her voice forced.

Of course. Oliver had told Ari, and he'd told Sage.

"But you knew that, right?" Piper shook her head. "What is going on, Sage? Who are these guys?"

"Piper, can you just come home, please?"

She frowned. "Are you in trouble? Forget all the shit between us, Sage. I'm your sister. I love you. If you're in trouble, I'll help you."

She felt her emotions bubble up. She was so frustrated right now. Something was going on and Sage was acting incredibly out of character.

"No."

"No? That hardly sounds convincing," Piper ground out. "I think these guys are trouble. Maybe you haven't connected the dots yet with Ari, but I'm following a lead and it's pretty shocking. Just... maybe stay away from them for a few days and then I'll tell you everything. Did you, er, go home?"

She didn't want to confess to breaking into her home, so kept that question short and sweet.

More silence.

Fuck.

"I've moved in with Ari, Piper. Look, just come home and I will introduce you to him and you'll see how much he loves me. I love him."

What?

Sage had only met him a month ago, and their first time had been with another man. She'd read about it in Sage's diary. Again, she wasn't going to confess to knowing those details, but *love?*

"Are you kidding me? You've known him five damn minutes!"

Was that a growl?

"Listen, sometimes you just know and with Ari, I knew almost immediately. He's... okay God, don't tell Mom I told you first, but he asked me to marry him."

Piper shot to her feet.

No, no, no, no, no.

Really slowly, her blood pumping loudly in her ears, Piper had asked, "And what did you say?"

"Yes. I said yes. I love him, Pipe." The use of her nickname filled her eyes.

"Oh, Sage." Fear had spread through her body.

Something was very, very wrong about all of this. Maybe she did need to get home and see her sister. If this man was manipulating Sage, using her sister's desire for love as a weapon, she was going to stop him.

"Please come home," Sage repeated, and she was starting to sound just like Oliver

Piper shook her head.

Her world was spinning.

Vampires could be real, and her sister was marrying a man who was friends with Oliver, who had the ability to wipe her memories.

How?

She was going to do her best to find out.

"Why did you leave BioZen?" she had asked.

"Congratulations Sage, I'm so happy for you," Sage said, mockingly. "Fuck's sake Piper. Given our history I would think you could find five minutes to put aside your career goals to just be happy for me."

Piper squeezed her eyes closed. "I am. If you love him, I am. Congratulations," she had said, and a part of her meant it because doubt was creeping in as she heard the hurt in her sister's voice. Perhaps she was wrong about all of this. "I'll be home in a few days. I'll try to make the dinner. I promise."

"Try."

"You can tell Mom and Dad on your own."

God, their father would be thrilled. Successful Sage getting married and achieving another life goal. One that Piper hadn't. It would be really fucking uncomfortable seeing the judgment in her father's eyes.

Yet again.

"I want you there when I tell them," Sage had said.

Piper had let out a long sigh. "Okay."

She would just have to work fast in LA, and maybe seeing Ari again would change her mind.

So, while the conversation had gone quite differently from what she'd expected, she was happy her sister was alive and safe.

Twenty minutes later, she stepped out of her hotel room and bumped straight into a huge chest.

"Going somewhere, gorgeous?"

"You gave me a heart attack." She slapped one of Oliver's pecs, mostly so she could cop a feel.

"Where are you off to?" he asked, holding the door open above her head with the palm of his hand and she shivered at the feel of him dominating her with his size.

"You look like shit," she said.

He didn't, but he looked tired around the eyes, as if he'd been awake all night.

"Headache. Now answer the question."

Before she could say anything, he scooped her around the waist, picked her up, kicked the door wide open, and carried her inside.

"Oliver, put me down. I need to get lunch and head out to a meeting." She squealed.

"Now we're getting somewhere." He placed her on her feet, smiling. "Where?"

She raised a brow. "I was thinking about the sandwich place on the corner. I fancy taco's but—"

"Piper!"

"You are so growly." She pouted but this time he raised his brows and crossed his arms, which just made his biceps bulge more out of the sleeves of the navy Hollister t-shirt he was wearing.

She swallowed.

"Like what you see?"

"Why are you so arrogant?" She huffed. "Look, I really have to go."

She turned for the door and he gripped her hips, pulling her back to face him. "Uh, uh, princess. You're staying right here."

"That would be called kidnapping. So no. Let go, Oliver, I have a job to do." She slapped at his hands.

His lips pressed together and he glared at her.

"Then tell me where you're going. I want to know you're safe. Address. Now." His piercing blue stare was full of genuine concern, and she let out a sigh.

Fine.

It was not a bad idea for someone to know where she was going. Piper whipped out her phone and showed him.

"Why do you care? Is this about Ari and Sage?"

"What about them?" he asked, but his poker face wasn't working on her this time. She wanted to ask if he knew about their engagement or where they had *really* gone on their holiday. She wanted some goddamn truth from someone.

But she knew she wasn't getting it from Oliver.

"Nothing. I have to go, or I won't have time to eat and I'm starving." Piper let out a small sigh.

It wasn't a lie. She *was* hungry.

A part of her, though, liked that he cared and even if there were other reasons behind it, she felt he genuinely did. She was going to hang on to that feeling.

"Who are you going to see? Who are the people at this address?" Oliver asked, taking her phone.

She snatched her phone back. "Jesus, Oliver, this is really overstepping the mark. You won't tell me anything about who you are, and you expect me to tell you what I'm doing? Well sorry, but I'm not going to. This is my job."

"What if something happens to you? For an intelligent woman you are being really stupid." He took a step closer.

She fish-mouthed it for a bit.

How dare he?

"Nothing is going to happen to me. And I'm not stupid. This is what journalists do." Piper slammed her hands on her hips.

He took another step toward her looking like the predatory tiger she'd envisaged earlier. She backed right into the wall and his hand slapped above her while those big eyes stared down at her.

"I have plans for us later tonight, so there better not be a scratch on you." His voice was thick with promise.

Oh.

Heat roared through her already flushed body as her lips stretched into a smile. "Now that I can get on board with."

His demanding mouth took hers and she knew she'd be changing her panties before she left the room again. Especially when his thigh pressed between hers. The hand above her dropped, cupping the back of her head, and their kiss deepened.

Gasping, they pulled apart.

"Fuck that, I can't wait." Oliver tugged her skirt up.

Thank God.

She ripped off her panties as he undid his jeans and tugged them down a little, then lifted her legs around him.

"Pull your breasts out," he ordered.

Piper glanced down and noticed one of her buttons had come undone. Oliver nudged his cock at her entrance.

"Faster," he growled as he pressed his swollen head inside her.

"Shit." She tried to unbutton faster, but he reached between their bodies and ripped open her top. Then he tore at her bra. Both her breasts sprung free, and he stared at them like they were the seventh wonder of the world.

Piper was just about to smile when he sunk further inside her.

"Fuck."

"God, I want all of you, all the fucking time," he ground out, lifting her so he could suckle on a nipple.

"Fuck," she cried out again.

She lost her goddamn mind when Oliver was near her. All her questions and concerns literally dissolved, and her body took over. He was the most dominant and demanding lover she'd ever had. In the most delicious but also scary way.

"Look at me while I fuck you, Piper. Eyes on me." His hands gripped her ass, and he began to pound into her. "I want to eat your pussy, but I know you don't have time."

Suddenly, she wasn't in such a hurry after all. He grinned at her as if he could read her mind. She went to smile back, but his cock hit the spot. *The* spot, and her body roared.

"Oli, fuckfuckfuckfuck."

"Jeeesus, Piper. Your pussy is so damn tight." He cried out and his cum poured into her.

Oliver staggered to the sofa, sat while keeping her on his lap, then leaned his head back against the cushions. She collapsed on his chest while his thumb rubbed circles on her hips.

"Can you just stay here, and we do this for a few hours?" he asked, not lifting his head.

Tempting, very, very tempting.

She sat up.

"I wouldn't survive. Are you trying to kill me?"

"No, you pain in the ass. I'm trying to keep you alive."

CHAPTER TWENTY-FIVE

After extricating her body from Oliver's incredibly gorgeous one, Piper changed into a new outfit, grabbed a coffee and muffin from the store on the corner, and was on her way to meet George.

Oliver had been unhappy at her leaving, but too bad.

She had a story to tell.

Since talking to Sage her motivation had shifted. Sure, she still wanted to prove to her father she wasn't a complete failure, but Piper had a feeling there was a link between her story and Ari Moretti.

And... Oliver.

She just wasn't sure how.

Hopefully George's friends were going to give her some answers today. The Uber pulled up outside an apartment building in Culver City which looked respectable enough. A young couple walked out pushing a baby buggy and began wandering down the street which relieved any remaining anxiety she had about walking into a home with four men she didn't know.

Knowing Oliver had the address put her mind at ease, but she wouldn't tell him that.

It was likely these guys were harmless, but it paid to be safe.

She pressed the buzzer.

"Yo."

Okay. "Oh hey, its Piper Roberts, I—"

Buzz.

Right. Thanks.

"Fucking introverts," she muttered.

She made her way to the fifth floor and to room 34B.

Knock, knock.

The door opened and George greeted her.

"Hey Piper, come in."

She stepped into a typical bachelor pad which was complete with ugly lounge suite and took in the three guys with laptops on their knees.

"Eric, Jack, Tyler. This is Piper." George introduced them all.

"Hey. Thanks for speaking with me." She waited for an invitation to sit but it didn't come so she lowered herself onto the arm of the beige sofa and hiked her bag off her shoulder.

Eric closed his laptop and picked up a can of Coke. "You're from *The Seattle Times*?"

She nodded.

"She's *VampGirl182*. The one commenting the other night," Jack said, lifting his spectacles onto the top of his head. He studied her. "You don't look like a journo."

How did he know who she was?

"They can hack and track anything," George said, reading her mind. He walked past her into the adjoining kitchen. "Coke. Green tea? Water?"

Green tea?

These guys looked like they lived on soda and Macca's, not herbal tea and kale.

"Ah, I'll have…"

"It's lemon-flavored green tea, by the way. And I'll have one, thanks." Tyler arched his neck to call out.

"Make your own!" George called back.

Piper smiled.

"Just water." She accepted the glass with a small thanks when George returned.

"So what makes you think vampires are real?" Eric asked, getting straight to the point.

Piper had thought about how to approach their questions during the ride over. She still wasn't confident her strategy was going to be the best one, but it was all she had come up with in the short time.

"Well, we all saw the breaking news a few months ago. I've been curious, reading the threads and blogs, and finally convinced my editor to let me do a story."

They all stared at her.

"Nope," Tyler said.

"Try again," Eric said.

Jack just shook his head.

Piper stared at them, confused.

"I told you they wouldn't talk if you tried to bullshit them," George said with a shake of his head. "Your account is new, Piper. Just this week."

Fuck.

"Look I can't tell you, okay. But my research and instincts have led me here. I'm hoping you'll share what you know so that *if* vampires are real, we can tell the world."

Jack snorted.

"Oh, they're real, all right," Eric said. "The question is whether you're the right person for us to talk to."

Piper pressed her lips together.

She needed these guys to trust her.

"What I have isn't solid. I'm looking for evidence I can take to my editor to continue my investigation. I'm not writing some ragtime piece. This is going to be front page news around the world."

Tyler sat back down with his green tea, and she took a closer look at him. He wasn't your usual hoodie-clad computer nerd who hadn't showered for three days. His board shorts, t-shirt, dirty blond surfer hair and silvery blue eyes may have fooled some people, but she saw a hint of money. Probably a trust fund, or he made a lot online and didn't like to show it off. Except for the expensive watch on his wrist. He lifted a Converse-clad foot onto his knee and tapped it, blowing into his drink and watched her watching him.

She looked away.

"Most of what we could tell you is already on the net," Tyler added, drawing her eyes back to him. "No one *wants* to believe it. That's the problem."

"True that." Eric stretched out his denim-clad legs. He wasn't a huge guy, not like Oliver, but his Volcom t-shirt fit snug across his chest, showing he was fit and active.

Jack was a little broader but appeared to be shorter, though it was hard to tell while he was sitting down.

"I guess that's why I'm here. I have a nose for these things, and I get the impression you have information you haven't shared publicly."

They all stared at her for a long moment.

"If you want us to trust you, you need to trust us back. Tell us what led you to LA and we can go from there," Eric said.

Piper understood their mistrust. Talking to them about Sage's diary, her sudden departure from her job, the long and mysterious holiday with Ari and her memory loss with Oliver felt like a risk. Yet, if she couldn't gain their trust, this entire visit was a waste of time.

These guys could provide her with the type of substance that made her story an award winner and once and for all proved the existence of vampires.

Making her career.

And changing human history.

Or they were full of bullshit and had absolutely nothing. She had to decide. Sharing her sister's information felt like another betrayal, but there was still a nagging concern in the back of her mind that Sage was being manipulated by Ari and he wasn't to be trusted.

And the same could be said for Oliver, but the more time she spent with him, the harder it was to think clearly and subjectively.

Tyler sipped loudly on his hot tea as her eyes darted from one face to the other, deciding her next move.

She let out a sigh.

"What I'm about to share with you is very personal and confidential. It could endanger my family, my sister, and me," Piper said firmly. "This information stays in this room."

They all nodded.

"My sister was an employee at BioZen."

Well, that got their attention. Not only were they glancing at one another, but they began shifting in their seats.

"Carry on," George said, leaning forward.

"She went missing. Or rather, she went on holiday with her new boyfriend, but… this is hard to explain. I don't think she went anywhere. I think she lied. I talked to her this morning, but while she was *missing,* I read her diary."

"Never a good move," Jack muttered and a few of the others cringed and let out a few *ooh no's.*

"Anyway," she continued. "Turns out it was a good idea. Sage, my sister—"

"Sage Roberts, aged twenty-five, lives at…" Eric read out her sister's address from his screen and Piper glared at him.

"The hell?"

Eric shrugged. "You come into my home; I want to know who you are."

Fucking hell, these guys weren't messing around.

"You sure you aren't the damn FBI or something?" She raised a brow.

"We've got access to far more information than those clowns." Tyler scoffed. "Unofficially."

Right.

"Carry on with your story." Eric shot Tyler a look.

"So, Sage overheard people talking about vampires and how they believe they're real. Something to do with her work. She got a promotion to work on this secret project and a few days later she leaves the office suddenly with a migraine. Sage doesn't get migraines."

"Yeah, this isn't solid evidence." Eric shook his head and stood.

"No, wait." Piper looked up at him. He was taller than he seemed while sitting. "So I go to the address she went to that day and its enormous. It's her boyfriend's but no one will let me in to see her."

"Not surprised. You sound like a stalker sister," Eric muttered from the kitchen. She heard the microwave beep.

Piper shot him a distant scowl and Tyler's chest wobbled in a silent laugh.

"Next thing I know, this guy takes me home and I cannot remember anything. Except over the next few days my memory starts coming back in bits and pieces. Then I start dreaming of him."

Piper wanted to slap herself. She hated that she was sharing this with a handful of strangers but equally she wanted their trust and the information they had.

Telling them about Oliver had silenced her, though. Heck, he'd been inside her just hours ago screaming her name.

George stared at her and she saw the penny drop. His mouth fell open. "The guy from last night. He's not your husband?"

Piper shook her head.

"Fuck me. Who are they?"

She shrugged.

"I don't know. He's a friend of Ari's. Sage's boyfriend. He's been watching me. He's... protecting me."

"That old chestnut," Tyler snorted.

George ran a hand through his hair.

Jack slowly nodded. "Okay, what else? There's more, right?"

"While Sage was missing, I went to BioZen, and they told me she didn't work there. A complete lie. Once I told them who I was and put some pressure on the receptionist, she let slip the head scientist has moved to Cali. So here I am. I rock up to their offices, but no one will acknowledge who he is."

"What's your theory?" Tyler asked.

Truth time.

"I think vampires are real. I also think my sister learned something she shouldn't have. I think Ari and Oliver are involved, but I don't know how," Piper replied. "Maybe they're protecting her. Maybe they aren't."

Saying it out loud made it all suddenly feel real. She knew most people would think she was crazy, but she hoped these guys wouldn't. Something wasn't right and even if she ended up not proving her worth to her father, if she could help Sage, this would be worth it.

But she still wanted the story.

"So what's your fake husband doing in LA?" George asked.

"I don't know."

"You're sleeping with him," Tyler stated.

"What? No—"

"Yeah, you are," George said, and her head swiveled to glare at him. "Piper, I'm a man. I know what I saw. That guy was possessive and territorial. If he's not sleeping with you already, he will be any minute."

Her mouth shut.

"He's sleeping with her," Tyler said again, nodding.

"Totally sleeping together."

"Oh yeah, they're fucking," Eric said.

Piper stood.

"Fine. I'm sleeping with him. Can we please focus here?" She walked into the kitchen and dropped her glass into the sink. "He admitted he's messing with my memory, but who has the ability to do that?"

Eric shrugged. "Honestly? Quite a few people. There's shit in this world that would freak most people the fuck out if they knew."

Jack nodded knowingly beside him, then stood and opened the sliding door and lit a joint. He offered it to her, and she shook her head.

"And vampires," Tyler said.

Piper's mouth fell open.

"What are you saying?"

"I'm saying vampires likely have the ability to wipe your memory. How else would they live amongst us undetected?"

Jesus.

"Do you know this for sure? What do you have?" She looked at Tyler and Eric. The latter held her gaze for a long moment, then stood and went to a PC set up on the table across the room and began powering it up. He tapped away for a moment.

She waited.

"Vampires," he said, tilting his head in invitation for her to view his screen.

She went around behind him and leaned in. What she saw was a number of bodies lying on steel tables as if they were in a morgue. Or hospital. They just looked like people. When she went to speak, Eric zoomed in on one section of the photo.

Clear as day she could see the BioZen logo.

"Oh shit."

More clicks and the mouse moved around, zooming onto one of the patients.

Was that a...?

"Fangs." Eric nodded. "In case you didn't work it out."

Piper stood straight and stared vacantly out the glass doors, then back at the screen.

"Are they dead?"

Jack closed the door and shrugged at her. "We don't know. That image was sent to us anonymously along with some documentation describing the experiments BioZen was undertaking. Cruel as fuck."

"So yeah, probably," Tyler said, confirming what she'd asked.

Holy shit.

This was huge. Not just that they had photographic and scientific evidence, but that, presumably, vampires could be controlled and killed by humans.

"Have you tracked the sender?"

Silence.

"That's a yes." She shook her head. "And you're not giving up your source. I get it."

"Actually, it's a no. But whoever it was is pretty clever to be able to prevent fancy pants over there from following the trail," Eric replied, nodding at Tyler.

Tyler smirked. "I'll find him or her. Do not doubt the master."

Jack snorted.

"Someone inside BioZen," Piper said, more to herself. "So I'm on the right track. Damn. BioZen is experimenting on vampires. No wonder they don't want the media sniffing about."

Eric shook his head. "What did you think they were doing? Having them over for cups of tea?"

"Don't be a dick, Eric." George frowned.

Piper ignored the asshole comment. Her mind was beginning to connect the dots. Had Sage found out and refused to work for them? She knew her sister had been active in changing the policies around animal experimentation, so this wouldn't sit right at all with her.

Still, what did Ari have to do with any of it?

"Can you look into a couple of people for me?" she asked them.

Tyler nodded and opened his laptop.

"Ari Moretti and Oliver Cambiaghi." She had to know who they were.

"Any other details?"

"They live in Medina." She read out the address from her phone.

"Fancy fucking address." Tyler whistled as his fingers fled over the keyboard. His brows dropped. "You might need to give me a few hours. Jeez, yeah, these guys do not want to be found."

Piper glanced at Eric, who was watching her.

"All right, Miss Journo. Looks like we can help each other out here," Eric said. "We'll be in touch tomorrow."

She smiled. "Vampires are real."

"Yup. Vampires are real," Eric said. "George, you headed back to downtown?" When he nodded, Eric tilted his head back to her. "Give Piper a ride home. Make sure she gets back safe in case she was followed."

She swallowed.

Followed?

"By whom?"

Eric stood. "Your fake husband, for one. Until we find out who these guys are, you need to be careful."

Piper chewed the inside of her mouth. Oliver hurting her seemed the most unlikely thing in the world. He was protective and seemed to care about her.

Nothing made sense.

She'd get her answers, though. She was determined. Meanwhile, she'd accept the ride home.

Piper's hair whipped around her as George drove them through the LA streets. With the top down and the palm trees around them she couldn't help but smile.

She loved the warmer climate even though she was yet to relax enough to feel like a tourist.

"Had you seen that photo before today?" she asked.

"Yes. Mind fuck though, right?"

"Hell yes. Vampires could be just walking around us. How crazy is that?"

"Or not. Maybe they can't go out in the daylight like in the movies."

"Maybe." Piper laughed.

George drove them toward Santa Monica Beach. They stopped at a set of lights and then turned to her and smirked. "Now that I know you aren't married, you want to grab an ice cream?"

Piper took in the swaying palms and bright blue of the ocean and decided, what the heck? It wasn't like she *was* married or even dating Oliver. They were just fucking. Both of them knew that.

"Sure."

Meeting George and the guys had changed everything. Oliver was involved. She just didn't know how. Did he work for BioZen as a type of security guy and was just trying to protect her before she got in too deep?

She thought about the conversation at the bar with Kurt and Ben about vampires. Had they been making fun of her with their answers?

Oliver had refused to answer… but then teased her body with talk of biting and fangs.

A shiver ran through her body.

She couldn't deny her desire for him, but if he was involved with any of this, she needed to keep away from him. From all of them. God knows BioZen weren't going to give her any information and now she knew why.

After ordering two double-scooped ice creams, they walked along the beach and George handed her one of them.

"Thank you," she smiled. "Boy, this is nice. We have beaches in Seattle, but obviously the weather's not this warm."

George laughed. "Yeah, I know. I have family up there, so I visit from time to time. Cali has its pros and cons. The weather is pretty nice, though."

"You work in corporate?" she asked, taking in his long pants and shirt open at the collar.

"Corporate sales." He grinned at her.

Piper laughed. "You totally have that salesman vibe." She laughed some more.

"Why doesn't that feel like a compliment?"

Piper finished her ice cream and tossed her napkin into the nearest trash can. "It's not a criticism. You are who you are. Just like I'm a journalist."

Suddenly, her phone rang. She pulled it out of her bag and stared at the number. Blocked.

"I need to take this." She apologized and swiped to answer. "Piper Roberts."

"Piper. This is Xander Tomassi from BioZen Pharmaceuticals. I hear you've been making some inquiries about our organization."

Oh, shit.

CHAPTER TWENTY-SIX

Brayden opened the door to his quarters, with the king following close behind.

"Whoa, where's the fire, Willow?" He caught her around the waist and pulled her up against his chest as he spun.

She smacked a kiss on his lips.

"You know where." She winked. "Now let me down, Mister Alpha. I'm heading to Bri's. We're video-conferencing with Sage in a few minutes."

He planted his mouth on hers and stole a few more kisses.

"Get a room." Vincent pushed past them.

"What are you, ten?" Willow asked the king, as Brayden dropped her back onto her feet.

"I'm the king," Vincent replied, shrugging.

"King of—"

"Stop." Brayden grabbed her lips with his fingers and then burst out laughing as her eyes bulged. She slapped his hands away. "Go. I'll see you in a few hours."

Willow patted him on the chest. "Love you."

Brayden watched as she danced off. He'd never seen his mate so happy. Nothing seemed to faze her right now—well, except for Vincent—and it wouldn't take long for the others to notice.

The door shut and he turned around.

"Anyway, what I was going to say is Ari called and they have tracked BioZen's scientist to a new facility. The team is moving in tonight, so we'll see what they find."

Vincent lowered himself into the large armchair and nodded. "They're producing something there. Why else would they create an entirely new location?"

Brayden shrugged and poured himself a whiskey.

He handed a tumbler to Vincent.

"Or a new lab to continue experiments now we've destroyed a few," Brayden said.

"There're not that many vamps in California," Vincent said.

"They can transport them from anywhere."

"Fuckers," Vincent said, shaking his head and taking a long swig of the golden liquid. "I'm tempted to just blow up the fucking place."

Brayden lifted a shoulder. "Let's do it. Put some real brakes on their plans."

Vincent nodded. "Information is more valuable right now. Let the team go in and see what they get."

The king was right.

Unfortunately.

Right now, Brayden was keen to eliminate every single risk to his family and race. He was feeling excessively protective, and it was only going to get worse.

"So you want to tell me what's going on with the princess?" Vincent asked. "Because she's dancing around like a fucking rainbow's pouring out her ass and that's not normal."

Brayden burst out laughing. "She's still riding your ass. That's normal."

"Spill."

Brayden placed his glass on the coffee table. Willow wasn't the only one on cloud nine, but until they were sure they'd kept it to themselves.

"We're pregnant," he said, knowing he had a stupid grin on his face.

Vincent stared at him. "Already?"

Brayden nodded.

"How the fuck?"

"I don't know. But we did a test. Three. And yeah, Willow is pregnant."

Usually it took fifty, sixty years before mates reproduced. Brayden understood his brother's shock because it had taken him and the queen over one hundred years to conceive baby Lucas.

Vincent threw back his whiskey and shook his head.

"Congratulations Brayden. I'm surprised, but happy for you. And Willow. Holy hell, our family is growing."

Brayden smiled, nodding. "That it is, brother."

Vincent stood and walked to the glass doors overlooking the castle gardens. Brayden left him to his thoughts, knowing his brother well.

"If Sage and Ari reproduce this fast, it will change everything," Vincent said, then turned. "I hope for all our sakes that doesn't happen."

God, Brayden hated all the politics.

He understood Ari's position and the anguish he must have felt his entire life. Yet, it was Vincent's job and life purpose to protect the Moretti throne.

As it was his.

Throw in the fact humans were on the precipice of learning about their existence and life was a little challenging these days.

"We need time to strengthen our bonds," Brayden said. "Let's follow through on the invite to have Ari and Sage visit. This doesn't need to be a threat to our lineage. You aren't King Francis or King Gio."

Vincent plunged his hands into his pants pockets. "We shall see. Eventually."

Brayden knew he was right. Perhaps he knew his brother better than he knew himself. Vincent wasn't a warmonger. He said stupid shit at times, but he had a solid heart and mind.

"I know you love our uncle, Brayden, but there must have been a reason our father and grandfather were so distrusting of him. I've been digging through the archives looking for something, but it's a painstaking task."

He had?

Brayden shook his head.

This wasn't at all going in the direction he was hoping. Was history going to repeat itself once more?

He fucking hoped not.

Willow sat cross-legged on the bed beside Brianna. Sage's face was streaming in from Seattle on the screen in front of them.

"So you kept just getting stronger?" Sage asked.

"Maybe I'm wrong, but it felt like it," Willow said. "Bri?"

Brianna shrugged. "For me it was as if I could control my strength and abilities more than becoming extra- powerful."

"Yeah, that could have been it. My best advice is to text us or call us if you have questions. Telling your mate will only make him more protective, and it can be smothering," Willow added.

Brianna giggled.

Willow rolled her eyes and nudged her friend. "She loves it. Craig all but carried her around for the first month."

"Nothing wrong with being strapped against that gorgeous chest. I encouraged it." Brianna laughed.

"She's not joking."

"Thanks you guys, this has been so helpful," Sage said. "Oh, one more question. Periods?"

Willow groaned and nodded.

"I'm afraid so," Brianna said. "Of all the damn things we have to put up with after becoming a vampire, we still get our damn periods."

"Unbelievable," Sage said, laughing. "So glad I asked because I wasn't sure. But then again, vampires can procreate, so it makes sense. Though, not all animals menstruate. Anyway, sorry I'm being a scientist."

Willow twisted her fingers together and saw Brianna give her an odd look. They signed off and promised to connect again with Sage soon, then Brianna turned to her.

"Spill."

"I can't. Not yet."

Brianna pinched her leg. "Spill. What is it?"

She had to tell her. She'd been dying for weeks to tell someone. Poor Brayden had been listening patiently to all her questions and pondering, but she really wanted to talk to her best friend and Kate, who had recently given birth to the new prince.

"I'm pregnant!"

Brianna's mouth gaped open.

"You serious? So quickly? Holy shit balls." Brianna launched herself at Willow and they tumbled over the bed. "Oh, my God, my bestie is having a baby!"

Willow giggled, and they both began to cry happy, ugly tears.

"Does Kate know?"

Willow shook her head.

"No one knows. I mean Bray knows, and I guess he'll tell Vincent, so we'll tell the queen next."

"I thought it took forever?"

"I don't know what to say other than I prayed nearly every damn day for this baby. Or perhaps I was already pregnant. We don't know how far along I am."

Brayden was going to speed up the plans to have a medical facility at the castle after Vincent had ordered it recently. This was the second royal baby and who knew how many more there would be?

Brianna glanced down at her flat stomach, and Willow wondered if her friend wanted one.

"God, I hope there's nothing in there," Bri said.

Obviously not.

"I thought you wanted children?" Willow asked.

"Sure, but I think we all know Craig is borderline crazy possessive with just me newly in his life. None of us want little Craig-a-kins popping out into the world for him to lose his mind over."

Willow snorted.

"Good point."

CHAPTER TWENTY-SEVEN

Piper dropped her bag on her bed.
"Oh, my God." She spoke out loud in the empty room.
BioZen had called *her*.
George had stared at her while she was on the phone, her face clearly paling during the conversation. The man had sounded threatening while chatting away in a professional but friendly tone.
She wasn't fooled.
Especially now she knew what they were doing.
She'd mouthed who the caller was to George, and he'd done all kinds of sign language that made zero sense. In the end she'd turned away so she could focus on the call.
Xander Tomassi.
A bigwig at BioZen Pharmaceuticals.
He had invited her to one of their new plants to view what they were doing. Not that she had told George that. She had to await his call in the morning, and someone would pick her up. She'd accepted the invite, but Piper was unsure if it was the best decision.
It could be dangerous.
She'd think on it overnight and decide before the call came through.

She spent the rest of the late afternoon typing up notes and sending an email off to Roger, her editor, to update him on where she was at. Loosely.

There was no way she was putting anything she'd found in an email.

After hours on the computer trying to find out more about BioZen and Xander Tomassi, Piper locked her laptop away in the hotel safe. She had a quick shower and changed into a short black dress and a pair of pumps, then headed downstairs for dinner in the hotel.

She sat at a table and ordered a drink.

Was she hoping to see Oliver?

Maybe.

She shouldn't be. After what she'd learned today, she should be moving hotels and keeping away from him, and yet all afternoon her mind drifted back to him.

What was he doing?

Was he thinking about her?

Did he want her again?

She was beginning to get a little addicted to his body and the way he made her feel. Not just horny, but… cared for. She had seen the way his eyes blazed with need, but when they held hers, there was more.

And if she was being honest, she thought her own gaze would reflect the same back.

The growing proof that he was involved with this vampire world and may not be who he said he was made things complicated.

Piper snorted into her vodka and soda. He *hadn't* said who he was. He never told her any damn thing.

"Can I take your order?" a waitress asked.

"Fish taco's please," Piper replied, and handed her the menu.

An hour later, she wiped her mouth with her napkin and dropped it on her plate.

No Oliver.

Fuck him. Not that he had promised her anything, but she felt disappointed and hated herself for being so needy of a man's attention.

Damn him.

Well, if he thought he could show up at her door tonight and have his way with her, he was out of luck. This was for the best. Until she learned who he really was, she needed to stop sleeping with him. *And* stop romanticizing that it was something it wasn't.

She glanced over at the bar where a well-built man had been subtly watching her.

Creep.

He winked at her.

She raised her brows at him, and he smirked and looked away.

Jesus, what a douchebag.

She took in his dark jeans and leather jacket and rolled her eyes. It wasn't that he was bad looking, but Piper was all out of patience with the entire universe of bad boys right now.

Standing, she decided to go for a walk and burn off the calories before having an early night. Tomorrow was likely to be a big day at BioZen if she went, and then she would head home the next day. She'd promised Sage she would be home for the family dinner, and she would be.

She stepped out of the hotel, turned right and began walking past the stores and hotels, taking in the night action of Los Angeles. It was busy at all hours of the day and night but being street smart she planned to keep to the main street and head back quickly.

She spotted a designer store across the road with a stunning window display and decided to check it out. Piper hit the crossing button and stood amongst a group of people waiting to cross.

"Hey gorgeous." A voice she didn't recognize spoke behind her. As she turned, she felt a hand on her lower arm and then a sharp prick.

The hell?

She looked up into the face of Mr. Bad Boy from the bar.

Oh fuck.

The world began to go fuzzy, and her legs turned to jelly as she crumpled to the ground.

"Honey, oh my God," Mr. Bad Boy said, and she tried to frown. "I've got you."

Liar.

Let me go.

She couldn't speak. Faces were watching her, and she felt the man grab her, but the world was fading in and out.

"Piper!" She heard a different voice call her name. A voice she recognized.

Oliver?

The last thing she thought as the world turned black was that she was imagining him. Oliver wasn't coming to save her. He'd warned her it wasn't safe, and she hadn't listened.

He was going to be so pissed.

CHAPTER TWENTY-EIGHT

Callan crouched by the edge of the water line and splashed his face. Scrubbing, he tried to wash away everything.
Every fucking thing.
The confusion, the memories, the pain.
He was different now. Nobody would remain unchanged after what he'd been through, but it wasn't just that. They had *changed* him.
They had fucking changed him in ways even he didn't understand.
Without this permission.
Like he was nothing more than a lab rat to cut, prick, take from and put shit in.
Whatever they'd done to him, he was changed. He could feel it in every cell of his body.
What had they fucking done to him?
Callan threw back his head and screamed.
Out here in the woods, nobody could hear him. He assumed. Actually, he didn't give a fuck.
That wasn't completely true. He did care.
He cared that he could hurt someone. As a vampire, he'd been taught to curb his bloodlust and ensure he was always fed. They all were. Their parents taught them these skills

from the moment they were born and able to comprehend. It was how they lived peacefully amongst humans.

Which they all wanted.

Right now Callan was wavering in that belief. He knew there was good and evil in the world in all species, but those motherfucking scientists had starved him, then given him fresh blood to gorge on, then starved him.

Rinse and repeat. Over and fucking over again until his natural predatory instincts began to rise.

That was just one of the cruel and disgusting things he'd endured for months, but his mind couldn't focus on it all or he'd go insane.

Right now, his focus was on retraining his body and mind so he could gain some equilibrium. He craved the blood lust while knowing it was dangerous. For him and those around him. The need to sink his fangs and cock into those who appealed to him was overwhelming.

He'd had a powerful sex drive before and it was getting even stronger. Some days he could barely look at the thing between his legs, recalling the way the scientist had run his hand up and down his shaft, until he was hard, and he eventually came.

The sick fucker.

He'd been restrained by Tungsten cuffs and straps. While he'd kicked and struggled the first few times, in the end he'd just let them jerk him off. It was just another bodily fluid they were taking so what the fuck did it matter?

His pride was shot to death at that point, but he knew their faces. Each and every one. The only one that had been scratched off his mental, *I am going to kill you* list, was the human female who had saved him. And she smelt like vampire.

No, Callan wasn't the same.

He was different, that's all he knew. His entire body ached, and every day it was getting worse. It was why he had to stay away from everyone.

Because he'd already fucked up...

Human and vampires—nobody was safe around him.

Until he knew what he was becoming or unbecoming, he had to lay low and hope he hadn't already started a chain reaction that couldn't be undone.

Then one day he would hunt out those on his list and destroy them.

CHAPTER TWENTY-NINE

Oliver watched Piper crumple to the ground.

He saw her walk out of the hotel just minutes before and ground his teeth. He had expected her to return to her room after dinner. Yes, he had been watching, but not engaging with her.

He had to keep his distance, although it had been difficult.

"We have to go," Ben had said when Oliver's eyes had tracked her as she left the hotel. He was about to ask them to wait while he brought her back inside and used his mind manipulation. A night in front of Netflix was exactly what she desired. It was a simple technique. Even he couldn't fuck *that* up.

He had opened his mouth to speak, when all three of them saw the same thing simultaneously. Two men, clearly from some agency, or private outfit, walked past them layered in weapons. In the same direction as Piper had just gone.

"Well, that's very fucking interesting." Kurt crossed his arms.

As they disappeared out the front entrance, Oliver shoved his bag into Ben's chest. "Ya'll carry on. I'll be right back."

"I'm on your six," Kurt said from behind him.

"I'll get a cup of tea then," Ben called.

Oliver couldn't help his grin.

Until he saw Piper falling to the ground.

"Piper!" he yelled as one of the men whipped her up into his arms.

Nope.

No fucking way.

His body tensed and his blood began to boil. The human needed to get his hands off his girl, or he'd skin the fucker alive.

He took a few steps toward them, his fists clenched and power rolling off him, when the man turned. Both the men froze. They were large for humans. AKA not as big as him and definitely smaller than Kurt. But they had skills and weapons. The one not carrying Piper had a scar on his forehead that was clearly a battle wound.

Kurt stepped up beside him. "Well, fuck."

He knew both the men were assessing the situation, studying him and Kurt. They were surrounded by tourists and humans. The two men had no idea they were facing vampires. Presumably.

"Clear the way please, gentlemen, we have to get this woman some medical care," Scar Face said, shifting his black jacket so Oliver could see his metal.

"Amateurs," Kurt mumbled, but they both knew they weren't. "Hand her over and we'll get her the care she needs."

"She's with us," Oliver said, his eyes taking in every single movement they made.

The two men raised their brows and glanced at one another.

"Is that woman okay?" a passerby asked.

"Yes." All four of them replied at once, not glancing at her, and she scurried off.

"You need to leave." The man carrying Piper's lifeless body made to take a few steps forward.

Oliver had to force his fangs to stay where they were, but he felt the moment his eyes vamped out and knew they were seeing red.

"What the fuck?" Scar Face went for his gun, but Kurt moved faster, gripping his hand on the human's weapon. He shook his head.

"Wrong move," Kurt growled.

"Ahh, fuck man," the man groaned as Oliver heard finger bones being crushed.

So sad. Never mind.

"Who the hell are you?" the other man asked.

"Your worst nightmare. Hand her to me. Now." Oliver growled, taking a step closer. "None of us want to draw attention and I get the feeling you'd like to live another day."

Which Oliver would allow, but only because snapping the guy's neck or stabbing him in public was frowned upon by the police.

"You need to leave. You have no idea what you are getting involved with." The man hiked Piper up into his arms as if she was nothing but a bag of potatoes.

And that was not okay.

"Three seconds," Oliver growled.

"Go find another girl. This one isn't yours," the man said.

Oliver grinned like a mad hatter. *That's where you're wrong, asshole.*

Oh good, the human had pissed him off enough that he now didn't give a fuck about consequences.

"You got that one?" Oliver asked Kurt.

"Go for gold, my man. Make it worth it." Kurt laughed.

Oliver quickly stepped forward, shot a punch under the man's jaw causing him to drop Piper. Oliver caught her as he kicked the man's legs out and watched him drop to his ass. Then he slammed his foot down onto his stomach, pushing him flat on his back. The man gripped his throat.

People around them gasped and scattered.

"Leave," Kurt ordered the two guys. "I don't give a fuck who you work for. Tell them they need to understand we are bigger and badder, and our tolerance has come to an end. So go home, fuck your girlfriends, and get a new job."

Oliver stood staring down at the lifeless body in his arms while Kurt implanted a few memories into the men's heads, and those who were still standing around. It was a hell of a cleanup job, and not perfect, but it would do.

Piper was pale, but he could hear her pulse beating gently. It was likely they'd injected her with Propofol to knock her out, so she'd wake in an hour or two.

"Keep your weapons holstered, asshole. I'm happy to let you remember this part so you can make better life decisions." Kurt gave Scar Face a fierce right-hand jab in his gut and the man bent over.

"Let's go." Oliver turned, knowing those men would follow Kurt's instructions and head home.

"She okay?" Kurt asked, glancing down as they walked back inside the hotel.

"Drugged. I'll take her to my room." Oliver saw Ben's eyes widen as they walked through the lobby.

"The fuck?" Ben asked as he joined them.

Oliver nodded, and they all stepped into the elevator. Kurt pressed the button.

"Jesus," Ben said. "Who were they?"

"I'd say they're part of Tomassi's security team," Kurt replied. "Same company we came across in Italy and here protecting Dr. Phillips. They have the same tattoo on their neck."

They did? Oli hadn't noticed that.

"I fucking warned her about this. I should've sent her home. Imagine if we hadn't been here?" He growled as his brain began to imagine all kinds of horrific scenarios. His fangs inched out.

"Okay big guy, go look after her," Kurt said as the elevator doors opened. "We'll head to BioZen and see what we find. We'll update you when we return."

Oliver glanced down at Piper's sleeping body, and shared a look with Ben. Right at this minute, he didn't give a fuck about BioZen or doing his job. Or anything. Nothing but getting her into his bed and knowing she was safe and alive.

"Oliver," Kurt said pointedly, holding his gaze for a moment. "Tell Ari."

He stepped out of the elevator, with Piper still in his arms. He nodded at Ben and Kurt as the doors closed.

Oliver lay Piper down on his hotel bed.

He examined every inch of her body. Well, except the fun bits. At least he'd seen the entire thing take place and didn't have to imagine or worry they'd harmed her in other ways.

There was no way they'd be breathing if they had. It was clear they weren't there to do anything but kidnap her, but what they intended after that was anyone's guess.

Fortunately, he had fucked up their plans.

Jesus, what if he hadn't been there?

The assassin in him knew they'd missed an opportunity to let them take her and follow them, but for Oli it had not been an option. Yes, it had crossed his mind and he knew Kurt would have thought the exact same thing.

He was grateful the senior Moretti warrior hadn't mentioned it.

It really hadn't been an option. His first and last instinct had been to rip her out of the human's arms and get her to safety.

With everyone wondering if Piper was his mate, he figured his decision to put her first was a sign it was possible.

It didn't matter.

It was unlikely the muscle was going to take Piper to the heart of the BioZen operation where they could bust it all open. She was just being removed because she was a nuisance.

Who knows, she could have been a dead body in the trunk of a car or thrown off the side of a boat by the end of the night.

Fuckers.

Oliver got a warm facecloth and wiped it over her forehead and face. It felt like the right thing to do. Then he took a look at the entry site of the drug. It was red. He wanted to lick it and heal it but knew that would raise questions when she couldn't find it.

Oliver paced the room for an hour, knowing he should ring Ari, but he wasn't ready. In the end he lay down on the bed and pulled Piper against his chest. Feeling her slow, steady heart calmed him.

He knew he shouldn't feel anything, but he did, and it was becoming increasingly difficult to ignore.

Every time he saw her, touched her, or was on the receiving end of one of her sassy smiles his emotions burst out of his chest. Yet, she was capable of throwing him off and destroying the most important thing in his life.

His job.

Ari's approval.

He pulled out his phone and called through to the mansion.

"Hey motherfucker, what's up?" Travis said in answer.

He closed his eyes. "Trav, I need you to organize the jet. Wheels up at five a.m."

There was a moment's silence.

"What happened? Did you not find anything out there? Shit, what time is it? It's still early."

"I've got Piper. She was drugged. I need to get her home. Kurt and Ben may or may not return with us."

"On it. Does Ari—"

"No. I'll call him in a minute. I wanted to get the jet booked."

"Got it. I'll have a car downstairs for you."

"Thanks, man."

He hung up and stared down at Piper. God, she was so peaceful and innocent-looking when she was asleep.

And drugged.

He groaned, shaking his head. How could he have let this happen to her? He moved her body and slid off the bed, throwing a blanket over her. Then stepped out onto the balcony, the noise of Los Angeles filling the air. Sirens, cars, people.

He hated it.

He lifted his phone to his ear and dialed the director.

"Oliver. Problem?"

Oh right. Calling while an assignment was underway was always a red flag.

"No. Kurt and Ben are at BioZen right now, scoping it out. I am at the hotel with Piper."

Silence.

"She was drugged by a couple of former military guys. Tomassi's security. We intercepted, and she's sleeping it off."

"Good work," Ari said darkly.

"Sounds like she's pissed off the wrong people at BioZen, finally. Fuck knows what they were planning to do if they'd taken her."

He heard the low growl.

"These fuckers need to be stopped."

Oliver nodded slowly, even though Ari couldn't see him. "I'm bringing her back to Seattle. It's too dangerous for her here."

"You have a job to do, Oliver," Ari said. "Alter her memories and stick her on the jet."

"No," he said firmly, surprising himself. "She's in too deep. I think she's being watched. Today she went to an address and met with some people. Could be related, I don't know, but it's not just about her memories now. And... I need to make sure she gets home safely."

There was a long silence, and he stood staring out into the night, knowing right in this moment he'd put a line in the sand.

Piper was on his side of it. His job on the other.

When the fuck had that happened?

He didn't remember making that decision.

"Bring her to the mansion and we will work out what to do. I need to speak with Sage."

Right.

Oliver pressed his lips together. Piper wasn't his. She was Sage's sister and Ari's sister-in-law. Those things might be true, but Piper was his responsibility. His to protect.

Where had these damn thoughts come from?

He wasn't going to fight the director on this. At the mansion, she would at least be under the same roof as him.

"Oli?"

"Yeah." He ran a hand through his hair. "We'll see you tomorrow morning."

"Alex is on his way to Los Angeles. He can stay with Ben and Kurt to continue the job," Ari said. "Obviously it's not my job to instruct Ben or Kurt, so just update them that Alex is replacing you."

"Got it."

"Was she hurt?" Ari asked after a moment.

Oliver walked back into the hotel room, closing the door behind him. He took in the female lying on his bed.

"No," he answered. "Aside from being drugged, they only took a few steps with her before we stopped them. There might be a little bit of fallout, from onlookers or the police, but it'll probably look like a bunch of jealous lovers."

Ari let out a dry laugh.

"That's fine. Get her home, Oli, and then we can talk."

He frowned.

Oliver wasn't ready to talk to anyone about his feelings for Piper. He didn't understand why he was so protective of her. Perhaps it had to do with Sage, but that excuse was fast becoming pretty weak.

Somehow, Piper had gotten under his skin.

Her sass, her complete disregard for her safety and her determination to gain acceptance from her father had resonated with him.

He understood her.

He wanted to help her.

But she'd chosen the one damn possible story that would hurt him, his race, and unbeknownst to her, Sage.

CHAPTER THIRTY

Piper felt something hard. Warm but hard.

Her head was foggy as she tried to clear her mind and make sense of her thoughts. What day was it? Where was she? Might help to open her eyes, but she really didn't want to. She was warm and safe.

Safe?

Fuck!

The needle. The men. She wasn't safe. Was she kidnapped and wrapped in a warm bundle of blankets, buried in an unmarked grave?

Holy shit, I'm going to die!

No. She would just lay here and pretend she was in Oliver's arms until she ran out of oxygen.

"Open your eyes, darlin'." A gravelly voice spoke right at her ear.

"Nope. Pretend Oliver, I'm not falling for it," she said, then coughed at her dry throat.

"Pretend?"

"Yes, I'm buried alive and hallucinating."

She heard a distant snort.

"Is she always this dramatic?" a man asked.

"Yes," Pretend Oliver answered with a sigh.

Piper began to blink and open her eyes. "I'm not in a grave?"

Oliver came into view. Real Oliver.

Or at least his chest and black t-shirt did. Then she felt her chin tilted up, and he gazed down at her. "Not today, sunshine, but I'm not saying it wasn't a possibility."

She closed her eyes again.

"I don't feel very good."

"I'll give you some privacy," the man's voice said. "Alex has just arrived."

"Okay, I'll join y'all shortly," Oliver said as the door closed.

"Who was that?"

"Ben."

She tried to nod against his chest.

"You saved me." A hand ran across her face, pushing her hair away and she opened her eyes again. "You saved me from those men."

He nodded.

"I knew you'd be mad." She sighed.

His brows furrowed. "I'm madder than a wet hen, Piper. You could have been killed or God knows what else."

She tried to sit up and look at him, but she felt weak, like her limbs were made of spaghetti and ended up just flopping back down.

"Yes, I'm mad." Oliver sighed, pulling her up against his chest as he sat up further. "I told you to go home because this story was dangerous, but you're so damn stubborn you wouldn't listen."

Suddenly, moisture filled her eyes.

"What are you doing?" He gasped.

"This is called crying, you moron," she snapped, and wiped at a tear.

"Why?"

"Because I nearly died!" she cried. "I was scared. Then I thought I heard you call my name and... I..."

"What?"

"I knew you'd save me." She spoke quietly, staring up at his beautiful face with his wild blue eyes.

He shook his head at her, pressing those eyes shut.

"I'm not safe to be around. You need to stay out of my world, Piper." His eyes opened and their gazes locked. "God damn it."

Her mouth parted at the intensity between them, but there was no need for words. His lips slammed against hers and his huge body swallowed her up. If she was going to be buried alive, underneath Oliver was a happy way to die.

Ninety minutes later, she found herself in a vehicle on her way to the airport. She'd given Oliver every argument she could think of, including, *you can't tell me what to do,* but aside from accusing him of kidnapping her—something she was getting rather sick of—she had decided to go with him.

Or rather, she hadn't had a choice.

She'd resorted to glaring at him from the backseat of their SUV while he drove.

"You sure about this?" Oliver asked Kurt in the passenger seat.

"Yeah, Ben can assist Alex and follow up those..." He shot her a look. "Leads. I want to make sure you both get home. I don't trust Tomassi. We're better off in teams, not going it alone."

Oli turned into the airport. "Thanks, Kurt."

Tomassi?

"I know him," she said.

"Who? Tomassi?" Kurt asked, turning. When she nodded, he asked, "How?"

"He rang me yesterday. Invited me to BioZen for a tour. Today. Guess I'm not going."

Oliver shook his head and slammed the steering wheel. "Shit, Piper. Why didn't you tell me?"

"They tracked her phone." Kurt cursed.

"I'm right here. Hello."

"Yup, they must have." Oliver ignored her. "God damn it."

"Give me your phone," Kurt said, holding out his hand.

"No. Nooo." She gripped her handbag, which contained her new iPhone.

"Okay, shallow grave it is then, Piper." Oliver growled and pulled the vehicle to a stop. Her mouth fell open. "You decide."

"Stop it. You're just trying to scare me." She glared at him.

"I'll let you deal with this," Kurt said and got out. She heard him giving people instructions and the trunk opening behind her.

"Why are you not already scared? Someone drugged you and tried to kidnap you. If I hadn't spotted them and followed you…" He growled and angrily opened his door. Hers opened a second later and he helped her out, grabbing her laptop bag.

Piper glanced up at him. His flaming blue eyes screamed possession and all she could think was, *kiss me.*

He blinked and glanced away.

Maybe she had read the vibe wrong. Now she was getting on the plane his job was done. Was that it?

"I want this story. It's important to me and I hate that these men have intimidated me." She focused back on her job.

Oliver took her chin. "Killing you is not intimidation, darlin'. I'm going to keep you alive and get you home safely. Once we're on that plane, I want you to tell me everything."

Well, she most definitely wasn't doing that.

"Okay," she lied.

Then she turned and took in the private jet for the first time. *Holy heck.* It was huge. She followed Kurt up the stairs, Oliver behind her, and nearly gasped as she looked around the luxury interior.

Large leather seats in soft gray lined the space. Some were like sofas and others were single seaters. There were tables and a door, which obviously led down to another section of the plane. On the walls were a few screens, and flight attendants were busy doing preparations.

Kurt went on ahead and grabbed a soda from a wall unit she figured was a fridge. Oliver's hand landed on the small of her back and encouraged her to keep moving.

"This is... very fancy."

"Yup," he replied, and placed her bag on one of the tables. "Sit anywhere and let Suzanne know if you want anything."

Suzanne.

Right.

The woman smiled at her. "Can I get you anything before we take off? Breakfast will be served in about forty minutes."

"Coffee?"

"Latte?"

Piper nodded, then selected a seat on the sofa so she could stretch out later. Not that the room was going to be an issue. She put her handbag down next to her and her laptop bag on the table.

"I'm going to go crash," Kurt said, giving them a wave and disappearing through the door. "Call me if you need me."

"Sweet dreams," Oliver said, smirking.

"Don't know how people can sleep during the day." Piper said.

"Hmm." Oliver crossed the space. She thought he was going to sit next to her when he lifted her bag. Her heart began to beat like a damn high school student. Instead, he ripped her phone out.

She gasped. "No, Oli. No!"

"Grave or iPhone?" he asked, holding it in the air as she jumped to her feet, grabbing at it.

"iPhone!" she cried.

He shook his head.

"Sit down. I'll buy you a new one when we land. You'll need a new number."

"It has all my contacts and details on it," she said, slumping back into her seat.

"We'll sort it."

He walked back to the door of the plane and she heard a strange crunching noise, then he returned.

"What did you do?" she asked.

How had he…? Oliver leaned in and told her to forget what she just saw.

So she did.

"Here's your coffee, ma'am."

Ma'am? How old do I look today? She guessed being drugged and nearly kidnapped could age a girl.

"Um, thanks."

Twenty minutes later, they took off.

CHAPTER THIRTY-ONE

Oliver sat across from Piper and his body physically relaxed as the jet lifted off the tarmac.

She was safe.

Safer than she had been in LA at least.

He had no idea what Ari would decide to do with her when he delivered Piper to the mansion, but that was out of his hands. She was Ari's sister-in-law, and he was the director.

Oliver's boss.

The male to whom he was trying to prove his worth.

And yet this damn sexy female was making him do stupid shit. Christ, he'd outright said *no* to Ari this morning. If he didn't get fired and booted out the front door he'd be surprised.

It wasn't like the ancient vampire didn't encourage independent thinking or empower them as assassins. He did. But Oliver's response had been purely based on Piper's safety and not taking into consideration the bigger picture of their job. His job. The job he was in charge of as head assassin.

He'd just up and left during the middle of it.

He'd chosen *her*.

And once again he looked like a young male choosing his dick over responsibility.

So why didn't it feel like that, this time?

Even when his father had judged him all those years ago, he'd never felt like it had been wrong. The guy was abusing her, so fuck him. She'd come to him wanting a moment of happiness—a reprieve from the abuse. In those days, it was extremely hard, nearly impossible, for a woman to leave her husband. Financially, there were few options for a female to look after themselves.

His father's disgust was out of proportion.

Oliver often wondered if his father had lived, and had time to think, whether he would have realized his reaction was over the top. Once he'd nearly asked his mother, but she was so deep in grief he didn't want to add to her suffering.

In the end, he'd just manned up and moved on.

Upon reflection, his father had always been tough on him. Oliver had always been more brawn than brains, and muscle was something his father didn't value. That wasn't to say Oli was stupid—an assassin wouldn't last five minutes if he didn't use his brains—but he'd had no desire to hold down a desk job and live a simple life.

Oliver thrived on adventure, danger and always aspired to do something that made an impact.

His father found it... irritating. Found *him* irritating.

All he'd wanted was his father's love and acceptance. His approval. He'd never gotten it.

Would he be proud of Oliver's role as head assassin at The Institute? It was as good as it got in his line of work. Becoming an SLC or Commander of the Moretti royal army was probably the only other role in the vampire world that was a step up, and Craig wasn't going anywhere.

He noticed Piper's fingers tighten on the leather of her seat. She was a nervous flyer.

His lips twitched.

Well, well, well, the sassy princess was finally scared of something.

Her eyes lifted to his and stayed there until the plane leveled, as if using his presence to feel safe. His chest swelled with happiness that he was the one that could do that for her.

And that's exactly what he was going to do.

Keep her safe.

She'd hate it, but it was too bad. Right now, she was on BioZen's radar and that was not okay.

"Okay, let's talk," he said, nodding at her.

"First, I don't want a cheap replacement iPhone. I want the latest model."

"Done."

He'd buy her ten if it kept her alive.

Piper's lips pressed together as if suppressing the argument she had planned, and he fought his grin.

"Why are those men after me?"

He let out a long sigh. "I'd say you know why after the lengths they went to get to you."

She stared back at him doing her best poker face, but he wasn't buying it.

"Let's start with what you know."

Her blue eyes shot to her laptop giving away the source of her information. Oliver stood and sat down beside her. He glanced at the laptop. "Is it all in there?"

"What?" she asked, surprised. He lay his arm along the cushions behind her and twisted his body while she reached for the laptop and pulled it onto her lap. "This is company property. You can't touch it. Its confidential."

"You won't need a job if you're dead."

"Stop with the threats," she snapped.

"God, female, what will it take for you to take this seriously? You still have their drugs running through your damn veins. I wanted to kill the man holding you."

She gasped.

"You would do that?"

He frowned, realizing he'd given her the wrong impression. Hadn't he?

Oliver watched the questions forming in her eyes. His words had told her more than he wanted her to know. It hinted that he cared. That he would protect her with his life. That this was a relationship.

There was no relationship.

At least, there couldn't be.

But he couldn't deny his growing desire—no, his need—to know she was safe. He needed to get her home and hand her over to Ari.

That's where things got a little tricky.

He was pretty confident Ari would be successful in wiping her memories and his body tensed at the thought of her not knowing him. His mind was like a damn yo-yo. He both wanted her home safe and out of his way and didn't want to let her go.

For now, she was here with him.

"You're out of your league here, Piper. You need to tell us what you know, and who's involved."

"Why do you care?"

He opened his mouth to reply, then shut it. There was no way he was going to start talking about feelings.

She swallowed.

They stared at each other in a stalemate and the air sizzled between them. In and out they breathed as their bodies craved one another.

Stay on task.

Don't stare at her breasts.

"Who is *us,* Oliver? Who do you work for? Is it Ari? How are you all connected?" Piper asked, and he nearly smiled. She was trying to ignore the arousal growing between them. He knew her voice. He knew when she was getting wet.

"I'm asking the questions, darlin'," he replied, leaning in closer to make his point, but all it did was make her lick her lips.

Don't kiss her.

She followed his actions, moving them just inches apart.

Snap crackle pop.

"I'm not telling you anything. My story is confidential." Her voice cracked with need. Both their hearts beat fast.

Thump, thump, thump.

His gaze dropped and found her fingers digging into the bag she held.

She needed him.

His cock pressed painfully against his jeans. When his eyes lifted back to hers, she was looking at it with such a raw craving Oliver lost control.

"Mmphhhf," she moaned as he grabbed her face and slammed into her lips.

He pushed the laptop onto the cushions and pulled her legs over his, so she was straddling him. His hands wrapped around her hips and tugged her against his hard cock.

"Oli," she breathed.

"Piper."

"Are you going to fuck me while we're in the air?"

"Yes, ma'am. I'm going to fuck you so damn hard you're going to scream into the heavens. You hear me?"

Her eyes widened, but she nodded. He pulled her top over her head, exposing her bra. One tug on the lace and her nipple popped free.

Lick.

"You have a problem with that?"

She gave him a husky *no.*

"Lock cabin doors," he said to the computer system.

"Cabin doors locked," it replied in a robotic voice.

Piper glanced around. "Shame, I quite liked the risk of someone seeing us."

He groaned.

"If you want to ramp things up a little, darlin', I'm happy to arrange it. I'm sure K—"

His heart slammed into his chest.

No. No fucking way.

Whether Kurt wanted to fuck Piper was not a question he wanted answered, and it was *not* an option. He wasn't sharing her. Not today and not tomorrow.

'Never mind," he said, slipping his hand between them and reaching between her legs.

"Damn you, Oliver," she moaned as his fingers slipped under the lace and circled her clit. "Why can't I say no to you?"

"You can always say no, and I will stop."

But she wouldn't.

One look into her eyes as he thumbed her nipple with his other hand, and she cursed, digging her fingers into his biceps.

She wasn't saying no.

He pressed his fingers inside her and she cried out, tightening around them.

"That's it, princess. Fuck my fingers." She thrust her hips against his hand, his cock now aching to get inside her heat. He rolled her nipple as she continued crying out and riding his hand.

He shouldn't care this much. He shouldn't be fucking her again. He shouldn't be feeling like he only wanted to please this female and no other.

He flipped her onto the cushions, laying her out. Then he slid her panties down. The skirt he shoved up around her hips. He wanted his mouth on her sweet honey pussy, but then his gaze locked on hers and his heart slammed up into his throat.

He swallowed.

"What is this, Oli?" she asked.

No, I can't do this.

"What do you want it to be?" It was an asshole comment, but facing his feelings for Piper wasn't an option for him.

Reaching behind him, he yanked his t-shirt off and then offed his jeans and boots. He lay over her, his taut arm pressed against the side of the sofa.

Then his eyes found hers again.

Rejection flashed across Piper's face, and she blinked it away.

Shit.

Oliver was a male in touch with his feelings. Sure, he was known to have lots of lovers, but that didn't mean he didn't feel anything. Even with Sage—which he should *not* be thinking about right now – there had been a connection.

With Piper, it was more.

It had always been more. More intense. More impossible to stay away, and more incredible.

He thought it would pass. Perhaps it still would once he got her home. Maybe this was about protecting a female that was sexy as sin and with a mouth to match. He couldn't deny that, right now, she meant more to him than he could allow.

What he didn't like was the sadness of his rejection simmering in those beautiful blue eyes. Oliver cupped the back of her neck and softly answered the way he should have the first time.

"I don't know. I don't know what this is, but I have a powerful need to protect you and have you in my arms."

Her eyes softened as her hands moved over his shoulders.

"When I'm deep inside you, there's this feeling that you are mine," he said, admitting the thoughts for the first time.

She arched into him, and their mouths collided once more. This kiss was different. It was passion and fire, promise and need. Their tongues scooped, danced, licked and demanded.

Pushing back the intensity, Oliver made his way down her body tasting and nipping at her. Then he crouched between her legs. "Legs up and wide darlin'," he said, taking in the pink flesh calling to him. "I want you wet and tight around my cock today."

His tongue swept lightly across her pussy. He knew it was a tease and smiled when she moaned and lifted to his face. Again and again he licked around the edges, slightly touching on her sensitive spots, and giving tiny bits of pleasure until she was wriggling and trying to take control.

He wouldn't let her.

He had her hips in a grip she couldn't break.

He needed control.

He needed possession of her.

"Oli," she moaned.

Then his tongue flicked against her clit and her cries got louder. Moaning for more. Around and around he circled and then slid his fingers inside her entrance, slowly adding a second one.

"Jesus fucking Christ," she cried.

His cock felt the same way. It was bursting to get out of his jeans and housed within her once more. It was time. He lifted her hips to his mouth and sucked hard until she screamed out her orgasm.

Sorry Kurt.

No he wasn't.

Dropping her hips, he fucked Piper with his fingers until he drew her last drop. As she lay gasping, he moved up her body and sucked her hard nipples into his mouth.

He stroked his cock, letting it know it was soon going to sink inside the gorgeous creature beneath him. Pulling her into position, she lifted her legs around his waist and their eyes connected.

"You with me, darlin'?" he asked, grinning at her flushed pink cheeks and glazed eyes.

"Yes. Get inside me."

"Yes, ma'am." He winked and guided his cock to her entrance.

"Why is everyone calling me ma'am... oh fucking God." She cried out and her little fingernails stung as they dug into his biceps.

Oliver reveled in the sweet pain as he drove deep inside her. Holy hell, she felt like heaven. Her pussy clung to his cock, sending raw pleasure firing through his body in a shudder. He gripped the arm of the sofa with one hand, and her hip with his other.

Thrust after thrust, he slammed into her, taking in the pleasure on her face. The *O* of her mouth, the hunger in her eyes, the flush of orgasm still rich on her face.

She was everything.

He wanted to please this woman more than any other.

Faster he moved, dominating her body, needing to see her succumb to his demands. Then his body tightened, and muscles bulged as he spilled his seed inside of her.

He let out a cry.

This was the fourth time he'd fucked Piper. When had he ever fucked the same female four times?

Had he ever?

Would this be the last time? Once Ari had her, this—whatever this was between them—was over. And he wasn't sure he was okay with that.

CHAPTER THIRTY-TWO

He'd kill? For her? Oliver had said he'd kill for her.

No one had ever said something like that to her before. God knows she had daddy issues. No one needed to spell that out to her. She was well aware.

Was that what she wanted? A man to protect her.

Sure.

Wasn't that what every woman wanted, even though in this day and age it wasn't necessary? Society no longer restricted women in the way they had in the past. She had a well-paying job, independence and a great family and friends, but it didn't change the fact she desired a masculine, sexy man.

Just not one who would tell her what to do all the time.

Like Oliver did.

He was constantly telling her to go home. Not to mention his favorite nickname for her was *pain in the ass*. Well, she was an embarrassment and pain in the ass to her father, too. And he'd all but written her off.

Yet… the way Oliver looked at her. The way his body moved closer and angled to protect her, even from someone looking at her, made her feel cared for.

It was such a foreign feeling she didn't know what to do.

Sage had been the one who sat on Daddy's knee being bumped up and down as a little girl while he called out to Piper for to tell her off for doing something naughty.

Now, the dominant way in which Oliver protected her was new and overwhelming.

The universe seemed intent on thrusting them together. He'd said it felt like she was his.

Mine.

No one had ever wanted to make her theirs before.

No man.

And he'd saved her life. It was hard not to forget that. Piper still had no idea of his involvement with everything, but she was beginning to wonder if he was worth letting her story go for?

When will I ever find someone else to feel like this about?

Oliver was sexy, protective, gorgeous, and clearly had an important job. And damn him and that southern accent. It was killing her.

He cared. She could see it in his eyes. Even when he didn't realize she was watching him she felt his eyes following her. The little things he did like getting her a bottle of water after a ravishing session or massaging her hips.

Did he know he even did that?

"I could've taken you into one of the bedrooms," Oliver smirked.

"That's not your style, cowboy." Piper nudged him to move. Oliver reached for the tissues, pulled out of her, and then handed her a bunch.

"How about a movie?" he asked when they had both cleaned up. He pulled her down onto the sofa as he flicked a switch. A whirring sounded as the furniture around them moved. The sofa now became a bed and the coffee table vanished into the floor. A screen fell from the ceiling.

"Do you have Netflix?"

"Everything. Name your poison," Oliver answered.

"Let's watch some vampire shows."

He groaned.

"What?"

"You really believe in vampires?" he asked.

"It's research," she replied, kind of testing him. If he was involved with all of this, she wanted to know before she let her feelings out and really fell for him.

Whether that was an option between them, she didn't know, but one thing was for certain: she was already losing control and falling.

And she had a feeling Oliver wasn't far behind.

"Well, at least in the air I know you can't get into any more trouble," he said, handing her the remote.

The cabin door opened. Oliver had unlocked them moments earlier.

"Are you ready for breakfast, sir?" Suzanne asked.

"Hell yes," Piper said, and Oliver smirked proudly, knowing he was the cause of her hunger.

He wasn't wrong.

He nodded to Suzanne and in moments, the cabin was filled with the aroma of poached eggs, bacon, grits, and hot coffee. Piper watched him out of the corner of her eyes as he was eating. Everything he did was sexy. Or maybe she was becoming obsessed. The way he lifted his fork to his mouth and his powerful forearms corded. When he reached for his mug and his t-shirt tightened around his biceps.

"If you keep looking at me like that, I'm locking those damn doors again." Oliver groaned, his eyes on the screen.

She blushed and looked away, but she felt the moment his eyes moved to her body. Heat pulsed over her skin.

"Finish your breakfast," he mumbled.

Twenty minutes later, Piper was snuggled against his chest muttering about Damon being hot and how she'd choose him, even though he was a bad boy.

"Go to sleep," Oliver growled quietly. "I told you, darlin'. You're mine."

As her eyes drifted closed, she smiled, imagining a life being in Oliver's arms forever. Safe, loved, and adored.

Maybe it was what she wanted.

Maybe it was possible.

After all, he was hardly a vampire.

CHAPTER THIRTY-THREE

"Fuck man, we're cutting it fine," Kurt said, ducking his head to glance out the windscreen.

It was about thirty minutes before the sun would begin to rise and they were both feeling it. Oliver pressed down harder on the pedal of his black Maserati.

"Yeah, I know, but I wanted to get her out of LA, so it was either this or waiting another day." He rubbed his brow with one hand and held the steering wheel with the other.

"I get it." Kurt nodded.

"Cutting it fine for what?" Piper asked, leaning forward. "And why are you going this way? My apartment is in the other direction."

Oliver groaned silently. He'd dodged this conversation so far and had been expecting her to figure it out as they drove through Seattle.

"I asked him to drop me off first," Kurt said, saving him from lying.

"Oh. I guess that's fine then." She slumped back in her seat. Oliver glanced at her in the rear vision mirror and a little smile hit his lips. She was so damn beautiful and annoying it blew his mind. He should want her out of his goddamn life, but he didn't.

Not for a single second.

"You're totally done for; you know that, right?" Kurt said, letting out a little laugh. "She—fuckkkkk!"

Kurt reached for the steering wheel as Oliver's head swung around but it was too late. He'd already heard the roar.

Fuck!

He wanted to scream a warning to Piper but there wasn't time. She didn't have the same reflexes they had.

A white SUV slammed into the side of the Maserati in a deathly crunch, sending them skidding. Then he felt them flip and become slightly airborne before the vehicle landed on its side. Metal groaned as they slid to a stop, glass shattering and blasting everywhere.

Oliver's head hit the steering wheel, then the side of the car as he was flung around like the inside of a clothes drier. Except less warm and cozy. Kurt was cursing, his hands braced on the roof and window, and he could hear Piper screaming.

When they finally stopped moving, the noise in his ears buzzed.

And he realized Piper had stopped screaming.

Shit.

"Port out," Kurt instructed firmly, knowing Oliver was going to try to get Piper. "Secure the environment, then get her."

He glanced in the back and saw her bloody, lifeless body, but there was a heartbeat. He nodded, and they both ripped the seatbelts from their bodies and teleported out of the vehicle.

The hell?

Two more white SUVs had pulled up and they were surrounded by military-style soldiers with machine guns pointed at them.

Then Oliver felt a pistol muzzle on the back of his head.

Travis SOS. He called for help, using his telepathic powers.

Where are you? Travis replied, responding with urgency to the call. They trained for this, and it wasn't the first time they'd had to use it. What they did was dangerous, and they'd all been working together for decades.

Track my vehicle. SOS.

Ari. SOS. We need help. NOW!

On my way. The director answered fast.

Nobody fucked around when it was an SOS call.

Nobody.

If Piper wasn't in the car, both Kurt and he would have turned this into a blood bath already. But she was.

How the fuck did they sneak up on us like this? he asked Kurt.

Good fucking question.

"Stay very fucking still." A voice spoke from behind him.

Another SUV, this one black, pulled up and two men got out and ripped the door open on the Maserati.

Oliver's eyes burned as they reached in and pulled Piper out.

Black GMC registration LMT-580. They're taking Piper.

How the fuck? Travis asked. *Tracking now. Ari is on the way.*

Then he felt a prick in his neck.

I've been injected.

"Mother fuckers," Kurt cried out, and then humans around him began to drop as the SLC took action. Bodies began flying and shots sounded.

Oliver smashed his arms out behind him and heard another gun go off.

Body check. He wasn't hit.

But the drugs were taking hold.

"Move. Move. Move!" someone shouted in a Russian accent.

He turned and saw Piper being carried into the black SUV. She was conscious again, and her terror-filled eyes widened. She reached out her arms to him.

"Oli!" she cried.

He wobbled on his feet, unable to move. When she saw that, she opened her mouth and screamed.

Oliver felt more useless than he ever had in his entire life.

"I'll find you," he said, but it wasn't loud enough for her to hear. Then his legs crumpled under him.

Out of the corner of his eye he saw Kurt collapsing.

Blackness crept into his consciousness and the last thing he saw was the sun beginning to rise.

Fuck.

CHAPTER THIRTY-FOUR

"He'll be fine. He's a vampire. He's not going to die," Ari said and Oliver nearly laughed as he began to wake up.

"Don't be mean, he still had a fright." Sage spoke from close beside him and then he felt her rubbing his arm. "Car accidents are scary."

A smirk hit his lips.

"See. He's fucking fine," Ari said pointedly. "Move away from him."

Ah, the insanity of a mated male.

"Plus, we need to find Piper."

Piper! Oliver sat up suddenly and Sage let out a little squeal.

"Told you to move." Ari laughed.

"Where is she?" he growled, and Ari shook his head.

The fuck?

He jumped to his feet, but Ari held out his hand.

Is she dead? he asked telepathically, so as not to freak Sage out.

"We were hoping you could tell us. What happened?"

Kurt?

He's fine. Ari glanced across the room and Oli followed his gaze to where Kurt lay on another single bed.

"We were ambushed. By fucking humans." Oliver pushed his fingers through his blond hair. "How long have we been out?"

"About six hours," Ari said. "What do you know? Any idea where they've taken her?"

Oliver cursed.

"No fucking idea. Same tattoos on the neck. I saw a couple."

"Shit," Ari said.

"Oh, my God," Sage said, her hand flying to her mouth.

Clearly, she'd been hoping he'd have some information to help them find Piper when he woke.

"This is all my fault," she cried, turning into Ari's chest. His eyes shot to Ari's face, and he could see the anguish as he comforted his mate.

Oliver cleared his throat. "It's not your fault, Sage. This is mine."

Ari looked up and Sage turned in his arms.

"I have been unsuccessful in wiping her memory many times and I should have told someone. I have been keeping an eye on her—"

"What does that mean? Keeping an eye on her. Where?" Sage asked.

"Just…" *Shit.* "At home, and places."

"Places?" Ari asked.

"Mostly at her home," Oliver confessed.

"You've been visiting her?" Sage asked accusingly.

Technically, no.

"Well, not by invitation," he answered, feeling sheepish.

Sage narrowed her eyes. "You were watching her? Did she know?"

Oliver ran a hand over his face and glanced at Ari.

"Sage, *mia stellina*, how about you try to get some rest? It's been a long day. The team are out there tracking Piper, but Oliver obviously doesn't know anything that can help us, or he would have said."

Of course, he fucking would have. Right now, his body was vibrating with the need to have Piper back in his arms.

Sage's eyes met his in question.

"Sage, I haven't hurt her. I swear. I will do everything in my power to get your sister back," he promised. "Every fucking thing."

"You care about her."

He nodded.

"Are you... did you?"

Oliver wasn't going to lie or betray Piper. What she wanted to share with her sister was over to her, and he wouldn't cross that boundary.

But it wasn't that.

Sage was asking for herself. What the three of them had shared was not uncommon for vampires, but for Sage it had been a sexual awakening of sorts.

They all knew that.

He was special to her. As she was to him.

It was one of the reasons he'd been fighting his feelings for Piper. He knew Sage would see it as a type of betrayal — especially after what Piper had done to her in college.

He knew.

He'd seen her memories.

"Yes."

As the single word slipped from his lips, Oliver found that his loyalties had shifted. He cared about Sage, and he still hoped like hell that his job hadn't been compromised because of his choices and actions, but Piper was important to him.

She was his priority.

"We'll find her," Ari said, pulling Sage against his chest and lowering his lips to her forehead.

Sage glanced at Oli, emotion rich in her eyes, as she left the room.

Fuck.

When Sage left, Ari turned to him.

"Before we go further into all that..." Oliver said, and Ari raised his brows. "We need to get blood samples. Right now. They injected us. Whatever they used, it must be the same shit they've been using to kidnap the other vampires around the world."

Ari stared at him.

"Look, I'm sorry about all this, but Ari, come on. I don't know how long this stuff will stay in our systems."

"Matteo is on his way with a kit," Ari said.

Oh right, Ari must have been telepathing with Matteo, his assistant, not glaring at him.

So hard to tell with Ari.

Then the director *did* stare at him.

"You're important to Sage," Ari finally said.

"She's important to me. It's not because of... you know," Oliver replied, and then realized that was a lie.

It *was* because of that.

Ari let out a grunt.

The truth was it had bonded them. Not as mates, but in friendship. Sage had been a big-hearted, affectionate human, and it wasn't going to disappear now she was a vampire. He and Ari had shared a moment in Sage's life that would always be momentous to her.

Sage didn't fuck. She made love. And in her mind, she'd made love to him. He'd felt it. Especially the second time. Though he would never, ever, fucking *ever*, tell Ari.

It wasn't necessary.

Sage was Ari's mate, and he was happy for them.

Oliver might not be her mate, but he had a tiny slice of Sage's heart, and he knew finding out about Piper would hurt her.

What Piper would think was another thing.

But as his mind returned to his mouthy dark-haired beauty, all he cared about was getting her safely home and then he would deal with everyone's damn emotions.

Fuck knows what those assholes were doing to her—if she was even still alive.

"We need to talk about Piper," Ari said.

"Yes. What's the situation? You haven't tracked her? What about the registration I gave you? Cameras? Fuck, we must have something?"

Ari plugged his hands into his pockets.

"Cameras were blacked out. Registration is a fake. Travis is working with Darren and the team. Logan and Elijah are tracking."

He was pleased to hear the other two senior assassins were back in town and able to help out. But the rest was not good news. Oliver felt himself pale and a sick feeling sunk deep into his belly.

Shit.

Knowing two of his team were on the ground made him feel better but it wasn't enough. He had to get out there.

"But that's not what I meant," Ari said, his eyes darting to Kurt then back to him. "Let's go for a walk."

A few minutes later they were heading down the hall to Ari's office. He pushed the door open, and they walked inside.

"Look, I know I've fucked up. I shouldn't have outright—"

"Oli." Ari pointed to a chair.

Fuck.

Was he going to lose his job? Did he care? Piper needed him. He had to find her.

"You've worked for me for a long damn time," Ari started.

"Yup," he nodded.

"I told you I selected you for this role because you're the best at what you do. You use your brain, common sense and all your skills," he said. "You were more than ready for this job."

He stared at Ari. "And now?"

"Now I need you to do your fucking job and stop doubting yourself."

Oliver stood.

Ari pointed to the chair again.

He sat.

"I have a question for you," Ari said. "One you may not have an answer for."

Oliver frowned. "What do you mean?"

His knee was bouncing, needing to get into action.

"First, for clarity. Are you fucking Piper?"

"Yes."

Ari nodded slowly.

"Kurt join in?"

His eyes widened. "No. *No*! Why?" He asked, then realized his mistake.

Ari wiped away the barest hint of a smile. "She your mate?"

Oliver stood and began to pace. "No."

"You sure?"

"No," he answered quickly. "Yes. Fuck. Maybe. I don't know."

Ari leaned back in his chair and swiveled, lifting his foot onto his ankle. "So if I was to say that Alex fucked her a few weeks back…"

Oliver turned, his body tensing and his fangs slipping out. "Did he?"

Ari stood and slapped him on the back despite, well, his enormous power and state, which was primed to kill someone. "No. But I think you should prepare yourself to be mated in the coming days."

Mated with Piper?

He stared at the floor, wondering if it was possible, when a knock at the door interrupted them.

"Come in, Matteo."

"I've just taken Kurt's blood, so if this is a convenient time, Master Oliver, I will take yours?"

He nodded and the old vampire came over and pulled out his medical equipment. Oliver sat down and held out his arm.

"Is Kurt awake, Matteo?" he asked.

"Yes, sir," he replied. "And not in a good mood."

Oliver grunted out a laugh. He could only imagine how Kurt was feeling. Humans getting the jump on a Senior Lieutenant Commander of the Moretti royal army didn't happen every day.

Nor the head assassin from The Institute.

His eyes found Ari's. "They need to die."

The director nodded. "Yes."

Elijah and Logan came banging through the doors of the training room and went straight to the fridge for a pouch of plasma.

Oliver waited for them to suck it down and then cross to join him and Ari.

"Sorry, man." Logan shoved his hands on hips and shook his head.

They both looked fucked off.

"Not a scent."

"They're pros. Aside from the debris from the accident and a few tire marks when they took off, there's nothing," Elijah said.

Travis walked in and the door banged closed behind him. "Darren said they've wiped out cameras for miles. All of them."

Oliver glanced at Ari. "That's some access they've got. Are we talking about government involvement here?"

Ari crossed his arms, those biceps outdoing all of them. The large vampire stared through them as his sharp mind ran scenarios.

"Nothing from her mobile?" Logan asked.

"Genuis over here destroyed it," Travis replied.

"That's head genius to you," Oliver said, giving him the bird. "And I destroyed it because Piper was being tracked by Tomassi."

Then he froze as an idea struck him.

He glanced at Ari quickly, then turned to Elijah. "Did you go through the Maserati?"

My poor fucking car.

Elijah gave him a quick shake of his head. "Didn't touch a thing. You said they pulled her out and put her in the SUV, so we followed the direction the vehicles went in and then did a five hundy mile radius search."

"Oli—"

"Back in a minute." Before he could 'port away, he heard Ari's voice. *Fuck's sake, wait.*

Oliver landed beside his Maserati and shook his head at the damage. He wouldn't think twice about exchanging it for Piper, but it still broke his damn heart. He loved that car.

"Oliver." He wasn't surprised Ari had followed him. "Talk to me."

Oliver gripped the door handle and yanked it as the steel groaned and croaked like it was the sound effects for the damn *Titanic* sinking.

Nothing.

He grinned.

"You want to tell me what's going on?" Ari demanded.

He turned and smiled at the ancient vampire. "They took her handbag and laptop with her. Darren will find her."

He knew it was a long shot, but their tech team was the best in the world. If there was a way of tracking her laptop and finding her, they would.

"You're assuming a lot," Ari said, then smiled. "But I think you might be right. Let's go."

Oliver grinned.

He would find her if it was the last thing he did. Hopefully, before she took her last breath.

CHAPTER THIRTY-FIVE

"Don't fucking shoot me, but I'm telling you, this is going to take a bit of time," Darren said, giving him a dark look. To be fair, the looks Oliver had been firing at the team were probably not the friendliest, either.

Nor were his the most patient.

He knew the drill, though. Leave the damn tech guys to do their work or they were not focused.

On the other side of the room, Ari was staring at his laptop, looking calm and collected, but Oliver knew better. The vampire might be more skilled at patience than most of them, but this was his mate's sister.

Sage would be on his case, constantly worried.

He knew the feeling.

He could barely breathe.

Kurt pushed away from the wall and pulled on his jacket. "Well, I nearly died today so I need a fucking beer."

A few sniggers filled the room.

Everyone knew it would be pretty hard to kill anyone in this room. Although, if Oliver hadn't reached out to Travis and Ari both he and Kurt would be ash scattered across the earth right now.

He shivered.

Instead, they were still powerful immortals. Or as close to immortal as any living creature on earth could get.

Hopefully, the blood samples taken would give them information about how humans were able to incapacitate vampires so easily. And stop them.

Ari had said Sage was going to order some equipment and set up a small lab. But they didn't have time for that right now, so somehow, they needed access to a non-BioZen scientist—because fuck no; she was not going near that organization again—to do the testing.

She was the perfect person, obviously as a lab assistant, and Ari said it would keep her mind busy.

Finding out what they were using to weaken vampires would be an incredible step forward in this war. Because it *was* becoming a war.

"He needs a beer, too," Darren said, looking pointedly at Oliver, in an obvious attempt to get rid of him.

Oliver frowned. No he didn't. What he needed was a certain sassy brunette, who wouldn't shut up, back in his damn arms.

"I'm not going anywhere," Oliver replied. "Unless y'all get a location, then I'm gone."

Ari looked up.

"Go. We can call you in seconds. You know that." It was an order. "Go and give these guys space to breathe and focus."

God damn it.

Kurt nodded at him. "Come on. Let's go swap war stories."

Oliver groaned and grabbed his jacket. "As soon as—"

"Go," Ari said, raising a brow.

Ten minutes later, the two of them were holding up the bar, or rather leaning their big-ass bodies on the wooden bar top of their local. The same one he and Ari had met Sage in not that long ago.

"Bit fancier than what I'm used to," Kurt said, lifting his bottle to his lips.

"Don't be fooled by the designer shoes and watches." He help up his own Piguet-clad wrist with a grin.

Kurt turned his wrist to show off his own oversized silver watch and shrugged. It went without saying that those in jobs like theirs were incredibly well paid by excessively wealthy employers.

They shared a laugh.

"Give it another hour and these rich assholes will have far fewer manners and class than a bar full of leather and denim," Oliver said. "Trust me."

Medina, where the mansion was located, was home to tech mogul Bill Gates and Amazon's Jeff Bezos, to name but a few of the billionaires in the area. While they were unlikely to walk through the door, many of their top executives lived in the area. Not that Oliver gave a shit about any of them right now. His mind was on Piper.

Was she alive?

Had they hurt her?

Was she scared?

He was only just holding it together, but Ari was right about giving the tech team space. No one performed at their best when someone was breathing down their neck.

"We'll get her back," Kurt said, reading his mind. "And it's time we showed these humans who they're dealing with."

Oliver nodded.

"I had the same chat with Ari."

"What did he say?" Kurt asked.

"He didn't disagree." Oliver replied. "What do you think the king will say?"

Kurt lifted his beer to his lips, thinking, and then dropped the glass heavy-handed on the bar. Oliver had a feeling it was on purpose to get the pretty bartender's attention. It wasn't the first time Kurt's eyes had lingered on her.

"I honestly don't know. He's strategic, you know. Not a warmonger," Kurt said, his eyes glistening as the female stopped in front of him.

She was a vampire.

"I'll have another beer and your phone number." Kurt smirked.

Good grief.

If he'd known Kurt was this bad at picking up females, he'd have brought some back up.

"Really? Is that—" The female froze her rebuttal and narrowed her eyes. "Oh my God. Are you…" Her voice lowered. "You are! You're Kurt Mazzarelli, one of the Moretti SLC's."

Kurt's lips stretched into a slow smile.

A knowing smile.

Well, then. Who needed moves when you had a fucking fan base? Oliver wanted to slow-clap the vampire.

Cute Bar Female leaned forward. "Are you from Italy?"

Kurt leaned an inch toward her. "*Si.*"

The female blushed and Oliver was sure that bounce on her shoulder-length blond curls was a sign of joy.

He tipped his beer and placed it on the bar. Not softly.

Neither of them noticed.

"You know, I think I'm going to wash my hair, do a pedimani, and have an early night after all." Oliver slapped Kurt on the shoulder and gave the girl a grin. "Y'all behave yourselves."

Kurt turned. "Night buddy. Don't forget to extricate. Or whatever that shit is."

"Exfoliate," the female corrected with a giggle.

Yeah, Kurt was about to have a really nice evening.

Oliver grinned and left the bar. Stepping out into the cold night air, he plunged his hands into his denim pockets.

Where the hell are you, Piper?

CHAPTER THIRTY-SIX

Piper wriggled her arms uselessly for the hundredth time and one of the security men shook his head at her.

"Just untie me, would you? It's not like I can get past you and run away." She pleaded again.

"Shut your mouth and I won't shoot you. How's that for a deal?" A dark-skinned man spoke, lifting a can of Red Bull and taking a long drink.

So far, they hadn't done anything to hurt her, but she'd seen Oliver fall to his knees and collapse, so she had to assume he was dead.

Which meant no one was coming for her.

And even if she was saved, Oliver was still dead.

The black streaks she assumed she had down her face were testament to the tears she'd cried—okay, screamed—until they'd shoved some crap into her mouth to silence her. The tears had continued to flow, regardless.

Oliver was dead.

She suspected Kurt was, too.

This was all her fault. Would they get to Sage, too? Were these men vampires?

"If you were going to kill me, you would have by now," she muttered.

A tall man wearing a long leather jacket glanced at her. "Stop watching all that Hollywood shit. I could just as easily kill you now as I could in an hour."

Gulp.

There were five men in the room with her, and she had a feeling they were waiting for further instructions. One of them was attempting to break into her laptop.

He wouldn't succeed.

All journalists' laptops were protected with an auto-destruct technology if it sensed a hacker. Or the journalist in question was forced to give up a password. A different one than your everyday one.

Once unlocked, it immediately dumped all data to the servers and sent a distress signal which anyone could pick up, but more importantly, it went to local authorities.

They would trace the laptop—and her—pretty soon.

Actually, she didn't know when.

But sooner or later.

Hopefully not before these terrifying men shot her, or however they planned to kill her.

This was bad. She knew Oliver had been right, and she had gotten herself involved in a dangerous story. Piper knew now that vampires were real, and it was clear they were powerful beings who did not want to be found.

These men could be vampires.

"Listen, I'm willing to drop this story if you let me go." She knew how pathetic it sounded but her life was worth more than the story. There would be another one. "Keep the laptop."

Oliver was right. If she was dead, there was no Pulitzer Prize and no proving to her father she was worthy of his love. Heck, if she wasn't enough as she was, then perhaps *he* didn't deserve *her*?

Oliver had seen her worth.

Hell, he'd fought to keep her off the story because he cared about her. She didn't know how he was connected and maybe she would never find out. If she got out of here alive, she would make sure Sage was safe and one day ask Ari about Oliver.

When her heart was less shattered.

Suddenly the man with her laptop slammed his hands down and hurled the device across the room.

"It's fucking wiped." He whirled to her. "You knew this was going to happen. Fucking bitch."

She recoiled from him, pressing into the sofa. "What? I, no, I didn't."

Okay, even to her ears, she sounded like a liar.

The man, who was clearly the leader, slowly pulled out his pistol. He pointed it across the space between them and unclicked the safety. "You have five seconds to tell me if we have just set off a tracker."

Four.

Three.

Two.

"Two seconds," he said as she gulped.

Piper's eyes darted around the room. It was her only hope of being saved. Yet...

"Yes."

He clicked the safety and put his gun back in his waistband. "Tape up her big mouth and throw her in the truck. We're moving."

Damn it.

As someone lifted her to her feet, she spotted a name on a notepad and memorized it. It may or may not mean something. Hopefully she lived to investigate it, or at least tell someone who may be able to do something about it.

It would keep her mind off the gaping hole in her chest, knowing she would never see Oliver again.

God, had she been falling in love with him?

The sound of tape ripping filled the air, and then it was slapped over her mouth. Her heart pounded. She wasn't a great nose breather, but these men didn't care.

She had no idea why they were keeping her alive.

"When is pickup?" someone asked.

"Ten o'clock."

Pickup? Of what?

"Thank God. If that laptop of hers brings this operation down, I'll slit her throat myself."

Someone was picking her up?

Piper began to kick and wriggle against the man holding her, even though she knew it was useless.

If only she had listened to Oliver.

Tears prickled at her eyes.

She was going to die.

She knew it.

CHAPTER THIRTY-SEVEN

"We've got a ping." Frankie, one of the tech guys, called out.

"Yes!" Darren cried out, then began tapping away. "Nice work, Frankie."

"Dude. You rock." Dave, the other member of Darren's team, said.

Ari nodded and stretched his legs. "Good job." They'd been working long hours, and they deserved the recognition. Now it was go-time.

Oliver, we have a location.

Be right there.

Ari would be lying if he said he wasn't concerned about his new head assassin. Not because he didn't think Oliver was capable, but the self-doubt he'd seen since Oliver took the job was a surprise.

He knew Oliver's history and understood the pain of being rejected by his family. Hell, in some ways he was still dealing with his own. Vincent had accepted him in part, but he saw the doubt in the king's eyes.

More so now that Ari had mated.

Soon, they'd have to talk. For now, they were just dancing around the damn subject. Both of them had had other priorities: the birth of Lucas Moretti, Vincent's son. And Ari meeting and mating Sage.

They would all be together later in the year for their nuptials, so perhaps there would be an opportunity then.

Vampires didn't marry like humans, but when he turned Sage without permission—something that occurred often enough—it had been his promise to her to provide her with a wedding.

He had once been human—heck, he was the original Moretti vampire, along with his now deceased brother, Gio—so he was happy to take part in the Christian-based ceremony. Especially as he had some knowledge of God's existence that no other living being had—as far as he knew.

What their vows would be, they'd decide together.

He just hoped he could bring her sister home in one piece.

To do that, he needed Oliver's head in the game. The male was motivated, there was no doubt, and he wouldn't deny Oliver the chance to get his girl—if anyone had tried to hold him back from Sage, he'd have destroyed them limb by limb.

Ari needed Oliver to step up and be the leader Ari knew he could be.

If Piper *was* his mate, they'd deal with it. He needed Oliver to show him he could be both head assassin and a mate.

If not…

He'd give him a chance, but the shit they dealt with every day was life and death stuff. Oliver knew that. And now they were partnering with the Moretti royal family, keeping the race protected. There was no room for half performers by those lacking in confidence.

He'd trained Oli better than that.

He just needed Oli himself to believe he was worthy.

Oliver teleported into the operations office, dressed head to toe in black and his body layered with weapons. He was ready to go.

Well, that was a good start.

"Where is she?" Oliver growled.

"Location in your device in three, two and one," Darren said.

Oliver looked at Ari for instruction as he pulled on his jacket and zipped it up. Elijah and Logan stepped into the room.

"Let's go," Ari said, and the four of them marched out the door and through the mansion to the front entrance.

Then they teleported out.

CHAPTER THIRTY-EIGHT

It had taken three jumps to reach the kidnappers' location. Finally, they were standing outside the building identified by Darren's team.

Oliver was ready to launch in there, but he closed his eyes and let his training kick in. Ari was with them, and he was in charge. Which was probably a good thing. And possibly on purpose.

Was it because he had lost faith in Oliver, or because Piper was his sister-in-law?

Right now, he didn't care. He just wanted Piper home safely. For some reason, when he envisaged her safe at home, it was in his room. In his bed.

In his arms.

Our connection has just died. Darren used the telepathic link.

Shit.

"Okay, we need to move," Ari said, keeping his voice low.

"Is it that building or this one?" Logan asked, his eyes darting around. Oliver stared at the original address and all of them realized the labeling on the buildings was all fucked up.

"It's confusing on purpose," Ari said. "Let's split up."

Oliver nodded.

"Logan, you're with me. Eli, go with Ari," Oliver ordered and his eyes darted to Ari, realizing he'd taken over leadership of the team while his boss was there.

Ari smirked.

Oh.

"We go lethal on this one," Ari said, glancing at them all. "These fuckers are dangerous. Remember, they have that serum so be on alert. I want Piper out in one piece."

"Got it," they all said.

Oliver nearly grinned.

Ari had just given them permission to kill.

They were assassins so they were trained killers and paid to do so. They killed bad guys—mostly humans—but it didn't mean they did so on the regular. But when they were dealing with people who were hired to kidnap and kill?

Nope, that shit wasn't okay.

Especially not women or children.

Tonight, the message was clear. Kill the assholes. Oliver was very on board with that.

He gave Ari another nod and pointed to the rear of the nearest building. Ari returned a sharp nod.

Check in every two minutes, Ari told them.

Logan followed his six as they made their way, in the shadows, around the apartment building. The complex also housed some businesses.

Stairwell on our right, Logan communicated as they passed a door.

He didn't bother turning, simply nodded. This was standard procedure, not a lunch time chat.

Out back there were parked vehicles of all different makes and models, and a roller door which led into a warehouse or garage.

Logan found a side door and tested it. It opened, so he glanced at Oliver who nodded. He watched the vampire slip inside, knife in hand down by his side.

We're out back. Logan has gone inside the garage. Oliver updated the others as he held the door ajar with his foot and looked around, his eyes taking in every detail as if it was just another day at the office.

This shit was what he did, and he did it well.

We're heading up the stairwell of building one, Elijah shared.

Suddenly, he heard voices in the garage.

I've got two males. Human, Logan said. *Hold.*

Hold meant to stay in location until advised because of potential danger to the target they were extracting.

Fuck.

Oliver's heart pounded, knowing Piper could be in there. Dead. Or suffering. Or about to lose her life. His fingers squeezed the door, and he felt the metal frame bend.

Waiting, fucking waiting.

Fuck this.

Oliver stepped inside the door and let it close softly.

Tick.

Hold. Logan repeated in a growl.

Fuck off. Is she there?

He couldn't see anything because of a goddamn wall in the way. Fucking wall. Who the fuck put a wall there?

The silence was deafening, but he'd worked with Logan for decades and knew he was one of the best assassins they had.

He pulled his cap down, if only to do something with his hands.

A car door opened.

Move now, Logan said, and Oliver silently made his way around that fucking wall and joined Logan, who was crouched under a stairwell.

Update, Ari ordered.

Oliver stared at the events unfolding in front of him. While his heart thundered in his chest, hope flared. One of the men was carrying a body wrapped in a blanket which was flailing around like a freshly caught fish. There was a mumbling noise, which he knew to be someone with their mouth taped.

They'd all heard it enough times.

But it wasn't the body or the sound that confirmed to him it was Piper. It was the scent of spring blossoms mixed with fear that reached his nose.

We've got her in sight, Oliver replied and nodded at Logan.

Elijah hold, Ari said, and Oliver figured they were close to entering the offices.

"In three." He mouthed silently to Logan.

Roger.

Oliver stood and felt Logan do the same beside him. They simultaneously teleported to the vehicle, and he grinned evilly as the humans turned in surprise. One of them nearly dropped Piper, but then gathered her hard against him.

"Hello, boys," Oliver said. "Y'all have something that's mine."

Before they could react, both he and Logan whipped into action and went straight for their necks.

Snap.

Snap.

Logan dragged the bodies around the vehicle as Oliver crouched beside Piper. She'd been dropped to the ground in the action but there was nothing he could do about that. She was moaning and wriggling.

"Stand guard and get Darren on the cameras down here," he told Logan who would know he meant to get them wiped, and fast.

"Got it."

I have Piper. Proceed. He told Ari as he peeled the blanket off her head. Not only was her mouth taped shut, but her eyes were wrapped with a scarf of some kind.

Oliver pulled her against him, and she continued to fight him.

"Shhh," he said, but she was obviously in such a terrified state she didn't recognize his voice. The scarf came off, and she blinked. Then he removed the tape. Fast.

It was the kindest way.

She let out a loud scream, but he silenced it with his hands.

"Sorry," he smiled, his eyes thick with emotion.

Her eyes blinked in fear and then shock and then filled with tears. Slowly, he removed his hand, and she gasped for air.

"It's me, Piper. It's Oliver." His voice croaked with emotion. "Baby, you're safe."

Fuck, he wanted to pull her against his chest and scream but until he knew if she was hurt, he had to be careful.

She was human.

I'm taking Piper home. Go back up the others, he told Logan, but made sure Elijah and Ari could hear.

We have a vehicle down here to load bodies. Logan dragged the two men into the trunk.

"Oli? You're alive?" Piper asked.

"Yes, of course..." He frowned, confused.

Oh shit.

The last thing she saw was him and Kurt collapsing. It was no wonder she thought he was dead.

"And so are you darlin'."

He lifted her into his arms and stood. Now he had a decision to make. He could teleport home with her and eliminate any further risk to her safety. But, hey, by the way, I'm a vampire who can move you through time and space.

Or he could find a car.

"I'm so sorry." She began sobbing and sunk her face into his chest. He cooed at her to stay quiet and tucked her tightly against his chest.

Fuck.

Think, Oli, think.

What if Ari couldn't wipe her memories?

"Oliver," she coughed, and he looked down at her. "I... I just want you to know... I love you." His heart roared open. "You don't have to say it back, but when I thought you were dead, I knew how I felt. I just knew."

He growled.

"No one is coming near you, darlin'. Not ever fucking again. I'm not letting you go."

"I just needed you to know," cough, "how I feel."

Fuck.

Decision made. He was teleporting. Then he'd tell her how he felt about her. His lips lowered to hers gently, and a tear slid down her face. "Let's talk when we get home."

"Okay."

"Close your eyes. We're taking a different form of transportation than you're used to." He placed a hand over her eyes. Whether it was fact, they were told it helped with the nausea for a first-time human teleporter. Tonight they were doing three jumps because of the distance.

He landed on a street corner and heard her gasp.

Next, he landed on a rooftop.

Piper's nails dug into him as she screamed.

"What the fuck is happening?" she yelled, her voice croaky.

The last destination was his room.

Thank fuck. She was safe. He placed her on the sofa and steadied her.

"You're safe, darlin'." Oliver gave her a reassuring smile and ran his hand over her forehead. "Take a breath and then I can answer your questions."

She let out an ear-piercing scream and scurried away from him to the other end of the sofa.

Oliver stood and rubbed the back of his neck.

Shit.

Sage, you better get in here!

CHAPTER THIRTY-NINE

Kurt waited at the bar for the sexy female to finish. Oliver had updated him that Piper was safely back at the mansion, so he'd called Craig with an update.

It was clear the girl was Oliver's mate. He'd seen enough of it recently to know the signs. Sure, he hadn't gone completely insane like some of the alpha vamps, but Kurt suspected it was because Oli was holding himself back.

There was something going on. He had a feeling it was to do with Sage and Ari—which made sense given the family connection—but he wasn't sure.

Right now, he was enjoying a little reprieve from all the vampire drama, watching the tight little ass of this petite blond behind the bar. It hadn't taken him long to spot she was a vampire. Then she'd recognized him. Kurt hated that side of being an SLC. They called themselves superfans, and there was a whole group on *VampNet*.

Brayden was ranked at number one. Because he was the fucking prince. Obviously. Craig was next, which he claimed was a technical error. Then Kurt.

Whatever.

He just wanted to catch the bad guys and protect the royal family. Okay, fine. He hadn't been unhappy when the cheeky little blond had recognized him and flashed her long lashes at him.

They'd flirted back and forth through the evening and then she'd disappeared. When he asked the manager, the guy said she was finishing her shift and usually left through the side door.

Kurt had nodded and finished his beer. The last thing he wanted to do was corner her or freak her out by going outside. He'd wait to see if she came to him.

And she did.

She had changed out of the short black skirt into a sexy-as-fuck pair of tight blue jeans and a black puffer jacket.

"You're still here," she said, tugging her handbag up on her shoulder and tilting her head.

Kurt liked her confident flirty nature, but he could tell she wasn't the wild type. Right now, she wasn't giving off the vibe that she was easy prey and for some reason, he was okay with that.

He kind of just wanted to talk to her more.

"You never told me your name." He stood. He grinned as her neck arched to take in his six-foot-three height. He had at least eight inches on her. "I couldn't leave without knowing it. Or getting your number."

If his height didn't intimidate her, the width of him would. And yes, he did mean *that* width.

"Madison," she replied, tucking her hair behind her ear and he could see she was a little nervous. He didn't want to scare her off, so he moved a step away and indicated to the door.

"Can I walk you home, Madison?"

She glanced at the door and then back at him. "My car is out back."

"Then I'll escort you to your car, milady." He waved his arm out royally.

She blushed.

"Yeah, that would be nice."

They walked through the bar and out the front door into the cool night air. Madison tugged her jacket around her, and Kurt had a sudden urge to give her his, which made zero sense. He definitely wasn't the knight in shining armor kind of vampire.

"Are you on holiday? Do you even have holidays?" She glanced up at him.

He smirked and shook his head. "No. Well, not officially. I guess if I wanted one, I could."

She stopped at her car. He leaned a hand against the metal as she backed against it and waited for him to kiss her. Kurt stared at her lips and when she swept her tongue across it, his cock hardened.

"You shouldn't do that," he said, his eyes darting back to hers. "Not unless you want me to act."

"Do I look like I don't want you to?" she asked, tilting her head.

He kicked her legs apart, gripping her hips so she didn't slip while his thigh slipped in between, and he tugged her up against him. "No, you don't."

Madison gasped as they stood, sharing oxygen. "Then kiss me, dammit."

"How old are you?"

"Fifty-five." She blushed. "Now kiss me."

A baby vampire.

He ran his thumb over her lips and felt her body tremble. Kurt wanted to devour this female. Take her back to his house and spend hours showing her the pleasure only an experienced powerful vampire could give her.

But something wasn't right.

Her scent.

It was wrong.

He'd been trying to ignore it because his cock, his body, wanted to feel her.

"Madison," he said thickly. "I need you to start talking. And fast. What are you?"

She gasped. "What? I'm a vampire."

Her head retracted and her jacket moved. That's when he saw it.

A mark. A bite mark.

A vampire bite.

"Are you mated?" he asked, taking a step back and releasing her. She shook her head. "Then who did that?"

It wasn't just a bite mark. It was red and looked infected. Something that wasn't possible. Vampires didn't get infections.

"A guy I met in the bar."

Shit.

"When?"

"A week ago." Her hand went to her neck. It was bothering her.

"Are you unwell?"

She shook her head, then nodded. "I feel... strange."

He cursed.

Call it instinct, but Kurt knew there was something wrong here. She needed his help, and he wasn't going to let her loose in the world where a lot of strange shit was happening right now.

"Madison, I need you to come with me tonight. I will keep you safe and we'll find out what is happening to you."

He hoped.

Her eyes widened. "What? I can't."

"Consider this an order from the king." He pulled out his phone and ordered a jet.

"I can't leave Seattle," she said. "I have rent to pay and..."

His eyes met hers. "And?"

She shook her head. "I just can't."

She had no choice and knew it. He'd played the royal card and wasn't letting her walk.

"So, this guy who bit you?" Kurt asked. "Was he your boyfriend?"

"No, I don't have a boyfriend. I'm a damn vampire," she snapped.

Semantics.

"But he got close enough to bite you. Was it consensual or not?" He tried to tell himself he was asking for investigative purposes, but part of him wanted to snarl at the thought of a wild male vampire near her.

Madison shook her head. "Yes. I guess. I didn't know he was a vamp. He cornered me by the bathrooms and kissed me. It was nice. He was cute, but then he suddenly lost control and next thing I knew, he bit me."

Nice?

No one ever described his kisses as *nice*. She'd never forget him if he kissed her. It would be fucking mind-blowing, not *nice*. That was, *if* he ever got to kiss her.

Focus, Kurt.

"He just bit you. Inside the bar?"

Madison nodded.

It was rare for a vampire to have that little control. Biting happened for three reasons. To share blood if a vampire was harmed or dying. For sexual pleasure. Or when bonding with your mate. The latter secured the bond and apparently it was a much more intense experience.

"Then he just disappeared."

"Teleported?"

"I don't know. He was just gone. I was focused on the bite. It stung."

Stung? A vampire bite was mildly painful for a human initially, but stinging was never used to describe it after that. Intensely arousing. Orgasmic. Delicious. Erotic. Never a sting.

"How long was it sore for?"

Madison looked at him for a long minute. "It's still sore."

Shit.

A shiver ran through his body and it was nothing to do with the strong attraction he had for the female.

"What did the male look like?"

He knew. He fucking knew what she was going to say before she said it. And as she began to describe him, Kurt silently cursed.

Callan.

CHAPTER FORTY

Piper's body trembled as she stared at Oliver.
What the hell just happened?
What is he?
The worst thing was, she knew. He was a vampire.
Unless there were some other damn magical species on the planet she didn't yet know about.
Oliver stood staring at her with an expression she couldn't place. He looked pained. What the hell was his problem? He knew what species *she* was.
Holy shit. She had slept with him. Many times. Nausea suddenly hit her, and her hand flew to her mouth.
Oliver's eyes widened and suddenly he disappeared and reappeared—or wobbled fast—or she was losing her fucking mind. And he was holding a bucket.
Piper didn't know whether she did it or he did, but when she vomited, the bucket was under her chin.
"Piper!" Sage came flying into the room and skidded to a stop on her knees in front of her.
Sage?
Her eyes darted between the two of them as she wiped her mouth. Oliver ripped off his t-shirt and handed it to her.
Don't look at his chest.

She wiped her mouth with the shirt and stared at her sister.

"Are you okay? Did they hurt you?" Sage asked, frantic.

When she glanced at Oliver, Sage shook her head.

"The men who kidnapped you. Did they hurt you?" Sage asked.

"What are you doing here?" Piper asked, confused.

"I live here."

"With Oliver?"

Her sister lived with vampires. Oh God, were they holding her hostage? If so, Piper was determined to get them both free and expose them all.

"With Ari," Sage replied. "Look, don't worry, just know you are safe."

Oliver groaned. "I teleported with her."

Teleported?

Is that what had happened? She recalled the feeling of her body particles screaming apart and being thrown back together again. Over and over and over.

"You did what?" Sage said, whipping her head around. "Why?"

He let go of the bucket and stood. Piper moved away further from him, up the back of the couch. Sage narrowed her eyes in concern.

Yeah, Piper was concerned, too.

It appeared Sage was fully aware of their vampire powers, or whatever one called them.

"It was too dangerous to drive, and I obviously didn't have a car." He crossed his arms. "I needed to get her home safe."

Piper glanced around the room, wondering where she was.

"This is my room," Oliver said in response, as if he knew her every thought and nuance. Maybe he did after what they'd shared, but that no longer mattered.

"You need to get away from me." She pulled the disgusting blanket from her kidnappers over her. "Get him away from me, Sage."

"I just saved you." He threw out a hand. "Come on darlin', stop it. I know this is scary, but it's me. Let me explain."

Was he joking?

"You *know* this is scary? Are you kidding me right now? What the fuck are you?" she yelled.

Oliver frowned and re-crossed his arms. "You know what I am."

"Just wait a minute," Sage said, holding up a hand. "Just stop. Wait until Ari is here. This conversation doesn't need to continue."

Oliver took a step forward in front of her. "No. He's not wiping her memories. She's mine."

What the fuckety fuck? She was most definitely not his.

"Like a slave? A pet? What on earth do you people—things—do here?" Piper cried. "I am not yours!"

Sage groaned.

"A pet?" Oliver frowned and shook his head. "Jesus."

Piper glanced at Sage, who appeared embarrassed by her reaction. Was she a part of this somehow?

"Sage? What the hell is going on? Is this a kind of vampire cult?" she asked.

"Oh, my God! Now we're a cult *and* keep humans as pets. I cannot believe this." Oliver threw his arms in the air.

How dare he! *He* was the vampire.

"She's scared. She doesn't understand. When Ari told me, it took me ages to accept. And I had far more knowledge than Piper does right now."

"Wait a minute. You've known all this time? I bloody knew it. Also, I'm right here, so can you stop talking as if I'm not. *And* I knew about vampires," she cried, then pointed at Oliver. "He told me I was an idiot."

Oliver leaned forward. "*He* is right here, and *you* told me you loved me."

The room went silent as that bomb dropped.

Sage gave her a look as Piper pressed her lips together, then a lightbulb went off in her head.

"Wait. Ari is a vampire too?" she asked, and Sage nodded. "I was right all along!"

"Nice deflection, darlin'." Oliver growled and walked over to a stool to sit.

Sage began rubbing her leg. "You really are safe here. I promise."

Piper didn't believe a word of it. Her entire reality had been blasted apart. Yes, she had said she loved Oliver. She had also thought he was a damn human.

Now?

No. She couldn't love a vampire.

Suddenly, he stood and began to walk out of the room. At the door, he stopped and turned. He looked directly at her with piercing eyes.

"By the way, if we choose, we can read minds. Thanks for sharing the truth about how you feel." He spoke calmly, but she could hear the hurt in his voice as the door slammed behind him.

His pain sliced through her, and she tried to tell herself it didn't matter. But it did. She just couldn't let it. She swallowed and turned to Sage. "Can you take me home?"

Then her last thread of hope was lost as her sister shook her head. "No, Piper. I can't."

Piper stirred awake and stretched out on her bed.

Nope, not her bed.

She sat bolt upright and every muscle and bone in her body screamed.

She groaned loudly.

Blinking away the sleep, she glanced around. She was in a different room. After Sage had refused to take her home, and it had become clear she couldn't leave, she'd asked if she could have another room. After all, this place was enormous. She'd seen it from the outside.

This was Ari's mansion, and he ran a private security company within the walls. Sage also lived here because she was mated to him. A vampire.

Piper groaned.

Oliver was also a vampire, and she'd told him she loved him.

She groaned again and fell back on her pillows, pressing her face into the feather-filled linen.

Jesus.

She'd also been kidnapped by very dangerous men and was lucky to be alive. Thanks to Oliver, but she couldn't focus on that right now.

Her tracker had been set off. Was her company looking for her? Or the local authorities?

She could be all over the news.

Missing journalist.

She climbed out of bed and on her way to the bathroom, she saw her bags. Piper needed to get to a phone. Her own had been crushed by Oliver, and she wondered if he would follow through with his promise to give her a replacement.

And what the hell did he mean by *mine*?

She didn't belong to him.

Piper had listened to her sister's explanation about their way of life and trusted Sage believed what she said. It didn't mean Piper did. As a journalist, it was her nature to ask questions and while she had expected the same from Sage—after all, she was a scientist—she seemed to have just accepted the status quo.

Now Piper had slept a few hours her mind was clearing. She had more questions. Namely, how the fuck would she get out of the mansion and find the authorities? Was there a way out of this life? Or, once you knew about vampires, like the Mafia, were you in it for life?

She wasn't sticking around to find out.

First, she'd find out just how brain-washed Sage was. If there was no hope, she was going to save herself. If that meant having to play along with this charade, then she would do that.

And hope these animals kept their teeth to themselves.

She didn't want to become anyone's pet in the meantime. Least of all Oliver's.

How dare he let her fall in love with him?

CHAPTER FORTY-ONE

Oliver glanced up as he heard Ari approaching.

"You know, you could hear her just as clearly from your room down the hall," Ari said, frowning at Oliver as he sat on the floor outside Piper's room.

"She's awake," was all he said in reply.

Ari nodded.

"She's a tough cookie. Give her time," Ari replied. "They aren't so different, you know."

Oliver arched a brow.

"Sage was no mean feat to turn around when she discovered my fangs." Ari shook his head, clearly recalling the memories of the recent past with his own mate.

Oliver pressed against the wall and slid his body up so he was standing. "Sage wasn't repulsed by you."

"You read her mind?" When he nodded Ari added, "The mind lies when it is in fear, Oli. Trust me."

He shrugged, not wanting to listen to reason. The rejection had hurt, and he wasn't vamp enough to admit it.

Ari patted him on the shoulder and indicated he follow. They walked through the halls and out the front door, following the path through the sizeable grounds. Above them, the stars were still twinkling but the sun would soon be rising.

"I'm in a predicament."

Oliver's stomach twisted. He'd been expecting this conversation at some point after the director had returned from the kidnapping site. He knew they couldn't keep Piper. Holding her against her will was illegal, and, well, it was technically kidnapping.

"I know."

"I can give you twenty-four hours. Max. You either claim Piper and begin the change, or if she still wants to leave, I will wipe her memories and return her to her human life."

"It's not safe. Whoever is after her will not stop until she is eliminated. I assume it is BioZen."

Ari nodded. "We'll put a team on her for protection. I've spoken to Brayden, and we're going to continue to act aggressively on this now. When you're ready, I'll update you."

Oliver frowned. "Update me now. I'm not exactly rushed off my feet."

Ari shook his head. "You need to focus on your mate. Forget work. Trust me when I say this is too important. We've got this."

Oliver looked away.

He knew what was happening. His job was being reassigned to someone else.

He nodded. "Sure."

Ari stared at him but left it at that.

"Tell her Darren intercepted the alert to the authorities so there's no manhunt out there. And Sage phoned her boss and said she returned to Seattle with a bug, and it had been her that set off the alert trying to get into her email to message him," Ari said.

"What are you talking about?"

"Her laptop set off a signal that alerted more than us. Looks like it's a safeguard on all *Seattle Times* laptops. Journalism is a dangerous business these days."

That was the truth.

Piper had proven that fact true twice over the past twenty-four hours. Yet he didn't think it was enough to stop her. He had a choice to make. He could forcibly change her into a vampire and know she was safe, but despite what Ari said, hearing Piper's thoughts of disgust about him was enough to let her go. No vampire wanted to hear his mate think of him like that. It had cut deep.

Still, some of the things she'd said had been ludicrous.

"Piper really wanted to break the story about vampires. Guess she learned more than she wanted," he said. "She thinks I want her as a fucking pet."

Ari smirked. "I heard."

Oliver let himself smile, then let out a long sigh. They stood staring toward the thick tree line knowing what would happen if she rejected him. Neither of them would find true love again. Piper would never understand why she had a hole the size of Texas in her heart.

Oliver, on the other hand, would have every single memory. Worse, it would drive him to madness and into the sun. That they hadn't yet bonded meant he had some time.

He stiffened. "My eyes?"

"No," Ari said, confirming his eyes had not yet shown signs of the dark ring around the outside which all bonded vampires had.

Thank fuck.

He had twenty-four hours to convince her he wasn't a monster, and she wasn't going to be renamed Lassie.

Or Fluffy.

"Any great advice?"

Ari shook his head. "Patience. Honesty. Mostly patience."

Oliver bunched his lips together and half laughed.

"And strength. She will test you over the next few hours. You must remain solid and strong in your feelings for her."

He let out a long sigh.

"And Oli, she may *not* be your mate," he said. "I have seen a few false starts in my long life. Be prepared for that."

"How will I know?"

"You'll know," Ari said. "There's a moment when nothing matters, nothing in this long fucking void of life matters as much as your mate. That's when you'll know."

A chill ran through his body, and he shivered.

"What if the memory wipe doesn't work?" he asked. "I've tried multiple times and for some reason, she's resistant to it."

Ari whacked him on the shoulder and laughed. "No, son, you were the one interfering. I was in there before she went to sleep. Trust me. She'll have no recollection of it."

Fuck.

And had Ari just called him son? For some reason, that meant the world to him.

Oliver blinked about seven hundred times.

"Go to her."

"Yup." He drew in a long breath, and ran a hand through his hair. He met the director's eyes. "Thank you."

At his nod, he teleported back outside Piper's room.

Then knocked.

Twenty-fucking-four hours.

Shit.

CHAPTER FORTY-TWO

Piper stepped out of the shower and squeezed toothpaste on her brush. Whoever had saved her luggage, she'd kiss them.
Unless they were a vampire. Then, no.
Spit.
Never.
Rinse.
Not fucking ever.
Spit.
She rummaged through the bags and pulled on a pair of jeans, a tank top and an oversized sweatshirt. She felt cold even though she knew the air temperature was mild.
For the first time in ages, she wanted to call her mom. Not because she had to, or any other kind of obligation. She just wanted to hear her mom's voice.
She had no idea of the time; all she knew was that it was still dark outside. Just. The sun was going to rise soon, and then she would find a way out. She walked to the glass doors which led out onto a balcony, and they opened.
Well, that gave her hope.
Clearly, security wasn't much of a concern here. Likely because of those big-ass gates she knew were down the

bottom of the drive. She'd climb the fence if she had to. She was getting out of here.

Would they come after her?

Probably.

But hopefully she'd make it to the authorities before that.

Or scream really loudly and hope someone heard her.

Could they even go out during the day? Sage hadn't told her everything earlier in the night, but when she thought about it, she'd never seen Oliver outside during the day.

So perhaps she could leave during the day and then they couldn't come after her. First, though, she had to speak to Sage again.

She closed the doors and began to make her way across the room when someone knocked.

She froze.

"I don't want to speak to you," she said quietly. Somehow, she knew who it was.

The door opened, and he stepped inside.

Click.

Now she was alone with the one person—vampire—she didn't want to see.

"Hi," he said quietly.

Piper wrapped her arms around herself and began to tremble. Oliver watched her as if she was an animal about to bolt, and maybe she was. "Please go."

He shook his head.

She watched him closely and spotted determination and pity in his eyes. She hated all of it.

"I don't love you," she said, and he winced.

"Okay."

Okay? Was that all he had to say?

Didn't he care at all?

Piper didn't know why she'd spat that out. She hadn't specifically wanted to hurt him. She just didn't want to encourage him. If he was here because she'd said that, then he could just leave.

"You can't keep me here."

Oliver nodded. "You're right."

"So, I can leave?"

"Tomorrow."

"Why tomorrow? What are you planning to do to me?" Fear raced through her veins, but he held his hands up.

"Nothing Piper, fuck. Nothing. Just talk."

She stared at him.

"Brainwashing. That's your plan," she accused. "Like you've all done to Sage. I'm not her. I won't be so easy to push around."

He let out a cynical snort. "You underestimate your sister. But then again, you always have."

What?

How dare he say such a thing? He had no idea about the relationship between her and Sage. They had a lifetime of history. He'd known them for a matter of weeks. Piper dropped her arms and placed them on her hips.

"You don't know anything about my relationship with *my* sister!"

Oliver crossed his arms. "I know Sage. Maybe better than you. You see her as weak, but trust me, darlin', she is far from that."

She narrowed her eyes at him, wondering what he meant. Was he right? She'd always had to fight for what she wanted in life, but for Sage things had always seemed to come easily. Sage had been adored by their father. She knew what it felt like to be loved but had never met the right man.

And Colin hadn't been Mr. Right.

Unfortunately, she'd never know how wrong he was now that Piper had been cast as the baddie in that storyline.

She'd never told Sage that Colin had been cheating on her. As far as Sage knew, the only time he'd done it was with her. And to protect her, Piper let her think that.

Perhaps Piper had been wrong and should have told her. Perhaps then Sage would have learned you can't trust men.

Had she blindly walked into Ari's arms?

Was this place a cult?

Maybe it wasn't. For all she knew, it was some human trafficking syndicate where they attracted single vulnerable women.

She glanced at Oliver. "Are you reading my mind again?"

She felt a blush of embarrassment cross her cheeks at her thoughts. Something about accusing him of sex trafficking felt very wrong.

"No, ma'am."

Piper crossed her arms but less defensively this time. "So then, put me out of my misery. What do you want from me until tomorrow? And be honest this time."

Oliver took a few steps toward her, and she had to force herself not to run. There was something predatory about the way he moved.

"I honestly just want to talk. To show you my life. You can ask any questions you want." He stopped a few feet from her and she stared at him, her eyes running over his solid muscular body. He was so perfect. Every part of her wanted to melt and run into his arms, even though fear was still simmering underneath the surface.

How could she make sense of the fear when those arms had held her? Those hands had pleasured her. His mouth had tasted her—all of her. Those eyes had seen every inch of her.

His... he'd been inside her.

She'd slept in his arms, against that broad solid chest. She had trusted him and felt things she shouldn't for a being that wasn't human.

But she had questions. Questions Sage refused to answer. If she was going to escape, then why not go armed with as much knowledge as she could?

Piper went to move, but her hip, which was in a lot of pain after being tossed around like a bag of peas, gave way. Before she could reach out to steady herself, Oliver had her in his arms.

"What is it?" Concern laced his voice.

She gulped.

Fear mixed with desire flowed through her body. "I hurt my hip," she said, her voice shaking.

She needed him to step away.

She needed him to hold her.

Oliver's eyes met hers. "You're still terrified of me?"

"Yes, I'm scared. You're a vampire." As the words fell out, a tear followed, and angrily she brushed it away.

He stepped back and held up his hands. But not before she saw the hurt in his eyes.

She hated all of this. For both of them.

She tested her leg and then walked over to an armchair.

"Fine. Let's talk then."

Oliver sat opposite Piper on the sofa and watched her. She looked vulnerable in the oversized sweatshirt, which swamped her figure.

Her face was free of make-up, and she played nervously with the rolled-up cuffs at her wrists. He didn't need to read her mind to know what her plans were. He was a trained assassin. He was trained to read people and situations in minute detail. Her eyes kept glancing out the window. Not because she was looking to run from him at the moment, but because she was planning to escape.

Just as anyone would in her situation.

He also realized Piper had agreed to chat because she was looking to get answers to her questions. For her story. Not to decide if she wanted to be his mate. Regardless, by the end, she'd learn there would be no Pulitzer Prize.

No matter which way their own story ended.

If she chose to be his mate, she would never write it.

If she chose to leave, she wouldn't remember a thing.

On that...

"You saw Ari this morning?"

Piper frowned at him. "No."

Well, fuck.

If he hadn't completely believed the director, he did now. It had been Oliver fucking up her memory wipes, after all. Which meant he was the cause of everything she'd been through.

The kidnapping.

The attempted kidnapping.

Her excessive desire for him.

Okay fine, some of it was natural chemistry, but the confusing manner in which her mind tried to process him would have created an appealing mystery.

She may not be his mate.

He'd soon find out. Only a true fated mate bond would hold them together. Especially now she knew he was a vampire.

"Why did you lie to me?" Piper asked, grabbing his attention back.

"About?" He frowned, and she waved her hand at him.

"Being a vampire?" he asked, astonished. "When exactly should I have told you? When I fell inside your bedroom that morning? Or while I was fucking you after you said you were investigating the existence of vampires so you could expose my race to the entire human population?"

Well, he'd failed the patience test.

Piper wrapped her arms around her middle. "There's no need to discuss the physical things we did, thank you very much."

The hell? He wasn't going to let her forget what they'd shared together.

"Why? They happened, darlin'. Don't you dare ignore what we've shared. I'm the same person. And you fucking loved it."

She stood. "You are not a *person*. You're a vampire."

Then she abruptly sat, and he knew it was because she was scared.

Oliver let out a low growl.

He'd done nothing but protect her since the day they'd met. He'd risked every fucking thing and now she could be the one living being on this planet who saw him stepping out into the sun.

And she was disgusted by him.

"Stop fucking doing that. I am never *ever* going to hurt you," he snapped, and she flinched. "Stop it, Piper. You know I won't hurt you."

He sat forward and pushed his hand through his hair. As he sat staring at the carpet, she was silent.

"Is this like the breakup conversation, then?" she asked quietly. "Like you want to talk this through to relieve your guilt and convince me not to tell anyone about your race?"

He sat back and let out a long sigh.

"Breakup? Ask me how many women I've had sex with more than twice."

Her lips parted.

"Ask me."

Those same lips pressed firmly together, and she shook her head.

"Zero," he said. "That's how many. Zero. And I'm over eighty years old."

"That's gross."

He let out a laugh. Their eyes met and a little smile formed on her lips, then disappeared. "I need to go home, Oli. I'm scared and don't feel safe here."

Unfortunately for her, this was the safest place on earth for her right now. She just didn't understand yet. But it was his job to convince her.

"Those men are still looking for you. Something you did in LA triggered them. You can tell me, or not. That's over to you. But it could help us to keep you safe."

She chewed her lip.

"Tomorrow, if you choose to go home, you will return home with no memories of me or any of this. Whatever you tell me today will help us to help keep you safe while you carry on with your life."

She gasped.

"You can't do that," she cried. "Anyway, it didn't work all those other times."

Oliver leaned forward on his knees. "Yeah, because I was doing it. Apparently, I wanted you to remember me. But another member of my team will do it, and this time you won't recall a thing."

The only technicality being that because Piper was family and would be exposed to Ari and Sage, it could trigger the odd confusion, but they would limit exposure to reduce the risk of that.

"Why?" she asked. "Why did you want me to remember me?"

"I don't know, darlin'. I wasn't aware I was doing it. I'm sorry. But it could be why you… why you were so attracted to me."

She barked out a laugh.

"What?" he frowned, sitting up.

"You might be a monster, Oliver, but that's not why I am… was attracted to you."

Am. She said *am.*

"Can we stop with the monster talk, please?"

Piper shrugged.

"You think I'm hot?"

"You *are* hot, Oli. Stop it. That's irrelevant now. You monster. Me human." She did the pointing thing.

He sighed.

One step forward. One step back.

Perhaps talking wasn't the best thing to be doing. He had to just show her he was normal and not going to hurt her.

"Hungry?" he asked, and she shrugged. Which was a stubborn yes.

"Not for blood or little puppy dogs."

He stood and gave her a berating look.

She shrugged.

He glanced outside and saw the shutters were going to close soon. It would frighten her. First, he ordered them some food by telepathing the chef in the kitchen.

"Breakfast will be here in twenty minutes." When she raised an eyebrow, he explained. "We have telepathic abilities."

Her mouth widened once more. Today there would be a lot of that.

"Before I forget and you scream again, the shutters in the castle are about to close. One thing your vampire movies got right is daylight. We cannot go outside."

Piper launched to her feet. "I'll be locked in?"

She was anyway.

"Yes," he said, though technically the doors were able to be unlocked. He wasn't going to tell her that. "I know you don't trust me, but please remember you did once."

Her eyes shot from the windows to him. "Before I knew who you really were. *And* you owe me a phone."

His hand went to his back pocket, and he pulled out a brand-new iPhone. He closed the gap between them and handed it to her, smiling at the surprise on her face. "All yours."

"What's the catch?"

"It will start working when I give the go ahead tomorrow."

She glanced up at him. "Thank you."

Seeing the warmth in her gaze once more spread happiness through him. He knew there was a long way to go in just twenty-three and a half hours, but he wasn't giving up.

"Can I see Sage?"

"Not right now." He answered truthfully. It was likely she was back, but Sage had been out breaking into a lab with Alex, who had returned from LA.

Oliver stared at the female who was his potential mate. She'd likely cost him his job. If he told her, she wouldn't care. He was about to cost her the story of her life.

And he wasn't sorry.

It was unlikely she would've lived to tell the story in any case.

Telling the story would impact millions of lives. The truth was, he didn't know Piper well enough to know how that would sit with her, ethically. Journalists were dogmatic in their need to tell the truth, and the world was a better place for it.

Most of the time.

Not in this instance.

Vampires were no threat to humans.

Humans, ironically, were a major threat to humans.

"Will you sit with me?" He indicated the sofa.

"Oli, I don't know what you want from me." She shook her head. "We can talk, but what we shared in LA, that's… it was a lie."

He turned away from her and walked a few paces.

The fuck it was.

"You said you were attracted to me."

"Yes."

"You said you loved me."

Silence.

He turned. "I said you told me you loved me."

She swallowed.

"You never said it back," Piper said quietly.

Oliver sped back to her and stopped just shy of touching her. He saw the confusion in her eyes. For a long moment, they gazed at one another, and he was too scared to speak.

She blinked and glanced away.

"You didn't mean to say that, did you?" he asked.

She shook her head and his hand lifted to touch her, then dropped. She followed the movement with her eyes, then lifted her gaze back to his.

"Let me touch you, please."

When she didn't say no, he carefully lifted his hand and laid it on her arm. She breathed more heavily, but he waited. When she didn't move away, he ran his hand up her arm to her shoulder and pushed away locks of her hair.

Time was one of the few things he couldn't manipulate. It could take her weeks to be okay with him being a vampire. Months even.

"Oli," she said, pressing her eyes closed.

"When I thought you were dead, I knew." Oliver spoke softly, his hand moving to cup her face. "The minute you looked at me when I fell to my knees, I knew I would do anything for you. Give anything to keep you safe and in my arms."

Her glossy eyes opened.

"But I was wrong."

She blinked and frowned. "You don't have to love me, Oli. It's fine."

"I was wrong because to keep you in my arms would mean taking away your free will," he said. "Many vampires, when they meet their mate, will take their life without question, and ask for forgiveness afterwards. It is always given."

He let that sink in.

"I know you, Piper Roberts. You would never forgive me."

She stepped away and gasped. "Turning me into a vampire?"

He nodded.

"Wait a minute. You think I'm your mate?"

He nodded again.

"No, no, no, no, no. This is even worse than the Mafia," she mumbled.

Oliver frowned. "The Mafia?"

"Oh, God. So much worse." She stood, shaking her head. "Promise you won't turn me," she demanded.

"I promise," he replied firmly.

He meant it. He knew on every level of his being that Piper would never, ever, forgive him for taking her humanity. It would need to be her choice or nothing.

It was who she was, and he wasn't going to force her into a life where she looked at him every day with the disgust she had shown over the past few hours.

Tick tock, tick tock.

The clock was ticking.

CHAPTER FORTY-THREE

When breakfast arrived, Piper felt too sick to eat, even though she knew she needed food to keep up her strength, so she spooned small bites of the scrambled egg into her mouth. Not that she could outrun or outmaneuver a vampire. Sage had rattled off a bunch of facts and figures, and basically, yeah, vampires were tons stronger and faster.

Not that it wasn't plainly obvious by the layers of sculptured muscle on the body sitting opposite her.

Oliver had been right. The shutters had whirred closed while the kitchen staff had delivered the meal and she'd given a little squeal. It was more psychological, knowing she was trapped, but when Oliver placed a comforting hand on the small of her back, it calmed her.

Though she wished his touch wasn't one of a soothing nature.

Mate.

Oliver thought she was his mate.

That just seemed insane. Sure, she'd fallen in love with him, but to learn she was the soul mate to a member of another species? Insane.

And yet, despite her fear, her defenses were weakening the more time she spent with Oliver. The shock of learning he was a vampire was beginning to subside, and that was partly due to the way he was chipping away at her walls with his reminders of their time together. Short as it had been. However, she had to admit the entire time he had been protecting her and had saved her life.

Twice.

When she saw the vampire on Eric's computer screen, it was vastly different from standing in a room with one or two of them. Sure, they were unearthly gorgeous, and the journalist in her was intrigued but it was only natural to want to run for your life, despite any trust that had been built.

Piper still didn't understand how Sage was so okay with all of this. She knew from reading her sister's diary that she'd met Ari randomly in a bar and not that long ago. She had to assume her sister truly loved Ari Moretti and perhaps vampires had normal relationships with humans.

Perhaps it wasn't all that different?

She'd obviously had sex with Oliver and there hadn't been anything weird. No extra body parts or sounds. But she hadn't seen his fangs, so that wasn't entirely true.

She stared at his mouth as he ate, then wiped a napkin over it.

No fangs.

Stop thinking about fangs.

"No coffee?" she asked when he finished his glass of water.

"No, ma'am." He let out a timely yawn. "I should sleep, but today I'm spending it with you."

"A vampire with a southern drawl. Shouldn't you be from, I don't know, Transylvania or something?"

Oliver let out a snort.

"Try Italy, but I was raised in the south here in the United States. But sure, if you want to believe we're hatched and keep humans for pets, then be my guest."

"Fine. I'm sorry." She dropped her coffee cup into the saucer. "I get snarky when I'm scared."

"No kidding." He arched a brow.

She let out her own yawn and smothered it with her hand. Despite the small amount she'd eaten it was enough to lull her into relaxing and her eyes wanted to close.

"You are tired. Given everything you've been through it's no wonder," Oliver said, standing. "Why don't we turn on Netflix and relax?"

Piper pushed away her half-eaten breakfast. "You want me to snuggle up with a vampire?"

"I want you to watch a movie with the same person you did yesterday on the jet."

He didn't wait for her to respond. He turned on the TV which was mounted on the wall and chose, yup, *Vampire Diaries*.

"Ha, ha." She shook her head and stood, then pushed her chair in.

"Would you rather a serial killer documentary right now?" he asked with complete sincerity.

"Well played, Oliver, well played." Piper laughed, feeling more relaxed. It nearly felt like he was… human again.

But he wasn't. He never would be.

He smirked.

"Come on," he said, and held out his hand.

"And let me guess… *You won't bite*?" she asked, as she moved closer to the sofa where he had flopped down.

"Well, now, I never said that darlin'." He grinned, patting the cushions. "You can sit on that side, and I'll stay over here."

She chewed her lip.

"What if Sage comes over—" Oliver shook his head, confirming she wouldn't. "And you won't—"

"I won't touch you. You can make all the moves, or none. The choice is completely yours."

A tug of desire flashed through her, surprising her. Did she *want* him to touch her? As her fear faded, the strength of the chemistry that was always constant was growing. That, and she was beginning to understand that love didn't disappear even when you found out the person wasn't human.

Go figure.

Piper sat and tucked her feet under her, then positioned two or three cushions around her.

The show started and the light in the room dimmed. Before long, her eyes closed, but she kept forcing them open. At one point she heard Oliver's heavy breathing. She felt her cushions slip and wriggled to get comfortable. A familiar arm fell around her and she snuggled into the warmth of his body, mildly aware of what was happening but not wanting to change it.

Denial was a comfortable space. Just for a little while.

Then she fell into a deep peaceful sleep.

When Piper opened her eyes, she was lying alongside Oliver on the sofa, and he was gazing down at her. She went to bolt off, but he held her with the arm wrapped around her hips.

"Let me go," she said quietly.

"No."

The calm stern manner of his answer surprised her. She knew without doubt there would be no budging him. It was as if he was saying, *you're mine and I'm not letting you go.*

"Oli."

Even as she protested her inner being knew she was in no harm.

"You're so beautiful when you sleep," he said thickly.

"Just not when I'm awake?"

"Take the compliment, Piper." He gave her a little frown.

"Can I assume my neck is bite free?" she asked.

"Why do humans always think it's the neck?" Oliver asked, shrugging. "I gotta tell you there are many other more delectable spots on the body."

"I'm sorry, did I offend your vampire-ness?"

A smile grew on his lips, and she forced herself not to grin back. The truth was, she was enjoying this banter and it was helping her feel more comfortable. Which was obviously his plan. Part of her felt he was just the same old gorgeous Oliver.

Yet, he *was* a vampire, and she couldn't forget that.

"What time is it?" she asked, craning her neck to see the shutters were still closed.

His smile faded. "Three in the afternoon."

"So, what do vampires do with their lives normally? You wanted me to know you, so perhaps you should show me."

Oliver stared at her for a long moment and then nodded. He wrapped his arms around her and lifted her off the sofa. His strength was more obvious now he wasn't hiding anything.

And God damn, it was sexy as hell.

"Go brush your teeth and I'll return." He patted her bottom.

"What are you trying to say? I have bad breath?"

"Two minutes," he called out as the door to her room shut behind him.

How rude.

Piper was only half honest when she'd asked him to show her his life. She'd just tricked him into a tour around the mansion.

Now she was one step closer to escaping.

CHAPTER FORTY-FOUR

"We lost the girl," Nikolay Mikhailov said, his voice dark and angry. "And I lost four good men."

Xander would be lying if he didn't admit the guy scared the living daylights out of him. Partnering with the Russian mob could be the worst or best decision he'd ever made.

Or both.

"I'm not surprised. They're very protective of their women."

The man let out a rough snort and made a dismissive *pfft* sound. "Why? They're often more trouble than they're worth. After they've spread their legs."

Xander let out a laugh and nodded. "Couldn't agree more."

He was really beginning to wonder if he should move Elizabeth, his sexy finance manager, to the United States. He'd had to have sex with his wife this week because he was getting sick of his own hand. He'd considered having women come to him at the house and had dismissed it, but after the vanilla missionary-style fuck with Suzanne, and no end in sight to his returning to Seattle or Italy, it was looking more and more like he'd have to.

He lifted his glass of whiskey to his lips and watched the mob boss light a cigar. He puffed out a mouthful of smoke and settled back in his chair.

"I want you to create a vampire vaccine," Nikolay said. "One every human will need to take if they want to be protected."

Xander narrowed his eyes in confusion.

"That's not how this works. They're a different species, not a virus."

"I don't give a fuck. You will tell them it is. Scare them enough and they'll be lining up on the sidewalks ready to be jabbed."

He wasn't wrong.

In fact, it was fucking genius.

"Twice," the Russian added. "Hell, make it an annual booster."

The two of them laughed as Xander's mind began calculating the enormous profit this could mean.

God, he could retire in five years.

Buy his own island.

Divorce his wife and have a lover for every week of the year.

Yeah, this had merit.

"I'll have to speak to the directors of the business. Our project isn't known to all of them, and this will take considerable resources." He scribbled notes down on a pad of paper as the ideas began to flow.

Why hadn't he thought of this?

"I don't give a fuck about your internal politics, Tomassi. Get this done and report back to me next week."

He choked.

"Ah, this isn't going to happen in a week, Mikhailov."

"Why not?" the man growled, blowing out more smoke as he loosened his necktie revealing a dark-looking tattoo.

"Because we have to develop it, then get it tested, and *then* FDA approved."

"No. You don't," he replied. "Whatever hoops you need to jump through; whatever walls you need breaking down, let me know. I accept it won't be a week, but you have months, not years."

Jesus.

He wasn't sure how he was going to do this, but one thing was for sure, now he had to bring a lot more BioZen people into his inner circle.

He'd speak to Cash Waltmore, Director of BioZen, and together they'd have to decide their future, because he knew there were owners and people on the board that wouldn't be okay with this.

"Let me be clear," Mikhailov said. "Anyone in the way can be… removed. You understand what I am saying?"

Xander did.

And it might just come down to that.

"*Si, capisco,*" he said, reverting to his native Italian tongue, to confirm he understood. "I'll need something in return."

The man was silent.

"I need a higher level of protection so I can move about and get out of this damn hell hole," Xander said. "Provide me with some of your men and I can get the ball rolling."

"Fine," he said. "I will have five of my best in the United States in three days."

Xander smiled.

Fuck the Moretti's.

They may be vampires, but the Russian mob were still dangerous assholes to mess with.

CHAPTER FORTY-FIVE

Oliver figured it was a good time of day to show Piper around the mansion. Most vampires, aside from the day skeleton crew, would be sleeping. They wandered from one area to the next, skipping the ops room and private quarters.

They made their way down to the training area, a space in which he spent a lot of time.

A couple of vampires were working out, and he watched Piper examine their power and physique. Just as jealousy began to raise its ugly head, she turned to him.

"Well, this explains your hot bod," Piper said, then shrugged. "Wipe that grin off your face. You know you have one."

He leaned down and whispered into her hair. "They can hear you. Keep talking."

She shook her head. "Boys! Whether you're a human or vampire, clearly, you're all the same."

He heard the vamps across the room snigger.

"Wow, those swords are amazing! Can you…" she faltered.

"Fence?"

"Is that what it's called?"

"Yes. Or dueling. Swordplay," he answered. "And yes. We're trained to use any and all weapons here."

At the start of the tour, he'd explained The Institute was a private security company but left out the bit about assassins. That was harder to explain. They were warriors at the heart of it. Not just killers.

Piper walked over to the swords, and he lifted one off the wall for her. She took it and let out a gasp at its weight.

"This is why you need to be strong." She nodded. "It looks so easy on the TV."

These weren't modern-day swords. They were the real deal and extremely heavy. She tried to lift it into the air and swing it around, but it began to dip. Oliver caught it just as it fell out of her hands, and swung it around, showing off.

And he didn't give a fuck if everyone knew it.

If there was anyone worth showing off for, it was the woman who was very likely his mate.

Piper's eyes shone.

For him.

He knew appreciation and desire in a woman and his female was looking at him with piles of it. It was working. After sleeping with her for a few hours during the day, despite the uncomfortable sofa, and now the playfulness that was re-emerging, hope was returning to his heart.

"Come," he said and stood behind her, wrapping his arms around her. "Give me your hands."

"Like virtual reality sword fighting?" she asked, laughing.

"Something like that, darlin'." He placed her hands under his. "Now follow my lead."

Sure, he might have been channeling his inner Patrick Swayze from *Ghost* and it was cheesy as fuck, but Oliver was willing to do anything to win Piper's trust and heart.

Slowly, he moved the sword through the air, taking all the weight and felt her body move with his. Cheesy movie aside, it was intimate as hell and surprisingly erotic.

Piper made a lot of appreciative noises and he let her take some of its weight. A few upwards and sideways swings through the air and then he spun them, keeping her pressed against his body so he could ensure her stability. She gasped sexily and he could feel she was loving every minute.

His cock hardened and when he turned her once more, her ass pressed against it. Their movements slowed, and he felt Piper's breath on his cheek as she turned to him.

He froze.

Leave. Now, he told the warriors in the training room and felt them teleport out a moment later.

Oliver threw the sword onto the mat away from them. Their eyes locked as the weapon clanged. Both their hearts thumped. Never in all his life had he felt such intense intimacy with another being. It was as if his breath, his very soul, belonged to her.

He could take, or he could wait. If he made the wrong move right now, he'd regret it for the remainder of his life.

Her eyes begged as her pupils dilated.

Then he knew.

He slammed his lips onto hers and she damn well melted in his arms as he engulfed her body.

Fucking yes*!*

Their tongues meshed together, familiar, and yet demanding to be reacquainted. Oliver lifted her, carrying her to a nearby bench, and spread her legs so he could wrap them around him.

"Wait."

"They're gone. We're alone," he said against her mouth, then pulled back. "Is that what you were asking?"

She nodded.

Suddenly, her eyes clouded. Oliver cupped her cheek. "Stay with me."

Bright blue eyes met his.

"How Oli? I don't understand how I can feel like this, knowing what I know."

"Sweetheart, it's just the unknown. You know me. Your body knows me. Will you trust me?"

"Stupidly, yes." She nodded and tears glossed her eyes. "I want to run, but if you walked ten paces from me right now, I'd probably chase after you."

He smiled.

"You're my mate," he said, surer now than ever. He kissed her gently. "I want to take you to my bed."

Oliver needed so badly to sink deep into her. To claim her. To dominate every inch of her. Having her safely in the mansion was one thing, but the bond was pulling at him. At both of them.

He knew Piper was feeling this, too.

Ari had been right. He knew. He knew Piper was his mate, above and beyond everything in his life.

If he lost his job, if he had to leave the mansion, he would.

Piper was his life.

Now he hoped she'd choose him.

She blinked away her tears and nodded.

Thank fuck.

He wrapped her legs around his body and lifted her. Piper looped her hands around his neck and played with the ends of his hair as she did every time.

"Close your eyes," he said and teleported into his bedroom.

When they arrived, he held her for a moment waiting to see if she felt ill, but all she did was blink and then gaze hungrily into his eyes. He lowered her onto the bed and lay over her. Fully clothed.

He was in no hurry.

"Your eyes," she gasped, reaching up to his face.

Oliver grinned. His eyes must have the mating ring around them now.

Holy shit!

"Piper Roberts," he croaked out, his voice thick with emotion. "I fucking love you."

She drew in a nervous breath and placed a finger on her lips. "Don't say anything. I just need this moment to revel in its perfection. God damn, I love you."

He knew they weren't out of the woods yet, but regardless of what happened from here, Oliver was taking the damn moment.

"Oli," she finally said, her eyes glistening as he peppered her with kisses.

"It's okay. You can say no at any point."

"Will you—"

He lifted his head. She thought he would change her, and that hit him hard in the chest.

"No. Never without your permission." He spoke firmly.

"Okay," she replied, touching his face.

Piper wrapped her legs around him and tugged him down for another kiss. Slowly he removed their clothing until they lay side by side, touching, kissing, licking. It was so intimate and intense, but soon his need to be deep within her began to take over.

He lifted her leg over his thigh and his cock nudged carefully at her entrance as he watched her respond. Oliver wasn't going to push, even though he was holding back his natural need to take, to own and to dominate her.

When she pressed her hips against him, he slid the head of his cock inside and let out a low curse. Her hot, moist body welcomed him in a tight grasp that set his body aflame.

Piper clung to his chest; her mouth parted as her own cries rang out.

Thrust.

He went deeper, and they moaned out their pleasure into the room together, fingers digging into flesh.

"Oli."

"I've got you."

Thrust.

Desire turned into desperate need. Oliver lifted her hips, going harder, deeper.

Thrust.

Piper gripped his shoulders, and her eyes demanded his mouth. He slammed his lips on hers as her pussy clenched around him, pulsing. Intense feelings flowed down through the bond, taking their pleasure to a whole other level.

He wasn't sure he would last. Or if Piper would come with him.

"Fuck," she cried, tossing her head back.

No!

Her neck, her pulse, the need to mate were overwhelmingly powerful.

Shit.

Oliver squeezed his eyes shut, knowing it wouldn't help.

Sharp nails dug into his chest, and Piper began to scream. "Oli, fuck me, Oli."

Just one small bite…

Her body demanded more from his cock, tightening as he thrust, desperately fighting to ignore his natural instincts.

Fuck.

Sweat beaded on his brow, and he pressed his eyes tight, but he could hear her pulse, he could see in his mind's eye that large pulsing vein. Piper's body convulsed around him, and he couldn't look away any longer.

Their eyes met.

Her orgasm rang out and when she began to relax, he gave her a painful smile. "I'm sorry."

Her eyes widened, and then he ripped out of her and flung himself across the room. "Oliver!" she cried.

He turned and flashed into the bathroom, slamming the door. Then sunk to the floor.

Fuck.

Fuck, fuck, fuck!

He dropped his head into his hands. He'd been so fucking close to biting her.

And losing her.

So damn close.

"Should I leave?" Piper asked. She'd been sitting on the other side of the door for the last twenty minutes. If he said yes, she wasn't sure how she *could* leave as she suspected Oliver's door would also be locked.

She hadn't forgotten she was a prisoner.

She just wasn't sure how much she wanted to leave now.

"No."

Relief spread through her, and it didn't go unnoticed.

"Was it something I did?" she asked. Oliver had pulled out of her with such speed and while it hadn't hurt her, it had given her a hell of a fright. The bang as he had hit the wall only added to that. Then he'd disappeared behind this door.

She didn't understand what was going on.

"I nearly bit you." He growled. "I told you. It's nothing you did."

Yes, he had told her that, but why was it a problem now and not any of the other times they had made love? Or fucked. Or whatever was going on between them.

She tucked her knees up against her chest. He sounded angry with her, but he *hadn't* bitten her, and she was grateful for that, but she wished he would come out and talk.

"But you didn't," she said again.

"No, but I wanted to. I still want to. Just give me a minute."

Piper wasn't a patient person, but no part of her could move from this space. Separating so quickly after she'd come had been emotionally disturbing more than anything. It was good she didn't have teeth, or rather fang, marks on her neck, but there was an empty feeling simmering within her.

She needed his arms around her.

She needed *him*.

It was beginning to dawn on her that even if she could get her head around him being a vampire, it wasn't going to be that black and white.

"Oli, could we be together if I'm a human?" she asked.

There was silence and after a long moment, the door opened. Piper fell backwards, and in a flash, Oliver caught her and lifted her to her feet.

Finally.

She fell into his chest, and he gripped her face a little hard and kissed her lips.

"It's complicated."

"How?" she asked in a whisper, not really wanting to hear the answer.

"I will not be able to restrain my fangs for long. The bond is calling me. It's our nature. I'm a strong alpha, so the pull is even more powerful than perhaps a less dominant vampire. I know I won't be able to hold back for much longer."

Piper's eyes dipped. Her mind was struggling to grasp what he was saying. What he wasn't saying.

"I want to say I'm sorry, but you're my mate. This is my nature."

"So you will have to turn me," she said, fear lacing her words.

Oliver nodded. "Yes."

Could she go through with this?

On one hand, she was horrified by the concept, but on the other, as she stared into Oliver's eyes full of love, desire and total possession, she felt… blessed that someone loved her enough to want to be her soul mate.

It both scared her and thrilled her.

"And what happens if I don't want that?"

"We will wipe your memories and you can live out your life. You won't remember me or any of this." He stepped away. "I won't stop you. You have my word. The choice is yours."

Piper stood there, naked and vulnerable before him, and nodded.

His eyes were dark, hiding something. They may not have known each other for long but it was if she knew him more intimately than she had before. She felt him. She felt deception but not toward her.

Oliver wasn't telling her something.

"And you? Will you just carry on with your life and meet another mate?"

His eyes flashed.

"No."

Piper's eyes widened at the harshness of his tone.

Then he shook his head. "You don't need to worry about me. You *won't* worry about me because you won't remember me."

If he wouldn't tell her, she'd find out. For that she needed to speak to Sage. She still loved Oliver despite knowing he was a different species, and he'd told her he loved her. Soon she had to choose what life she wanted.

A human one.

Or an immortal one.

To make a decision, she needed all the information, not just the bits he chose to tell her.

CHAPTER FORTY-SIX

Oliver slid down the headboard and rearranged the sleeping body in his arms. Piper had quickly fallen asleep mumbling about loving him and dying after he'd pulled her into his arms and taken them back to bed.

He'd sat frowning for ages, worrying about what she was dreaming about. She had a big decision to make, and he wasn't taking it lightly. For him, being a vampire was a gift. Being human, a weaker species, held no appeal whatsoever. Yet, he tried to imagine the tables turned.

For some reason, humans valued their short mortal lives. What was it about being human, vulnerable, and living a short life that made it so desirable?

Piper had gotten very close to a truth he didn't want her knowing—his future should she not choose him. He wanted to be honest with her, but she needed to decide what she wanted, not be pressured by the dire consequences on his life of her decision.

Oliver needed her to choose him because it was what her heart desired.

The shutters began to whizz open.

Damn.

Usually he looked forward to seeing the night sky, but tonight all it represented was the ticking clock.

He had about ten hours left.

Sage would like to see Piper. Ari telepathed, interrupting his thoughts.

She's asleep, but I know she wants to see her sister. Give us thirty minutes.

Thank you.

Oliver smiled. It wasn't often the Ari used those two words. It was likely Sage was pressuring him.

He ran a hand over Piper's hair and got a sexy little noise in return for his efforts. Shuffling down, his hand roamed along her back and over her soft, curvaceous bottom.

"Piper." Another little moan escaped her lips, and he had to stop from telling Ari they needed an hour. "Hey, darlin'," he drawled.

"Oli?"

"Sage wants to see you. Do you want to wake up?"

Her eyes blinked open.

Please don't panic. Please don't regret what we did.

That would break his damn heart.

He lowered his lips gently to hers, keeping his eyes open, and she pressed into him. He relaxed. *Thank God.*

"Sage? When is she coming?" Piper asked, sleepily.

"In half an hour," he replied, reluctantly pulling his body from hers and getting out of bed. He collected her clothing from the floor and placed it on the end of the bed. "I'll let you shower and meet you out in the living room."

Piper was pacing the floor when the short knock sounded. She gave him a look and when he nodded, she flew to the door as it opened.

Ari gave him a nod over the heads of the two women while they embraced, then nudged them inside and closed the door.

"Let's all sit down," Ari said firmly.

"I want to speak with Sage alone," Piper replied, and Oliver shook his head when she glanced at him.

"We have a lot to discuss," Sage said, squeezing Piper's arm and giving her a pitying smile.

He knew she'd hate that.

And panic.

"You can have time with her afterwards. There are things you need to know right now," Oliver said, standing and guiding Piper down on the sofa next to him.

"Jesus, what now?"

Sage and Ari sat down in the opposite sofa and the big vampire draped an arm around his mate. They were so comfortable with each other, as if they were one unit.

Oliver wanted that.

With Piper.

Sage glanced at him, and he nodded. "Go ahead."

Piper's eyes darted between them.

"Sage? What the hell is going on?" Sage reached blindly for Ari's hand, and he was instantly there, his arm enveloping her with his support. Oliver realized this was a big deal for Sage. She didn't want to feel rejected by her sister when she told her the news.

He wasn't surprised when Piper worked it out before words were even spoken.

"No," Piper said, shaking her head repeatedly. "No fucking way."

Sage nodded.

"I'm sorry for lying to you. Ari changed me, but I don't regret it, Piper. I love him." Sage's eyes filled.

Piper stared, her mouth gaping. "You're a vampire."

Sage nodded. "Yes. But I'm still me. You're still my sister."

"Fuck," Piper finally said quietly, her hand flying to her forehead and rubbing it. "Fuck. Fuck!"

She stood and then sat. Oliver placed a hand on her back, and she melted into him.

Ari gave him a look, a warning that he was about to take the floor. Oliver nodded and drew in a deep breath.

It was truth time.

Well, mostly.

"Sage is my mate. We love and honor our females. Whatever you think about our race, whatever you decide today, I want you to know that I love your sister with all that I am," Ari said, his voice strong, calm, and sure. "She will always be my priority. Above all else."

Hearing the director say that was a bit of a shock. Ari had created The Institute and recruited every single vampire that resided within the walls. Oliver didn't doubt he would give it all up for Sage if it ever came to it.

The power of the mating bond was sinking in, and it was a reminder of just how important this moment was in his life. He had to win Piper's heart.

The funny thing was, he had her heart; it was her mind he had to win over. And therein lay the challenge. She was a very strong-minded woman, and he was asking her to push past fears that were natural.

It was why most vampires changed their mates and then dealt with the repercussions afterwards. Some, like him, felt that was unwise. Or that their mate would never forgive them.

He'd be lying if he said the thought wasn't lingering in the back of his mind.

"This was your decision?" Piper asked, and Sage nodded.

Technically, that was a lie. Ari had changed Sage and then begged forgiveness. It had taken weeks for her to speak to anyone. He'd been lucky. Some females, or males, took far longer.

Piper chewed her lip and glanced at him.

"We will let you two chat afterwards, but right now we need to talk about where we go from here," Oliver said.

"This is about me becoming a vampire, then?"

Ari shook his head.

"No. That is for you to discuss with your mate. With Oliver," he said. "I want to talk to you about your media story. Piper, you need to understand we can't let you announce the existence of our race to the world. It would have devastating repercussions for millions of vampires. Not to mention a substantial and irreversible impact on the human race."

Piper's jaw tensed but her eyes darted around the room as she processed this perspective.

He hoped she was coming to realize this wasn't just about her breaking a huge story and proving to her father she wasn't useless. The impacts were far greater than her own personal gain.

It also impacted her family now that her sister was a vampire. He was a vampire. Oliver hoped that meant something.

"BioZen have been experimenting on vampires. Torturous experiments, Pipe. It would only get worse if knowledge of the race was made public," Sage said.

Piper glanced away and his body tensed. Their bond wasn't complete, but he felt something through the link, and he didn't like it.

"You knew?" he asked, his voice rising.

She whipped her head around. "Yes, but…"

"What?" Sage asked in surprise.

"You knew about the experiments?" Ari asked, his own brows tight. "How?"

That was a good fucking question.

How the hell did she know? His mind raced back through their timeline in Los Angeles and the information in Sage's diary. Something had changed the day she'd been kidnapped. It had triggered a lot of things, and none of them had been good so far.

"Who did you meet with that day in LA?" Oliver demanded. "What triggered BioZen?"

He could hear Piper's heart pounding and the scent of fear rushed from her.

"Oli, you're scaring her." Sage frowned.

Piper pulled away from him. "I... it's not like I could tell you. I didn't know you were a damn vampire."

"Tell me what?" he pressed.

Piper shook her head. "I can't tell you. People have trusted me with their information. How do I know you won't hurt them?"

Ari growled, and he felt Piper tremble.

Jesus, they were going backwards, but if she knew some information, she had to start talking.

"We're not going to fucking hurt anyone," Oliver said, running his knuckles over his forehead. "You just need to tell us who they are."

Fuck me.

"These people could destroy the peace on this planet and millions of lives. We may be vampires, but we're also mothers, fathers, brothers, husbands—or mates, as we call them." Ari leaned forward. "I can pull your memories from you, or you can tell us."

Piper's fists clenched the edge of the sofa tightly. "Don't you think we have a right to know? It's our planet too."

All three of them let out a resounding *no*.

Oliver loved her sharp and intelligent mind, and it was the reason she pushed boundaries and asked questions. There was nothing wrong with that unless it was going to unleash a series of events that even the warriors in the vampire race couldn't control or undo with their memory wipe abilities.

It would be far too big to contain.

Even the human leaders on the planet who were in the know realized how dangerous this information could be if it was unleashed.

"This is a dangerous time. The information is already in the wrong hands and they're doing exactly what our race has feared they would do," Oliver said, placing his hand on her thigh. "Which is why you need to drop the story."

"Am I going to have a choice?"

"No," Ari said firmly.

"Your sister was harmed by these people. *You* were nearly killed. Twice," Oliver reminded her.

"I get it. I get it. Okay," Piper said, sitting back on the sofa. Then she glanced at Ari. "What did you mean by *whatever I decide today?*"

Ari glanced over at him.

"You know what it means. It's time to decide if you are staying with me or returning to your life with your memory wiped," Oliver said, turning to face her. "If you want some time with Sage, we'll give you some space."

Oliver had done as much as he could in the short amount of time available. He'd told her he loved her. While it was clear she didn't understand the deadly consequences at his end, Piper had a decision to make.

CHAPTER FORTY-SEVEN

Piper felt so many emotions right now she didn't know where to start.

Her sister was a damn vampire. That was pretty enormous. She had stared at Sage's body and hair and eyes looking for a change and didn't see anything visible. Piper guessed there were fangs behind her lips, but she wasn't going to ask to see them.

Fuck that.

Her brain could only handle so much in one go.

Also, her story was dead. And while she was less upset about that than expected, because their reasoning was pretty sound and there was a lot she didn't know, it was still disappointing.

Sure, she wouldn't get her Pulitzer, but part of her was beginning to not care what her father thought of her anymore. Oliver's love was changing her. She felt protected and deeply cared for. Just one glance into those big blue eyes and she felt like his love surrounded her in an embrace.

Never once had she seen emotion from her father, except perhaps judgment and disappointment.

But it was all too soon.

They wanted her to decide on whether to turn vampire *today*.

Were they nuts?

Piper wanted to speak to Sage on her own, but now it was clear where her priorities were. With Ari. They were clearly in love but a little clingy for her liking. Still, she liked the way Ari had assertively expressed his loyalty and protection of Sage.

Their father would approve, she thought cynically.

He'd make some snide comment about Piper never being able to find a man as good as Ari.

Hadn't she, though?

She shot Oliver a glance. He was watching every single move she made.

God, he was sexy. He looked so confident with the way his arm lay along the sofa behind her, the other leaning on the cushions. His thick denim clad thighs were spread wide.

Her eyes traveled over his navy t-shirt, which did nothing to hide the layers of taut muscles underneath. He rubbed a hand over his square jaw, now covered in scruff due to the long few days they'd had.

When their eyes met, he tilted his head a little in question and a small smile hit his lips. Despite his natural confidence he still seemed vulnerable and full of doubt. A look she imagined very few people, if any, had ever seen on this power man—vampire's—face.

He trusted Ari and Sage.

"Tomorrow, before sunup, you need to decide if you will mate with Oliver. If not, I will erase your memories and you will return to your human life," Ari said. "You won't remember him, but you will retain a memory of sorts in your heart. There will be no other love for you in this life."

She turned to Oliver.

"It's true," he said. "Humans never choose another partner after they have rejected a vampire mate."

Ever?

"That seems unfair." She frowned.

"I don't make the rules." He shrugged.

"Why do I have to decide so quickly?" she asked, turning to Ari.

"Things are too dangerous right now. This is for your safety as well as ours," Ari said. "Plus, Sage has chosen to remain in her family's life for the next decade or so. This means we need to integrate into the family now. The longer we leave it, the more potential damage to your memory and mind."

"Remember your headaches?" Oliver asked.

She nodded and groaned. Pain aside, she'd be living a great big fucking lie. That didn't sit well with her. But it was that or give up her human life.

"So, I'd think you were my sister, but you'd be a vampire. Awesome."

"I *am* your sister!" Sage snapped.

Oliver groaned beside her.

"I told you she'd be like this!" Sage cried, tears filling her eyes. "She's so selfish. Just wipe her memory and take her home."

Shit, she hadn't meant to upset her. "Sage, I'm sorry."

Sage stood, and Ari joined her, pulling her into his arms. "That's not our decision and not one I would make for Oliver or Piper, sweetheart. Not with the consequence for my head assassin."

Piper whipped her head up and glanced between Ari and Oliver. "What consequence."

Oliver groaned.

"What?" Sage asked, obviously not in the know either.

Ari's eyes flew to Oliver and darkened.

"That is not up for discussion," Oliver said. "I think you two girls should chat. I'm going down to the training center and will be back in an hour."

Oliver stood and Piper suddenly felt panic race through her.

"No—" she said, standing and gripping his arm.

"Talk to Sage. She's your sister." He dropped a kiss to her lips. "We will talk when I return."

Sage nodded at Ari when he looked at her in question and the two large vampires left the room.

Piper stared at the door when it closed, and she felt as if someone had sucked the soul out of her. Her chest tightened slightly, and she found her hand going to her breast.

Sage flopped back on the sofa, snapping her out of her funk.

"Sorry," she said again. "I didn't mean you aren't my sister. Of course, you are."

"Thanks. This has been hard and lonely. I love Ari but not having anyone to speak to has been difficult. Then… the look of fear and disgust on your face, just…" Tears filled her eyes and Piper raced across the space and pulled her sister into her arms.

"God. This is so flipping weird."

Sage sniffed against her shoulder and let out a little laugh. "Yup."

They held each other for a long moment then Sage pulled back and smiled at her. "I truly forgive you now, Piper. I need you to know that, no matter what you decide today. I love you."

Then stupid tears were falling down her face and they hugged some more.

After a time they both stretched out their feet on the coffee table and just sat in silence, kind of snuggled up, leaning on each other, like they had when they were younger.

"So what's it like?"

"Being a vamp?" Sage asked and she nodded. "Honestly, it's weird and great, but none of it matters. Only Ari matters."

Piper nodded slowly.

She could see that in the way they were with each other.

Is that what she was feeling about Oliver right now? The hole in her chest that ached so much she kept wanting to rub it.

"Ari changed me without permission," Sage admitted, "so I was saved the process of deciding. I was furious, of course, but when I realized I couldn't live without him, I forgave him."

"I'd be furious."

"Oliver won't do that to you. For Ari, it was different. If you become a vampire, I'll tell you more."

Could she do it? Let Oliver change her?

"I don't know if I like the idea of being so dependent on a man. What if I fall out of love with him? Is there a vampire divorce?"

Sage let out a laugh.

Okay, clearly not.

"No." Sage smirked at her.

"What?"

"Are you wearing his shirt?"

Piper waved off her sister. "My clothes were dirty."

More smirking.

Fine, she'd wanted to wear his stupid shirt. He'd helped her tie it in the front, so it fit her, and she was seriously considering keeping it forever.

Speaking of forever, where the hell *was* he? And why was an hour so friggin' long, anyway?

But while he was gone, Piper had to ask the question that was on the tip of her tongue. She knew Oliver wouldn't tell her, so it was her only hope.

"What will happen to Oliver if I leave?"

Sage's teasing smile disappeared, and she shook her head. "I don't know, but if Ari hasn't told me, it can't be good."

A chill ran through her body.

That wasn't good. Why would they hide whatever it was from Sage? Surely these things were common vampire knowledge—not that she was a vampire culture expert all of a sudden.

Was it unique to Oliver?

Ugh, her brain was going a million miles an hour.

Then something hit her.

"You care about him," she said, but it was more of a question. When she saw the blush on Sage's cheeks, she narrowed her eyes. "Why?"

Sage lifted her hand. "It's not what you think? Okay, yes, it is but—"

Piper stood and glared at her sister.

"Jesus. Do vampires go around fucking each other? Is that what you all do for fun around here?"

Sage shook her head. "Let me explain."

Explain? As in, give her details about how Sage had made love to Oliver.

No, thank you very fucking much.

"Is that where they are right now? Fucking a room full of people. Vampires. Whatever." She could hear herself spiraling out of control, but was unable to stop.

"Piper."

"Where the hell is he?" She marched to the door and tried to open it, but it was locked. "Oliver!" she screamed. "Oliver, get your damn ass back here now!"

She turned to see Sage staring blankly, then blink and cross her arms.

A moment later Oliver appeared in the living room wearing a pair of black sweatpants and… nothing else. His chest was heaving and sweat dripped from him.

"What's going on?" he asked, staring between the two of them.

Piper couldn't take her eyes off him. Testosterone seeped from every pore of his body. His hands shot to his hips, biceps bulging, his pecs moving as he panted.

Even inch of him was pure raw masculinity and Piper was transfixed.

"I telepathed Ari," Sage explained as she walked to the door. "You both need to talk."

Piper continued staring at Oli. Had Sage left? Did she walk out and close the door? No idea. Did she teleport? No friggin' idea.

Her eyes were locked on Oliver's heaving, sweaty body.

"Piper?" He strode over and lifted her chin. Her eyes flicked up to his.

"Huh?"

"You've seen every inch of me. What—"

She laid her hand on his pecs and he stopped talking. "Is this some kind of vampire magic?"

"My body?"

"No. Yes. Whatever you're doing to *my* body?" Her hands ran down his abdomen as her panties moistened.

What had she been thinking before?

She couldn't remember.

"Oh, that's my natural charm." He smirked.

She slapped his chest playfully and he gripped her wrists. "No. These are your true feelings. I can't manipulate them."

Piper nodded, pleased she could trust what she was feeling. Oliver lowered his mouth to hers and they stood kissing and tasting one another. Then her mind began to clear.

"You were training," she said.

"Yes, ma'am." He nodded, then frowned. "Why? I told you where I was going."

The mix of emotions she'd felt just moments before came rushing back. "You slept with Sage."

"She told you?" he asked, surprised.

Piper felt a little chip of her heart break away. Oliver had no intention of ever telling her.

She stepped away. "Yes. She did."

"It was before I met you, Piper. It was the first night Ari met her."

Piper recalled the entry in Sage's diary.

"That was *you*? The threesome." Her brows rose. When he frowned, she explained. "I read her diary."

"You shouldn't have done that," Oliver said. "But yes, that was me. And before you ask, no, I haven't slept with anyone else since the moment I laid eyes on you."

Well, that was nice to hear because she hadn't either. Even though she had barely remembered him. Which was his fault.

But that wasn't what was bothering her.

"Do you love her?" she asked. "Was she Ari's and you couldn't have her?"

Piper didn't understand how this mating business worked, but she knew her sister, and the way Sage had spoken about Oliver was with affection. And since Piper had met Oli, he'd been protective of Sage as well. She needed to understand their relationship.

Did she like that they'd had sex and shared something so unique? No. But if he loved Sage, that changed everything.

"Not like I love you. I care for her."

That wasn't a *no*.

"Were you going to tell me?" Piper asked, her heart aching from the unspoken truth.

"Eventually. Does it change how you feel about me?"

Did it?

She didn't like that he was lying. Or omitting the truth. She didn't like that he was upset with Sage for telling her. Not that she had. Piper had worked it out.

Could she give up her life—her humanity—for a man who would lie to her?

"What else don't I know?"

Oliver sighed and ran a hand through his hair as he took a few paces away and then turned back to her. "There was a second time. With Sage," he said. "It's complicated though, and…"

Her mouth dropped open. Was he kidding right now?

"How? I thought this mating stuff was all rainbows and fucking unicorns. How did Ari let you fuck Sage *twice*?"

Oliver shook his head.

"Do you really want details?" he asked, holding his hands out in question.

Did she? No. She let out a groan and turned away.

"You need to understand single, or rather unmated, vampires, Piper. Which I *was* at the time. We are highly promiscuous. When we met Sage, this was something she desired. Then… Piper, I really don't want to make this worse by describing what happened."

God, why did she care so much? He was a vampire. It wasn't like she was seriously considering giving up his life for him, was she?

"I didn't finish. The first time," he added.

Jesus, just the thought of Oliver and Sage together made her ill.

"Then when I—"

Nope. She couldn't listen for a minute more.

"Stop. Oli, I can't. Stop." She turned away but felt him at her back. His hands landed on her hips.

"Piper, trust me when I say it wasn't… I mean, I cared. But it wasn't like it is with us. At all."

A mix of fury, jealousy, confusion, and nausea fled through her. Any moment, she felt like she was going to vomit and burst into tears.

"I need some space." She turned. "Can you take me back to my room?"

"We don't have much time left."

Piper let out a long sigh. "It's the middle of the damn night and I'm trying to deal with the fact I'm in love with a vampire who's shagged my sister—twice—and if I don't let you change me into a vampire too, then I'll never love again."

She crossed her arms.

"So forgive me if I want a moment alone to catch my breath."

Oliver glared down at her.

"What?" she grated.

"I love you. You love me. I can see it in your eyes. I can feel it in our mate bond. Stop resisting it, Piper."

What the hell? How damn invasive.

Was there no privacy in this world?

"I'm trying to give you space, but if all you're doing is looking for excuses not to be with me, then fine. Follow me, princess, and I'll take you to your damn room." He turned and stormed to the door, ripping it open.

Her heart pounded.

Seeing his anger and the way he was eager to get rid of her, she suddenly didn't want to leave as much as she had a few moments ago.

Oliver raised a brow.

Stubborn pride sliced through her, and she dropped her arms and stormed past him. The door closed, and he overtook her, then led her along a hallway, down a set of stairs and then another hallway. He stopped at a door, pressed his thumb on a panel and it clicked open.

He waved her in. She turned and watched the door close.

She was alone.

Just as she'd asked.

Tears sprang to her eyes, and she collapsed on the ground, sobbing.

CHAPTER FORTY-EIGHT

Oliver stood on the other side of the door, his head leaning on the doorjamb.

Fuck.

He'd heard this mating business was hard all his damn life, but this was beyond anything he could have imagined. Of course he had to fall in love with the most stubborn, independent, and frustrating female on the planet.

But God, he fucking loved her.

Just when he thought he'd been making progress, the topic of him sleeping with Sage had come up. He'd planned to tell her when they were fully bonded, and she was a vampire. Their bond would be stronger, and she'd understand the difference.

As a human her feelings were weaker than his, or so he'd been told, just by the nature of her species.

He hadn't exactly kept it from her. Things were moving very fast between them. He just hadn't thought it was a priority, but he'd been wrong.

Of course it was important to her.

Still, Oliver couldn't help feeling it was just another excuse she was clinging to, to leave him.

He'd snapped.

He realized that. But he couldn't stand looking into her face a moment longer as she rejected him. He felt her desire; he felt her love, and he felt her rejection.

It was painful.

He loved Piper with all that he was.

Taking her back to her room had been hard. It went against his very nature. What he wanted to do was rip his shirt off her, slam his mouth down on hers and press her against the wall while he thrust into her.

He wanted her to acknowledge she was his, but what she needed was space to truly feel his absence and work out what she wanted.

It would hurt them both, but he understood it.

He knew what was at stake.

He listened to her sobs and squeezed his eyes shut.

Fuck.

Every part of him wanted to go to her and pull her into his arms to comfort her. Instead, he straightened, and teleported back to his rooms, then punched a hole in the wall as he let out a yell.

Every vampire in the mansion knew what was going on. They would have heard him. When a mating was underway, everyone knew about it.

He had to go against his very nature and give Piper space to feel this pain and make her decision. She would either want him when he returned to her, or leave.

Oliver teleported back to the training center and found Ari leaning against the boxing ring. He threw Oliver a pair of boxing gloves.

Without saying anything, he slipped them on and climbed under the ropes.

"Don't go easy on me."

"Wasn't planning on it," Ari replied.

Piper picked herself up off the floor and climbed into bed. She tucked the covers around her and curled into a ball.

What a mess.

Part of her wanted to run home and get away from this entire situation, but the rest of her really wanted to be wrapped in Oliver's arms. To feel safe and loved. It was the only place she had truly ever experienced that.

She felt his love in every cell of her body. She felt the gaping void of his absence.

But he'd lied.

He'd slept with Sage. He wasn't telling her the consequences to him of what would happen if she remained human.

So many lies.

This wasn't about just deciding to date someone, or even marry them. She had to decide in a matter of hours if she would give up her humanity and become a different being altogether.

Tears rolled down her cheeks.

Deep down, she knew she couldn't choose him.

In some ways, she'd always known she'd remain on her own and unloved in this life.

Now she knew why.

Punch.

Omphf.

Oliver side-stepped and then ducked. When he'd asked Ari to not go easy, he probably should have thought it through a little more.

Punch.

Fucking hell.

He knew what the guy was doing, though. Distracting him. It was working to a point, but the mated vampire knew it would take a lot more, especially at this vital point.

"She's not going to change. I know it," Oliver said.

Punch.

"Jesus, Ari."

Then Ari tried to kick his legs out from under him but Oliver teleported to the other side of the ring.

"Breach of rules," Ari exclaimed, spinning.

"I don't give a fuck." He growled.

Ari nodded and gave him an understanding dry smile.

Oliver stood straight and held up his gloves. "Time out. I can't concentrate."

Ari stepped forward and tapped him with a glove; just a nudge. "Well, I'm trying to help you with that."

Oliver shook his head. "It's the bond. She's pulling me back. I can feel her anguish."

Ari stepped back and dropped his arms.

"Yeah, they do that. Let her experience the void for as long as you can resist. It will help her understand the nature of the mate bond. Or you could just change her." Ari shrugged. "You don't need to live without her."

Oliver ducked under the ropes and began removing his gloves. Ari did the same, and they both tossed them in the ring to be sorted.

"Piper wouldn't forgive me. She's like a wildcat. Stubborn and protective." He shook his head. "I need to let her choose. Even if she doesn't understand what will happen to me."

Ari cursed. "You won't last long without her, Oli. Fuck it."

Oliver nodded. He knew. Every male vampire knew.

For powerful alphas such as himself and many of the males in his world, mate rejection was a death sentence.

Eventually.

How long it took was up to the individual.

There was no way he could remain in his role as head assassin. He couldn't even be an ordinary assassin. He'd be unable to focus, and every part of him would grieve the loss of his mate.

The same mate who would have no memory of him.

She would continue with her life and build new memories, but she'd never love again. Humans often dated, had sex and married, but the relationships were hollow and missing any true love and intimacy.

For a vampire, the utter loss and grief drove them to suicide. If Piper chose her humanity, it was just a matter of time.

Tick tock, tick tock.

"Hey," he said, suddenly realizing he hadn't seen the Moretti SLC around. "Has Kurt left?"

Ari let out a sigh. "There's been a development, and he's returned to Casa Moretti in Maine."

Oliver crossed his arms.

"There's been a close contact situation with Callan."

His eyes widened. "We've found him?"

"Not quite," Ari said. "He bit a female. And its infected her."

What the hell?

"Change your mate, Oliver. Then come back to work. We need you. Things have just gotten very fucking serious." Ari slapped him on the back. "She'll forgive you. Have faith."

Oliver stared at the back of the ancient vampire as he walked away.

Jesus.

What the hell had they done to Callan?

What was he?

CHAPTER FORTY-NINE

Oliver listened outside Piper's door, then gave a short knock before letting himself in. They only had a few hours left before Ari would expect an answer.

Hell, *he* wanted an answer.

He'd left Piper for a few hours, every second of it painful, but now it was time to talk.

It was crazy to think this sassy pain in the ass held his life in her hands. She didn't know, of course, but Oliver was determined to let her decide her future, regardless of this situation with Callan.

Did he want to help the race? Yes.

But he couldn't live every day with the woman he loved despising him, knowing he'd taken her life. It would be worse than hell.

He'd decided. He would give up his life for her.

If Piper wanted to remain human and live out her life as a mortal, then Oliver would accept her decision. At least with Sage and Ari in her life, as family, he knew she'd be looked after as she aged.

Who knew what the afterlife would bring? Even vampires didn't know the answer to that. If soul mates were a thing, perhaps they'd get their shot together in the next life.

He glanced around the empty space and made his way to the bedroom where he found Piper curled up on the top of the covers with a wad of tissues.

She was dreaming fitfully.

Oliver sat on the bed beside her and rested his hand beside her head.

"Hey." Gently, he brushed the hair from her face.

Slowly she opened her eyes and rolled toward him. "Hi."

"I'm sorry," they both said at the same time.

Oliver smiled sadly as she shuffled into a sitting position, and he adjusted, keeping his arm over her.

"It hurts so much," Piper said. "When you're not with me."

He nodded. "It gets better when the bond is in place solidly. So I hear." He shrugged. "It doesn't go away. Mates can't live with—"

Shit.

"With?"

"Yeah, it's just hard. You're right," he added, leaving it at that but big blue eyes scanned his face.

"Will it be like this if I leave?"

Oliver wiped his hand over his face and sat away from her an inch. He felt her edge toward him and then relax back. The tug and pull was so evident he wanted to tell her it was okay.

But it wasn't okay.

Suddenly he knew. Every bone in his body knew she was going to reject him. It was time for some cold hard truths.

Or some of them.

"It's the essence of who you are, our souls, which have connected. Not our memories," he answered. "Over time, it will lessen but, as Ari said, you'll always feel the loss and never love another."

Unlike him. He would feel the void grow until he could no longer breathe without her.

Nor would he want to.

This was the curse of being vampire.

"God. I never asked for this," Piper said, shaking her head. "I'm sorry, that sounds so horrible. This is just… crazy. I shouldn't have to die to be with someone I love."

And yet he would die if she wouldn't be with him.

"What did you say?" His eyes flew open.

"Oh—"

He grabbed her legs and dragged her to him. She let out a laugh he could tell she hadn't been able to contain.

"You love me?" He cupped her face, brushing her hair back. "Say it again."

"Oli."

"Just say it, please."

"I love you." Her eyes dropped.

"Just look at me and say it, goddamn it." He pleaded, gripping her tighter.

Her eyes flew back to his and held. "I love you, Oliver Cambiaghi. I do."

His lips slammed down on hers and she turned to jelly in his arms. He forced his way inside her warm wet mouth and took possession of her tongue, entwining them in a passionate dance.

He'd told her when they made love after the sword play, but she'd not said it back. Not since she'd learned he was a vampire. He sensed strongly she was going to leave, but right now he wanted to relish in this moment. She loved him, despite what he was and if this was all he had of her, he'd take it.

He'd take fucking anything.

"Don't give me your answer yet. I just want to have this moment with you."

She nodded, tears springing. He pressed his thumb against one and wiped it away. No, he wasn't facing any of that yet. He wanted to just focus on those three words.

They both removed their clothes and then came together like desperate lovers. Clinging awkwardly, biting, sucking, licking. All they both wanted was the intimate connection.

"Oli."

"I know," he ground out, wrapping her legs around him and reaching to slide his fingers through her moist entrance. "I want it too, darlin'."

His cock wasn't waiting, it twitched toward her, needing to be inside her now. Laying down over her, their eyes met as he pressed against her pink wet flesh.

He smiled. "You are the most beautiful person I've ever met, Piper Roberts."

Fuck.

Fucking emotions. They sped through him like a speeding bullet. Her arms wrapped around his neck and their lips collided as he entered her. Her warm channel immediately wrapped around him as if she was made for him.

Because she was.

He slid in fast, and they both groaned, holding their bodies close together. Oliver grabbed her hips and began to move rhythmically, kissing her, staying so close as if it was the last time he'd ever have this beautiful annoying woman in his arms again.

Because it might be.

"I love you," Piper cried. "I'm sorry, Oli. God, I love you."

Fuck. He heard her apology and knew what it meant and still he ignored it.

Their bodies slapped desperately as the pressure grew, both of them not caring how good the lovemaking was, just that they were connected. Touching. Together.

Oliver arched and growled as his orgasm began. "Come, darlin'. Come with me."

"I—"

His eyes dropped to hers. Tears were pouring down her face, but she clung to him and clenched her pussy muscles as she began to come. Her eyes never left his.

It was heaven and hell.

Heat shot up his shaft and he came in a rush inside her, panting, groaning, and thrusting to milk every last drop. For the very last time.

Rolling over, he pulled her against him and rested her head on his heaving chest. If only he could freeze time.

Piper returned from the bathroom and snuggled back into Oliver's arms.

Five more minutes.

Then she would tell him.

"Those weren't my best moves," Oliver said and she could hear the smile in his voice.

"Sure they were, big guy." She grinned up at him and he smirked back. Then the mood turned serious.

"We need to talk."

She let out a sigh. "I know. Let me get dressed."

Five minutes later they were both sitting on the edge of the bed and staring at their feet.

"Just say it," Oliver said, taking one of her hands and entwining his fingers.

Emotion built in her throat, tears stinging her eyes. How could she love him so much? And how could she live without him?

But she had to.

"I'm going home," Piper said. "It's not you. Oh God, that sounds so cliché. But it's not you. I just can't wrap my head around becoming another species. If—"

"If I was human?" he asked, and she could hear the clench of his teeth as he spoke.

She had to tell the truth. He deserved that.

"Yes," she whispered.

They sat there in silence for a long moment. A really long moment. Then suddenly he slapped her on the knee and nodded.

"Okay."

Okay?

Her head shot up as Oliver stood. "Okay? Is that all you're going to say?"

He nodded. "Yes. You've made your decision and I love you so I will honor it. You're an intelligent woman, so I trust you think this is the right thing for you."

She stared at him.

That was it? He was accepting her rejection just like that. Was that how much he loved her? She'd been prepared for a huge debate, and maybe for him to try and change her mind.

Okay.

That was all he was going to say?

Well then, perhaps she had made the right decision.

So much for soul mates, fucking fated mates, and all that bullshit.

Oliver plunged his hands into his pockets. "If you want me to fight for you and change your mind, just fucking say it. I'm trying to do the right thing here."

Oh.

"I guess I do, but that's selfish. I'm not going to change my mind," she admitted.

He nodded. "That's what I thought. I know you, Piper Roberts. You make up your mind and you are stubborn. So if this is what you want, I accept your answer."

Yes. It appeared he did know her.

Her heart began to splinter as she stared into the face of the man who loved her enough to accept her rejection with a straight back and nod of his head.

For her.

He was doing it for her. She could see that as plain as day.

Tears slid down her face like rain on a windowpane. They seemed to never end. She didn't know if she wanted them to end.

Oliver nodded and kept nodding, then took a step away.

She clenched her fists to stop from reaching out and asking him to stay, but instead a sound left her body that seemed to come from her very soul.

He stopped and looked at her like she'd ripped him open.

"I have to leave. This is too painful to stay here with you now, Piper," he said, as if apologizing. His hands ran over his head and then his arms in a confused and chaotic way. "Ari will see that you get home, and your memories are erased."

Piper stood.

His eyes shot to hers. "Stay there. Please."

Would he not let her touch him again? He couldn't just leave. A flush of panic spread through her.

"Oliver, please. At least kiss me goodbye."

The eyes that looked back at her were not ones she recognized. They were primal and wild. He blinked a few times, took the few steps toward her, slammed his lips down on hers harshly, and then lifted his head.

"Goodbye Piper. I will love you with all that I am until my very last breath."

Then he took two steps backwards and vanished. A guttural cry left her body and for the second time tonight, she collapsed.

This time, though, she felt like she'd lost a huge chunk of her soul.

CHAPTER FIFTY

"So they'll be outside, and I won't even know?" Piper asked, setting her bag down on the kitchen bench in her apartment.

She was all cried out and basically feeling like a walking zombie.

But it was good to be home.

No, it wasn't.

Everything sucked.

In some ways she was looking forward to not remembering, even if they kept telling her she'd still feel sad.

She didn't feel sad. She felt like she was a potato that had been grated and was a sad heap of slush lying on the chopping board.

Dramatic much?

Stupid love. Why did she have to go and fall in love?

Ari nodded. "Yes."

"They'll keep you safe," Sage said. "And I'll come around regularly to visit."

"Won't I think that's suspicious, given we hardly hung out before?" Piper raised a brow, even though knowing she'd see more of Sage was definitely a nice thing.

Out of all this, mending the relationship with her sister was something she was grateful for. And if she was being honest, the time she had had with Oliver was something she'd cherish.

Even if she only remembered him for another few minutes.

"I'm getting married, so I'll just say it's wedding planning. You'll be my bridesmaid, won't you?" Sage grinned.

And wouldn't you know it? Apparently, she hadn't run out of tears.

"Oh my God, *yes*!"

Sage threw herself at Piper and they hugged like it was the last time.

Ari cleared his throat, but they ignored him.

"I'll be your bridesmaid, but if you make me wear pink, I swear I will haunt your vampire ass when I'm a ghost," she said, and they both grinned stupidly at each other.

"Okay ladies," Ari said. "I have to get back to The Institute, so let's wrap up this love fest. You will be in each other's lives for a long time to come."

"Ari," Sage admonished.

"Sorry sweetheart, but I have a meeting with the king."

Sage nodded and gave Piper an apologetic look.

"Let's begin," Ari said, indicating she should sit.

This was it.

This was the end.

Panic flew through her body, and he frowned at her, clearly picking up on her tension. "You need to be sure."

She nodded, pressing her lips together firmly.

"Piper. Are you sure?" he asked, and she wondered why he was pushing.

She nodded again but gripped the bench as nausea and dizziness hit her.

Shit.

Was she making the right decision?

"Will Oliver be okay?" she asked.

"He'll be fine. I'll keep an eye on him," Sage said, rubbing her arm, but one look at Ari's face and Piper knew she didn't have the last piece of the puzzle.

"What? Tell me. He told me he would be okay."

Didn't he?

Ari walked up to her and took her chin. "Oliver has chosen, just as you have. Now, focus on my eyes…"

Oliver stuffed a few things in his duffel bag and began to tidy up his rooms. He was strangely calm under the circumstances.

No, that wasn't true.

He felt dead. Robotic. Life had no meaning now. It was just a matter of hours, days, weeks, or perhaps months.

Not if he was lucky.

Every minute would be one of absolute suffering.

Like right fucking now.

Piper was gone. She'd made her choice and Ari had taken her home. His body was like a tight coil, ready to burst. The need to protect her, possess her and fuck her was dominating him to the point of obsession.

Yet, he remained where he was. Tight, restrained, and clenched.

Like a ticking time bomb.

His phone rang.

"Hey."

"I heard," Ben said, not wasting time with niceties.

"Yup. Laughable really," he replied, and they both knew there was nothing funny about it at all. "How many women have I fucked over my long life and had to turn away?"

"Mr. Lover-lover," Ben said in a sing-song voice, reminding him of a nickname they used to have for him. The humor was strained so they both went silent. "I wish I could fix this, Oli. You're my fucking best friend."

He nodded, even though Ben couldn't see him.

"Just go and change her. This is fucked up. I'll come and fucking talk some sense into her," Ben growled.

Oliver ran a hand over his face.

Their decision was impacting many other people. It would have far-reaching implications, and yet Oliver hadn't considered anyone else. Only Piper.

As any mate would.

"I'm sorry, buddy. You never know, I could get past this." They both knew it was a lie, but it was the best he could give his longtime friend.

"Fuck off, Oliver. Did you even fight for her?"

Anger pulsed through him suddenly. "Yes, I fucking fought. No. Wait. What? I told y'all I was letting her decide."

Ben cursed and Oliver heard some noise in the background.

"Oliver!" a commanding new voice said across the airwaves.

What the hell?

"My lord?" Oliver said, becoming suddenly alert.

"Sorry, he stole the phone," Ben called out from a distance.

"I heard what happened," Brayden Moretti said.

The prince of the vampire race was on the phone, speaking to him about his failed mate-ship. Excellent. Could this get any worse?

They may have worked together on a few things recently, but that didn't mean they were friends. The Moretti captain was still the prince of the royal family.

"Yes, my lord. It's... unfortunate."

"Listen. Willow was human, so I know what you're going through. Get your ass back to her right now and do not give up. Tell Ari you need more time. You're a good male and a strong warrior, and I will not allow you to step into the daylight. You got that?"

Oliver blinked.

What the hell was happening right now?

"And," Brayden said. "If either of you fucking repeat this, I will push you out into the sun myself... but I was wrong. Willow chose me, thank God, but it was my job to show her that. If I had my time again, I would change her and patiently wait for her forgiveness."

What was he saying?

"Go get your mate and turn her, for God's sake," Brayden ordered him.

Or at least, it sounded like an order.

"Yes!" Ben shouted in the background. "And my lips are sealed for eternity. Jesus. Willow would have your balls for saying that."

Oliver let a smile creep onto his lips. He didn't know the princess well, but he was pretty sure Ben was right.

"I'll have yours if you ever repeat it," Brayden said, and he heard the phone drop on a surface, footsteps, and a door close.

Oliver stood staring at his bed, shaking his head.

"Um, so that just happened," Ben said, now back on the line.

"Jesus," Oliver said. "What the hell do I do?"

"Go get your girl or it sounds like Brayden Moretti is going to kill you." He laughed.

They both knew it was an empty threat, but he'd heard what the prince said.

Had he made the wrong decision?

Was it too late?

Piper waved her hands in front of her face. "No wait a minute. What has he chosen?" she demanded as Ari closed in on her. "Sage, stop him."

"I don't understand," Sage replied. "Ari, what will happen to Oli?"

Ari cursed. "Can you both for just one day be—"

"Be?" Sage asked, crossing her arms and glaring at her mate.

Piper was just about to jump off the stool when a crashing sound came from her bedroom. The door flew open and Oliver raced in.

Panting.

Looking all kinds of crazy.

"Jesus Christ," Ari said, throwing his arms up.

"Is she? Are you…?" Oliver began, slowly walking toward her.

"Am I what?" she asked, confused.

What was he doing here?

"Oh, God. Am I too late?" His eyes darted between her and Ari.

"No," Ari replied, and stepped back.

Oliver physically relaxed and let out a sigh, coupled with a curse.

"Yet," Ari said, then whipped out his phone that had begun ringing. "Bray, what's up?"

Oliver stared at him, and the two enormous vampires glared at each other for a long moment.

"Is that right?" Ari growled and then walked down to the end of the apartment and continued talking on the phone.

Oliver walked to Piper and glanced at Sage.

"I'm going to go do… things… in another room," Sage said and wandered off awkwardly in the direction of her mate. Piper half-grinned but turned to Oliver, who was standing in front of her. His eyes were full of determination.

"Piper—"

"I have a question." Her heart pounded with knowledge. She had no idea how she knew.

Oliver nodded, and she noticed he had a wild, predatory look about him.

"What will happen to you?" His eyes closed for a moment. "Please tell me the truth. I know you're hiding something. I can sense it."

"How?" Oliver opened his eyes.

"Will you die?" she asked, ignoring his question.

He stared at her a long time, then took a step closer, cupping his hand gently around her face.

"Yes," he finally said.

Panic slammed into her, and she began to breathe erratically. Their eyes locked together, and tears welled. His and hers.

"No. No, no, no. Oliver, noooo." Her voice grew louder. Then she threw her arms around him. "No!"

"It's okay." He scooped her up and moved to the sofa. "Shh, shh."

It wasn't all right at all.

He was going to die because of this.

Her life for his.

His life for hers.

Except she would live, and he wouldn't.

Oliver shifted her onto his lap and toyed with her hair. "Piper, I came to change you, but I still can't do it. I love you too much. I need this to be your decision."

Her eyes widened.

Then she imagined him standing up and walking away, vanishing, like he had before. Every inch of her heart shattered like glass and suddenly she knew.

"Will it hurt?"

His eyes shot to hers and widened.

"I don't know. Maybe." His eyes were full of question.

"Do you truly love me?" she asked.

"More than my life. Obviously." A little smirk hit his lips.

"If I do this, will you be okay if I keep being a journalist and doing human things?" Piper asked.

His body stiffened, and then he began nodding.

A lot.

She watched the life seep back into his eyes and that wildness subside. Warmth spread through her entire being in a way she hadn't felt for hours. Somehow, in some crazy, ridiculous way, she knew this was the right decision. As terrifying as it was.

Perhaps she'd find her place in a vampire world. She had certainly found a man who loved her for who she was. It didn't matter what she did, Oliver loved her completely and utterly.

Not even her father had been able to love her unconditionally.

She'd be a complete fool if she walked away from him.

And really, now she knew his life would end, it wasn't a choice.

She loved him.

She'd always loved him.

"Really? Are you fucking kidding me? Fuck yes, anything. Wait. What kind of human things?" Oliver asked.

She shrugged.

"Piper, darlin', there are limits."

She grinned. "Excellent. I love pushing boundaries."

He groaned, and she laughed as he flipped her underneath him. Then their laughing stopped.

"Ari, I need you and Sage to disappear right now," Oliver said, and when she was about to tell him they couldn't hear from down in the bedroom, she remembered they had vampire hearing.

"See you soon, Piper," Sage called out, and then there was silence.

"Are they gone?"

"Yes, ma'am." Oliver's voice was thick and sexy, and her body began to tremble under his gaze and touch.

"What's happening?" she asked, even though she knew.

"I'm going to bond us."

Moisture pooled in her panties as his fangs extended and his bright blue eyes glistened as little red lines appeared in the whites of his eyes.

He looked primal and sexy, hovering over her, his enormous shoulders dominating her. She needed to feel their bodies connected and his mouth on her.

Now.

CHAPTER FIFTY-ONE

Oliver ripped open her top, and she did the rest, pulling it off.

His body was on fire. His fangs ached like a motherfucker. He'd never felt this powerful an impulse to bite like he did right now.

He stood and, using vamp speed, tore his clothes from his body.

"Holy shit." Piper gasped. He froze, worried. "You," she said in explanation, waving her hands out. "Your body is all pumped and my God, look at those veins."

Oh. That.

Yeah, he was ready to bond with his mate.

"Get it all off." He pulled her skirt off and could smell her need. It had only been hours since they'd last had sex, but she was ready. Slipping his fingers under the lace of her panties, he slid them off.

"I don't know how this is going to go or feel, darlin', but I'll take care of you."

Piper nodded, her eyes on his cock.

He took her chin. "Piper."

"Hmm?"

He grinned and lifted her into his arms, wrapping her legs around his waist. While he spotted a dozen different surfaces on which he would love to fuck her right now, this was an important moment. He carried her into her bedroom, to the place he'd watched her all those weeks ago, and lay her on the bed.

Big eyes stared at him as he crawled over her.

His fingers slid through her pussy. She was ready. She needed no preparation. He circled her clit and watched her mouth part and pleasure spread across her face.

There would be time for playing afterward.

"Are you sure?" he asked one last time.

"Yes," she answered, arching into him. The energy between them was electric and impossible to ignore.

Oliver nodded, guided his cock between her wet folds and then thrust inside. Deep inside until he could feel his balls slam against her ass.

"Oli," she cried.

Fuck, yes!

His body roared, knowing they were bonding.

"Piper Roberts, you're mine," he cried, slamming into her again and again. "My mate, my fucking mate."

"Yes," she screamed, and his fangs extended as he leaned down to her neck. He punctured the skin and then bit. "Holy shit!"

Her cries, the taste of her blood, and her tight pussy around his cock set him off. He shot cum inside her as blood rushed down his throat. It was the most erotic and overwhelming feeling he'd had in his life.

Every bone in his body felt like it was on fire, but it was delicious. Orgasmic. When he lifted his gaze, Piper's eyes were half-rolled back in her head.

Yeah, that's how he felt.

"Piper, darlin', are you okay?"

"Holy hell," she said, one hand gripping his arm in a death grip while the rest of her body looked like jelly.

She was okay.

"Your body will start transitioning soon, and I will start giving you my blood," Oliver said. "I'll be here when you wake. I won't leave you."

Nothing would tear him away.

"Okay," she said. "That felt amazing, but I'm not going to lie. I'm scared."

He was, too. But there was no way he was telling her that.

"Relax in my arms, darling. Let me taste you again." Oliver leaned back in, following his natural instincts and sinking his fangs into her again.

His cock hardened, and she clenched around him once more. He slowly moved in and out of her as he sucked her blood and came inside her over and over. It was like childbirth, he figured. His body and hers knew what to do.

Then Piper slid into the transition coma and his heart began to pound.

To distract himself, he cleaned her up and dressed her in a pair of PJs. Then he flashed them both to his bedroom in the mansion where he knew she would be safe, and tucked her into bed.

This could take hours or days. Every human was different. All he knew was that he wasn't going anywhere.

He had his mate, and she was his everything.

She had chosen *him*.

Finally, he knew his father had been wrong. He was a good male. He had nothing to prove.

Ari had known. He'd known all along.

Even the prince had crossed a boundary to fight for him, and that spoke volumes.

But it really hadn't mattered because, at the end of the day, he'd had to work it out for himself.

Oliver had to feel worthy of his mate before he was willing to fight for her, and while Piper had chosen him in the end, it had taken his decision to come and get her, for her to do it.

Three weeks later, Oliver drove his new Maserati through the gates of the mansion.

"Mom seemed to like you," Piper said, shooting him a glance from the driver's seat.

"Your father doesn't," he said, shrugging. "Then again, I don't think he's all that impressed with Ari either."

The first family dinner with the Roberts had been painful. Not only had Sage and Piper had to introduce their parents to their mates, but they were also learning to hide their vampire selves at the same time.

Twice, Ari had to wipe memories when fangs slipped out or one of them used excessive strength.

Oliver had found it amusing, though they all knew it was dangerous. This would be their life for at least the next few decades, and they needed to limit how often they adjusted human memories.

"I think he's intimidated by Ari."

"Most people are. Especially humans," Oli replied.

"How old is he?"

"Ancient. But you should ask him about that. There's more you need to know but in time," he said, parking.

Piper had only been awake for a week, and she had a million questions. Her journalist nature was alive and well, but despite knowing she had a lifetime or ten to learn everything, it wasn't slowing her down.

He opened her door and she hopped out, wrapping an arm around his neck, and kissing him.

"Well, don't worry about Dad. Finding out both his daughters are getting married at once probably gave his bank account a seizure."

"He's not paying for a thing," Oli replied, squeezing her against him. He was ready to sink inside her already. It had been five hours—far too long.

Yeah, he was getting married. Like a damn human. When he'd found out Ari proposed to Sage and how important it had been, he'd assumed it would be the same for Piper. The idea of her wearing his ring had appealed to him. Hell, whatever way he could mark her as his was fine with him.

When she'd finally awoken and gotten her bearings after a couple of days, Oliver had filled his spa bath and scattered red rose petals around the place. He'd spent weeks researching romantic ideas, but most of them felt too clichéd. What he and Piper had always shared was a raw, primal intimacy. It had always been physical with them. Sure, there had been an initial lust, but their love would always be a sexual one.

He'd carried her into the bath and poured them a glass of champagne while she nibbled on decadent chocolates, telling him how much she loved her new vampire life.

He'd grinned, waiting for her to finish the damn bubbly liquid and hoping she didn't swallow the extremely pricey diamond ring at the bottom of it.

How had she not seen it already?

When she did, the whole world heard her squeal and water had gone everywhere as she'd thrown herself at him.

"We're already mated." He'd laughed.

"Don't care!" she'd cried. "Put it on me. Put the enormous thing on me."

She'd thrust the ring into his hands, and he'd pulled her onto his lap, then slipped it on. And yeah, there had been some magic in that moment, so the humans were onto something.

"Now say it. Say the words."

He'd laughed. "Will you marry me, Piper Roberts?"

"Um…"

His brows had risen as she mock-considered his proposal. "I guess. Okay, yes. But only because you're so hot."

"And you love my cock."

"And that. Yes." She nodded, holding out her hand. "Oh my God, I'm getting married."

Ari had been right. It was important.

Oliver felt like Superman for that one special moment. It was different from when he'd bitten her and bonded their mating, but both were special.

If only to see the utter joy on her face.

And yes, he loved seeing his square-cut diamond sitting on her finger every single day.

In the week since she'd been awake, Piper had shared her research and Darren had looked into the humans she'd met with in LA. They were smart guys. There was not a lot they could do about them but keep an eye on their activity. The king had a communications team who were actively monitoring and countering social activity, so they'd passed on the details.

Piper told Oliver she'd asked Tyler, one of the online guys, to look into him and Ari, but they weren't worried. No one at The Institute had a digital footprint. Thanks to Darren and his team.

They were interested in the documents that the men had on the experimentation. Now more than ever, they needed information to learn what BioZen were up to.

Ari had met with Brayden, Vincent and Kurt who had shared what they knew about Callan and the female vampire he'd bitten. She was in Maine being closely monitored.

And by the sounds, not very happy about it.

Oliver couldn't believe it was the flirty young bartender they'd met when Kurt was in Seattle.

What a damn lucky break. For her and them.

There had been something else. A name. Piper had seen it on a piece of paper when she'd been kidnapped. The memory had resurfaced only yesterday.

They'd walked down to the Operations Room and mentioned it to Ari and Darren who were leaning over a tablet.

The name had sounded familiar, but he wasn't sure why.

Both of them had barely looked up when the two of them had walked in, but when he asked them if the name Nikolay Mikhailov meant anything, their heads had shot up.

"Why?" Ari growled.

"Shit," Darren said, tapping way.

"He's got something to do with Piper's kidnapping," Oliver said, and explained what they knew.

Turns out, the guy was the new head of the Bratva—the Russian Mafia. New as in, he'd inherited the role after his father was assassinated. Rumor had it, Mikhailov had been the one holding the knife.

Knife. Not gun.

The guy was a cold-hearted killer.

Oliver knew about killing. He was trained. Killing a living being was no easy feat, but a parent? Yeah, that fucker was dangerous.

That act had gained him a global reputation in all the circles that were important.

"Do we think they're in bed with BioZen? Acting as security? Or independently?" Oliver asked Ari.

The director simply shook his head. "I knew Nikolay's father, and his grandfather. This isn't good. The Bratva don't mess about. Whatever their involvement is with BioZen, it is *not* good. Not fucking good at all."

Oliver had pulled Piper closer, realizing how lucky they were to have saved her before she was handed over to the Russian mob. Seriously fucking lucky.

He was glad she was a powerful vampire now, and fully intended to get her into the training room to show her how to defend herself.

Meanwhile, Sage was working on the blood samples he and Kurt had provided to learn what the humans were using to weaken vampires. If they could create an antidote and distribute it globally, it would go some way in protecting their race.

Because this was a war.

One with bio-weapons.

And by the sounds of it, super-soldiers. Now they had to wait to hear what the king had decided to do next.

If it was up to Oliver, they'd bomb every BioZen plant on earth. But the human fatality would be huge. He respected the king wasn't as bloodthirsty as he was.

But then again, that's why he was an assassin.

Head assassin.

Still.

And he was worthy of the role.

"Dad will probably try to pay," Piper said, snapping him back to the present moment.

The wedding.

Oliver snorted. That was easily solved with a few memory shuffles. In any case, the less involved the parents were, the better.

Oliver scooped her off the ground and grinned as she let out a squeal. He teleported them into his rooms and carried her into the bathroom.

"Shower sex? Really?"

"Every day." He made fast work of removing their clothes and nudging her under the water. When Piper slid to her knees and took his member in her mouth, he changed his mind.

"Make that twice a day." He groaned. "God, yes." He watched her lips slide over him. "Touch yourself, darlin'. Push your fingers inside your pussy."

Her eyes locked on his as she did as he'd instructed. With her legs wide and her fingers sliding in and out of herself, she began to struggle to suck on him.

Jesus fucking Christ, his mate was everything.

He pulled out of her mouth after a few more minutes and lifted her around him, pressing her against the shower wall.

"Oli, shit."

"You want to come, darlin'?"

"Yes," she said as he shoved his cock into her.

"Beg me to come," he said, slowing his movement.

"No, move. Fuck me," she demanded.

God, he loved hearing her talk like that. His cock swelled and tightened. "Beg."

"Please, fuck me. Make me come. Damn you."

His finger stretched to her ass as he thrust hard in and out of her, pressing against her hole. He knew just how sensitive she was there, and when it hit the right spot and her body spasmed, his cock exploded.

Together, they cried out.

Oliver slapped the wall with his palm, holding her with his other arm, and lifted his head to find Piper grinning and panting. Her new fangs had extended.

"You going to bite me, mate?"

She nodded and when she dug into his pecs with those sexy, razor-sharp teeth, his cock sprung to life again.

Fuck, life was good.

I hope you loved Oliver and Pipers story. **Turn the page to read** the first steamy chapter of Kurt and

Madison's romance - The Vampire's Wolf– **the next installment in the Moretti Blood Brothers series**.

OR click HERE to buy now.

JULIETTE N. BANKS
THE VAMPIRE'S WOLF
THE MORETTI BLOOD BROTHERS

THE VAMPIRE'S WOLF

CHAPTER ONE

Kurt Mazzarelli walked through the halls of the Moretti royal castle. His eyes were peeled for... well, you'd think as one of the five Senior Lieutenant Commanders—or SLCs as they were known—in the king's army he'd be looking for threats to the royal family. Or danger. Or trouble.

Hell, even keeping an eye out for insubordination by any of the hundreds of soldiers who reported up the chain of command.

There were only two higher than him and the other SLCs and that was Craig, the commander, and Brayden, the captain. Brayden Moretti was also the prince.

Kurt wasn't looking out for any of those things. Well, perhaps he was. He'd been doing this so long it was second nature now.

Which was why he hadn't hesitated when he saw the red, swollen bite mark on Madison's neck. He'd ordered a Moretti jet and flown home to Maine from Seattle with the little flirty blond.

She was somewhere within these great walls, but he needed to keep away from her. At least when he was on his own.

Three young female Moretti soldiers, dressed in top-to-toe black just as he was, walked past him and shot him blushing smiles. He nodded at them in acknowledgment and continued *not* looking for Madison.

When he got to his room, he shut the door and drew in a chest full of air and let it out loudly.

Fuck me.

It had been two weeks of physical hell.

No one knew what was wrong with her and, while she wasn't technically in isolation or quarantine, she'd been told it was best if she restrained from any sexual activity.

Well fucking hell, he should have thought of that...

Kurt pulled off his large black boots and kicked them into his wardrobe. Pants, jacket, and black long-sleeved Moretti t-shirt came next. He threw them on the armchair in the corner of his room.

Unlike some of his colleagues, he didn't do commando. He liked his junk tucked up nicely in a pair of briefs. Leaving them on, he flopped his enormous muscular body down on the bed, face up, and let out another sigh.

Running a hand through his dark hair, his mind, yet again, returned to the flight home with Madison.

They had boarded just before daylight after teleporting to her home so she could pack a few things. She clearly wasn't a wealthy vampire, and at only fifty-five years old, he wasn't surprised. They'd jumped in an Uber, because teleporting into an airport unless absolutely necessary wasn't recommended with all the security and cameras.

Their teams could clean it up, but it was just another job. They'd had time, so it was no biggie to order a car via the app.

What he hadn't factored in was his reaction, even just sitting next to her in the back of the sedan. The proximity had set off sparks between them he'd not been expecting, and his fingers had twitched to touch her. Instead, he had jammed his hands between his thighs.

When he'd followed her up the steps of the plane and his eyes were glued to her ass, his cock growing ready for action, she had suddenly spun around, and those green eyes had captured his.

"I've never flown before," Madison had said.

"Ever?"

She shook her head.

Kurt had taken a few more steps, her ass now out of his eye line, and placed a hand in the small of her back.

"There's nothing to worry about. Most people would love a private jet as their first flying experience." He winked down at her. "Come on."

He'd led her onto the jet and the crew had made sure they had all they needed while Kurt unpacked a few of the weapons he had on him and tucked them into a cupboard.

Madison knew he was an SLC, so she hadn't reacted when the handgun and two knives had appeared. In fact, it had been the opposite. Her eyes had glistened with obvious need.

Before he spotted the bite on her neck, he'd been about to kiss her. Both of them had built up tension and if she looked down and saw the bulge in his pants, she'd know he was on the edge, too.

They had the entire jet to themselves, with the exception of the crew. Did he go sit on the other side and give her space?

No.

Did he sit opposite her to see where the sizzling chemistry might lead?

Yes.

Given he'd whipped her away from her home and she was in a new territory, he wasn't going to be assertive about it, but Kurt had no intention of making it difficult.

An hour into the five-hour flight, the sexual tension was off the charts.

Madison had asked him about his job with the royal army, and about his training.

"You must work out *a lot* to keep all that going on," she said, waving her hand around in a circle at his body and grinning at him.

"We work out. The job is physical, so there's not a lot of sitting around." He leaned to the side, his head tilting as he took in her lithe tight body. "What we do is dangerous."

Her eyes sparkled.

Kurt knew this shit got females wet, and he was playing it up.

"Were you on a job in Seattle? Is that why you were there?"

Now that he couldn't answer.

"If I told you that, I'd have to kill you, wouldn't I?" He winked.

She blushed, but grinned. "You wouldn't hurt me, Kurt Mazzarelli. You're one of the good guys."

He let out a snort.

"Oh, sweetheart. I'm not all that good. Don't mistake a warrior for a knight in shining armor. I am no Lancelot."

It was a bit of an inside joke. Lance was one of the SLCs and had always been a ladies' man. Then when his mate,

Sofia, came along, that is exactly what he'd done. Pulled a "Lancelot" and saved her.

"So, you're a bad boy."

"If what you are thinking is the same as what I'm thinking, then yes. Very, very bad."

She'd bitten her lower lip and his cock had jerked right up. Their eyes had locked and burned as his mind completely stopped working.

"Come here," he'd said.

When Madison slid her things away and stood, Kurt reached to press a button, locking the crew out of the cabin. Then he unzipped his jeans.

Her eyes had shot to his cock as he pulled it out.

"Is this the kind of bad you're looking for?" he asked, gripping one of her hips with his other hand as he began to stroke himself.

More licking of her lips.

"Take off your clothes," he said.

Her eyes had locked with his, nerves beginning to show. He smiled.

"You want to play with bad boys, Madison, you need to be brave. Are you brave?"

She nodded without hesitation and began to undo her jeans. He stood and removed her top, running his hands over her lacy bra.

"We don't need this." He pulled down the straps and she helped him by undoing it at the back. When her breasts were bare, he groaned. "Gorgeous tits."

"Is this what you usually do?" Madison asked. "With females you meet?"

His smile grew as he removed the rest of his clothes. "Did you think I was a virgin, Madison Michaelson?"

He took her hand and planted it on his cock, hissing out at her touch.

"No," she replied, lust thick in her voice.

She wanted to know she was special. He was surprised. Humans asked these questions usually, not vampires. But she was young.

Kurt had long ago decided he'd never mate. If he ever met the one, he had a plan. He would move to the Antarctic or some shit so he couldn't bond with them.

That love shit wasn't for him.

He'd seen too many things and lived a hard life since he was young. Love wasn't something he wanted or desired.

Tugging her with him, he stepped back and sat on the leather seat. Without coaxing, she fell to her knees.

On glance at him, where he nodded, and she took him in her mouth.

Oh, yes, fuck!

Her mouth was warm, wet and not entirely skilled at what she was doing. Yet, it felt incredible. She fumbled away, sucking, licking, stroking, and watching him for a reaction. He was reacting, all right.

When she reached and gave his balls a squeeze, he had to make a decision. Come in her mouth or no.

He decided no.

Gritting his teeth, he pulled Madison off him and up to her feet, nudging a knee between her thighs. She gripped his shoulders.

"Man, you really are built."

"And it's all yours right now." He grinned and her little hands ran over his skin, down to his pecs and over his biceps like she was a kid in a toy shop. His ego, he wasn't ashamed to admit, doubled.

While he glowed under her touch, he slid his fingers along the seam of her panties and then tugged them to the side.

"You wet down here?" he asked, and she moaned in answer, her legs going a little weak. His fingers moved further and struck her creamy moisture, and his mouth watered.

He got rid of her panties and tugged her closer, planting his mouth on her clit. She cried out, gripping his body.

"Holy shit."

Had she come already?

He slid more fingers through her pussy and then inside her. She was so damn tight he had the feeling she wasn't all that sexually active despite her flirty bar girl act.

Fuck, she was going to feel incredible around his cock.

He worked her a little more and stared up at her face. She looked like she was in heaven, her teeth clenched around her bottom lip.

God, he could play for hours with this pretty baby vamp.

His cock was impatient, though. It was dark red and leaking, needing to sheath inside her center.

Kurt pulled his fingers out of her and, as she watched him, he licked them slowly.

"Still like a bad boy, sweetheart?"

"Yes," she breathed.

"Good," he said, tugging her onto his lap. "Let me feel you on my cock."

"Go slow. You are bigger than I'm used to."

A sliver of annoyance rushed through him. *Who else was touching this female?*

"We can go as slow or as fast as you want," he had said, lining his cock up at her entrance. Then Madison had lifted one of her hands from his arm and flicked her hair back.

The bite.

Red, swollen, pulsing.

She tried to slide down onto his shaft. He held her firm.

"Kurt," she groaned.

His eyes had locked onto the wound.

"Fuck, Kurt. I need…"

With vamp speed, he lifted her, dumped her back on her seat and then fled to the door of the cabin.

"Get dressed," he had ordered her.

As he exited the cabin to take a cold shower and change, he heard her questions behind him, but couldn't stop. If he did, he'd plunge into her.

What had he been thinking?

God knows what that bite meant.

The vampire who had bitten her was on the run after they'd assisted his escape from BioZen, a pharmaceutical company who were doing experiments on vampires.

Callan had been with them for months after being captured. They had no idea what had been done to the male, but after seeing the wound on Madison's throat it didn't look like anything fucking good.

Until he knew, he couldn't touch her again.

If she ever let him.

Kurt blinked, coming back to the present, and found his hand inside his briefs, stroking his cock.

Again.

For two weeks it was all he'd done, and it was never enough. Every time he saw Madison his body flared with desire. She barely looked at him, but when she did his fangs ached like a mother fucker.

She was distracting and too pretty for her own good.

And right now, she wasn't going anywhere, so he was going to have to learn to live with her being in the castle.

He jumped up.

There was a female in the castle he shared body juices with from time to time.

Fiona.

It was time to go see her.

One good fuck and Kurt was sure this aching need would subside. He should have done it earlier.

Then he could forget about wanting to sink balls-deep inside the little blond bar girl once and for all, and get back to focusing on his damn job.

To keep reading Kurt and Madison's steamy and deeply romantic book, THE VAMPIRE'S WOLF, click the title.

ALSO BY JULIETTE N. BANKS

The Moretti Blood Brothers
Steamy paranormal romance
The Vampire Prince
The Vampire Protector
The Vampire Spy
The Vampire's Christmas
The Vampire Assassin
The Vampire Awoken
The Vampire Lover
The Vampire Wolf

Realm of the Immortals
Steamy paranormal fantasy romance
The Archangel's Heart
The Archangel's Star
The Archangel's Goddess

The Dufort Dynasty
Steamy billionaire romance
Sinful Duty
Forbidden Touch
Total Possession

LET'S STAY IN TOUCH

To receive information about my new or upcoming releases, new series and free giveaways join my **VIP BOOKCLUB.** Click HERE to join.

I'd love to invite you to join my private Facebook Group. I'm very active in there and share a lot about my writing process, what's coming up, plus sneaky (and spicy) excerpts from my current manuscripts before they publish! Click the link below to join, answer the group questions and just remember its R18!

PRIVATE READERS FACEBOOK GROUP

Plus…

FOLLOW ME ON INSTAGRAM

FOLLOW ME ON BOOKBUB

FOLLOW ME ON GOODREADS

Printed in Great Britain
by Amazon